The Prodigal

BEVERLY LEWIS

The
Prodigal

DOUBLEDAY LARGE PRINT HOME LIBRARY EDITION

BETHANYHOUSE
PUBLISHERS
MINNEAPOLIS, MINNESOTA

The Prodigal
Copyright © 2004
Beverly Lewis

Cover design by Dan Thornberg

Published by Bethany House Publishers
11400 Hampshire Avenue South
Bloomington, Minnesota 55438
www.bethanyhouse.com

Bethany House Publishers is a division of Baker Publishing Group, Grand Rapids, Michigan.

Printed in the United States of America

ISBN 0-7394-4731-9

This Large Print Book carries the Seal of Approval of N.A.V.H.

Dedication

For
Carolene Robinson,
with happy memories
of our "baby days" . . .
and laugh-out-loud Mark Twain nights.

By Beverly Lewis

www.beverlylewis.com

ABRAM'S DAUGHTERS
The Covenant
The Betrayal
The Sacrifice
The Prodigal

❖ ❖ ❖

THE HERITAGE OF LANCASTER COUNTY
The Shunning
The Confession
The Reckoning

❖ ❖ ❖

The Postcard
The Crossroad

❖ ❖ ❖

The Redemption of Sarah Cain
October Song
*Sanctuary**
The Sunroom

❖ ❖ ❖

The Beverly Lewis Amish Heritage
Cookbook

*with David Lewis

BEVERLY LEWIS, born in the heart of Pennsylvania Dutch country, fondly recalls her growing-up years. A keen interest in her mother's Plain family heritage has led Beverly to set many of her popular stories in Lancaster County.

A former schoolteacher and accomplished pianist, Beverly is a member of the National League of American Pen Women (the Pikes Peak branch) and the Society of Children's Book Writers and Illustrators. She is the 2003 recipient of the Distinguished Alumnus Award at Evangel University, Springfield, Missouri, and her blockbuster novel, *The Shunning,* recently won the Gold Book Award. Her bestselling novel *October Song* won the Silver Seal in the Benjamin Franklin Awards, and *The Postcard* and *Sanctuary* (a collaboration with her husband, David) received Silver Angel Awards, as did her delightful picture book for all ages, *Annika's Secret Wish.* Beverly and her husband have three grown children and one grandchild and make their home in the Colorado foothills.

Prologue

Winter 1956

Sometimes in the midst of gray fog and drizzle, especially at this time of year, it's difficult to tell where the day ends and the night begins. Alas, mud clings to nearly everything—buggy wheels, horses' hooves, and work boots. But in a few short days, when the predicted cold snap arrives in Gobbler's Knob, all this sludge will freeze hard, and hopefully everyone's footing will be safer once again.

Yet even now the long night of separation is past. My repentant sister, Sadie, has returned to the open arms of the People, and my heart is tender with love for her. Nine-year-old Lydiann privately asks me why Sadie ever left us to live in the Midwest. 'Tis a prickly subject with little hope of being understood by a girl so young and one who scarcely knows Sadie. I can only pray that dear Lydiann will set aside her curiosity and enjoy her eldest sister for who she is now . . . for who she is becoming.

Little by little, Sadie and I have completed the task of sewing her new dresses and aprons—all black for the one-year mourning period—since the few she brought home in her suitcase definitely reflected the style and pattern she wore while living in Nappanee, Indiana. Even the head coverings are quite different out west compared to here in Lancaster County—lots more pleats to iron than we have in our prayer veilings. We boxed up all of Sadie's former clothing and sent it back to Nappanee, hoping some of her deceased husband's family might be able to put it to good use. For sure and for certain, she intends never to need it again.

Along with tending to my youngest sister and only brother, I have been going to plenty of quilting frolics, where joyous fellowship fills the day now that I've learned to tune out the tittle-tattle and simply concentrate on making tiny quilting stitches. With Adah Peachey Ebersol, my best friend and cousin by marriage and, at times, Aunt

Lizzie by my side, I am ever so content. Aunt Lizzie has an amazing ability to swiftly sew many little stitches, and straight ones at that. Sometimes she and I make a game of seeing who can sew the smallest ones, and she always wins with seven or eight per needle. Naturally she would; she's been quilting for many years longer than I. Yet it seems to me finishing well in this life is not so much about who is the best or greatest at something, but rather who embraces lowliness of heart. Laying down one's rights—meekness—is a blessed virtue, one that must surely come straight from the Throne of Grace.

In the nearly seven years since Mamma's death, Aunt Lizzie has become a mother to me, though I have yet to refer to her as Mamma. Still, in my heart she is now just that, and I know she senses the affectionate tie that binds the two of us.

On quilting days, Aunt Lizzie and Sadie take turns staying home to cook and clean and look in on *Dawdi* John, our elderly maternal grandfather, who still lives in the cozy Dawdi *Haus* adjoining our farmhouse. But neither Sadie nor Aunt Lizzie will ever consider letting *me* stay behind, and they're rather outspoken that I should be the one getting out of the house, even though winter is surely creeping up on us. I don't have to remind them that I do have ample opportunity to leave the Ebersol Cottage and have a change of scenery, since I work for the English doctor, Henry Schwartz, and his wife, Lorraine. Truth be told, sometimes I think Lizzie is concerned that too much of my free time is spent with fancy folk, though she brings this up only rarely. Probably in the back of her mind—and *Dat*'s, too—is Mary Ruth's leaving the community of the People behind for the Mennonite church, though I believe Dat has begun to temper his displeasure with Mary Ruth, speaking out less strongly here lately. Dawdi John, too, says he's seen "a whole other side" to Dat in recent days.

Secretly I've been reading Mamma's old Bible and searching out the underlined passages, coming to understand why dear Mamma was so patient and kind—walking the way of true humility. Such qualities seemed to come second nature to her, as she had a servant's heart, just as I desire to have before the Lord. If I continue to follow diligently the path God has set before me, though sometimes as prickly as nettles when I find myself alone, I believe I will be most joyful.

Patience is yet another virtue, one that grows stronger through the practice of waiting, and I've done much of that in recent years, come to think of it. I often linger near the school yard for Lydiann and Abe, whom I happily view as my own little ones. Young Abe, surrounded as he is by a houseful of women folk, is dearly treasured by each of us. He brings such delight to our lives that it's truly painful to contemplate how terribly close we came to losing him along with Mamma on the day of his birth.

I must also admit to waiting, with some measure of hope, for a letter from Grasshopper Level, praying that one day Mamma's cousins Peter and Fannie Mast might wake up and realize they have a whole family of folk who love them here. And it would be wonderful-good, if the Lord wills, to get word from someone—anyone at all—telling of Jonas Mast and his faraway life and family.

Most of all, I longingly wait for Sadie's six-month Proving to come to an agreeable end. Bishop Bontrager's choice of an older woman to oversee her during this time is Mamma's dearest friend, Miriam Peachey. The Proving means my sister can't be alone with a man for the time being, except male relatives. Of course this means she's not allowed to be courted until next April. Still, though she's but twenty-eight, I can't imagine her even being interested in another man—or at least not for a good long time.

So there is nothing to do but go along with the minister's stern decree and look ahead to a happier season—next springtime—when Sadie will be reinstated as a member in good standing, if she keeps her nose clean. We can only hope and pray she will; otherwise, she will no longer be welcome in Dat's house or the community of the People. As harsh as her shunning was, what with no letters allowed all those years she was gone, I sincerely hope the severity of this second Proving has not caused further distress in my widowed sister.

Before long the shortest day will darken the hours at both ends of the clock, the celebration of the Lord's birthday will come and go . . . and soon after, our little Abe will observe his seventh birthday. Then, too, my sister Hannah will bear her third wee babe.

All of this in the space of a few short days, Lord willing.

For now I'm content to push split logs into Mamma's old wood stove and help Sadie and Aunt Lizzie cook and bake the family recipes, though in doing so, I am ever mindful of the constant ache in me, living life without dear Mamma. Keeping busy is one way of getting by, I daresay. Although Sadie now shares our parents' former room with me, it is in the night hours, when the rest of the family is snug in their own beds, that I am most threatened by profound loneliness as a *maidel.* Nonetheless, I remember always to count my blessings, moment by moment . . . day by day.

Part One

♦ ♦ ♦ ♦

The entrance of thy words giveth light . . .
—Psalm 119:130

Chapter One

Early morning winds pressed a row of saplings nearly flat to the ground, and the stark contrast between a dreary sky and the eerie whiteness of a snow-sleek earth created a peculiar balance of light.

Leah pulled her woolen shawl tightly against her as she made her way back to the house from the barn, where she'd gone to take a tall Thermos of hot coffee to her father and brother-in-law, Gid.

" 'Tis terrible cold out," she told Sadie, making a beeline into the kitchen, eager to warm her chapped hands over the wood stove.

Sadie looked up from Dat's favorite rocking chair, her needlework in her lap. " 'S'pose the men were glad for the coffee, *jah*?"

Leah nodded. "I like seein' the smiles on

their red faces. Besides, it's the least I can do for Dat and our new preacher, ya know." She smiled. Truth was, Dat needed a bit of fussing over, still floundering at times without Mamma. So did Gid, what with Hannah so great with child she could scarcely shuffle to the kitchen to cook a meal for their growing family. Both Lizzie and Sadie had been taking turns carrying hot dishes up to the log house on the edge of the woods, helping out some. "What do ya think Hannah will have this time—girl or boy?" asked Leah.

"I'm sure Gid's hopin' for a son, just as Dat did all those years back. But it wouldn't surprise me if Hannah has another daughter. Girls seem to run in the Ebersol family," Sadie said.

"Jah, prob'ly so." Leah didn't care one way or the other. So far, young Abe was the only male offspring, and a right fine boy he was.

◆

Hours later, when the time came to call the family together for dinner, Leah headed to the front room, where Lydiann was dusting the corner cupboard. Stopping to watch, Leah was struck by how sweet the girl's face was. Nearly heart shaped, truly, and pretty blue eyes much like Sadie's. She sighed, thinking what a handful Lydiann could be, yet at the same time, she brought a wealth of affection to the whole family. Lydiann was especially attentive to young Abe, her only close-in-age sibling.

"Sadie says the stew's ready," Leah said softly, so as not to startle her.

Turning, Lydiann smiled. She laid the dust rag on the floor and fell in step with Leah, slipping her arm around her waist. "Our big sister has that certain touch, ain't so?" Lydiann sniffed the air comically. "I daresay her cookin' oughta bring her another fine husband someday."

"Now, Lyddie," Leah chided her.

"Well, Mamma," whispered Lydiann, "you know what I mean."

"S'posin' I do, and Sadie does have that special something every cook yearns for." Leah went to the back door and rang the dinner bell while Lydiann washed her hands at the kitchen sink. Quickly Leah pulled the door shut, keenly aware of the bone-chilling cold, the bitter kind that crept up through long skirts and long johns both.

The present cold snap was expected to linger for a while, according to the weather forecast, which wasn't always so reliable. Dat, however, took both the weatherman and *The Farmer's Almanac* quite seriously most days, especially here lately. Leah wondered if her father simply needed something to hang his hat on, but the weather was the last thing a body could count on, as unpredictable as winter was long.

She went to help Sadie carry the food to the table. Along with stew, there were cornmeal muffins, a Waldorf salad, and a tray of carrot sticks, pickles, and olives, with plenty of hot coffee for the adults and fresh cow's milk for Lydiann and Abe. The children much preferred the taste of the milk when the cows were barn fed instead of pasture fed, so she knew they'd be draining their glasses tonight.

By the time Dat and young Abe dashed indoors, got themselves washed up, and sat down at the table, Dawdi John and Aunt Lizzie had come over from the Dawdi Haus, commenting on the delicious aroma of Sadie's stew. Lydiann was swinging her legs beneath the long table, clearly restless as Leah slipped in next to her on the wooden bench.

"What's takin' everyone so long?" Lydiann whispered to her.

"You must be awful hungry," Leah replied. "But how 'bout let's be willin' to wait, jah?" She bowed her head as Dat motioned for the traditional silent prayer.

After the table blessing, Leah noticed Dat's gaze lingering a bit longer than usual on Aunt Lizzie, who was smiling right back at him. *Well, now, what on earth . . . Is it possible?* For a moment she contemplated the idea Dat might be taking a shine to Mamma's younger sister. She couldn't help wondering how peculiar she'd feel if Dat were actually sweet on her own birth mother.

And what might precious Mamma think?

Sadie dished up generous portions of the stew as each person in turn held a bowl to be filled. Abe's eyes were bright, apparently pleased at the prospect of his favorite— "plenty of meat and potatoes." He smacked his lips and dug a spoon deep into his bowl.

"I'll be takin' Abe with me to the farm sale

come Thursday," Dat said, glancing at Leah. "Just so ya know."

"Yippee, no school for *me*!" Abe exclaimed, his mouth a bit too full.

"Aw, Mamma . . ." Lydiann complained, looking at Leah with the most pitiful eyes. "Can't I—"

"No need askin'." Lovingly, she leaned against Lydiann.

"But *you* always went with Dat to farm auctions growin' up, Mamma," Abe said, surprising her. "Ain't so, Dat? You told me as much."

Their father had to struggle to keep a grin in check, his whiskers wriggling slightly on both sides of his mouth. Truth was, Abe was quite right, and Leah was somewhat taken aback that Dat had told about those days when she had been her father's substitute son.

"Jah, Leah was quite a tomboy for a *gut* many years." Here Dat turned and, for a moment, looked fondly at her. Feeling the warmth in her cheeks, she lowered her head. It had been the longest time since Dat had said such a thing in private, let alone in front of everyone.

"I daresay our Leah has herself a higher callin' now," Aunt Lizzie spoke up.

"She's our sister *and* our mamma," Abe said, grinning from ear to ear.

Lydiann muttered something, though just what, Leah cared not to guess. Best not to make an issue of it. No, let Lydiann simmer over having to attend school on the day of the farm sale. She needed not to miss any more school, having recently suffered a long bout with the flu. Even if Lydiann hadn't missed at all this year, there was no reason for her to go traipsing off to the all-day farm sale with Dat, Abe, and Gid when her place was at school or home.

Mamma must've thought that of me, too . . . all those years ago.

"You go 'n' have yourself a fine day of book learnin' on Thursday, Lydiann," Dat said just then. "And no lip 'bout it, ya hear?"

Dat must have sensed the rising will in his youngest daughter. He was becoming more in tune with his family's needs as each year passed, in spite of the grief he carried over him like a shroud.

Lydiann buttered her cornmeal muffin and then asked meekly for some apricot jam. Sadie hopped right up from the table to get it, and Dawdi John smiled broadly at the preserves coming and asked for a second helping of both stew and muffins. "Won't be a crumb of leftovers." He patted his slight belly.

This got Abe laughing and leaning forward to look down the table at their grandfather. "Maybe Dawdi oughta be goin' with us to the sale," Abe said. "What do ya think of that, Dawdi John?"

Dat murmured his concern. It was anybody's guess whether or not Dawdi, at his feeble age, could keep up with the menfolk, since a full year had passed since Dawdi had made any attempt at going. In fact, Leah recalled clearly the last time Lizzie's elderly father had decided to push himself too hard and go down to Ninepoints, where an Amish farmer was selling everything from hayforks to harnesses to the farmhouse itself. Dat had soundly reprimanded Aunt Lizzie for suggesting that her frail father go. Leah knew this because she'd unintentionally overheard them talking in the barn that day. Turned out poor Dawdi had gotten right dizzy at the sale, sick to his stomach, and later that night, he'd suffered with a high fever and the shakes. The illness had put an awful fear in not only Dat, but all of them.

Thankfully Dawdi was now saying no to young Abe's request, his white beard brushing against the blue of his shirt as he shook his head. "*Ach,* you and Abram go for the day. Leave me here at home with the women folk."

Once again Leah felt a warm and welcome relief, and she realized anew how deep in her heart she carried each one of her family members.

◆

Sadie and Dat hitched up the open sleigh to the horse the next morning, which took far less time than the usual half hour or so when the job was to be accomplished by only one person. With weather this nippy, Sadie couldn't see letting Leah start out with frozen fingers and toes from having to hitch up and then drive Lydiann and Abe to school, stopping for all the neighborhood children who attended—Amish and English alike. It had been her idea to surprise Leah, getting Dat from the barn so the two of them could prepare the sleigh.

Since returning home in October, she hadn't found the courage to open her mouth and tell the whole truth to her sister, but she *was* awful sorry about the part she'd played in keeping Jonas from marrying Leah. The letter from Leah to her beloved, the one Sadie had deliberately and angrily discarded so long ago, continued to haunt her. But she worried that it might cause another rift between herself and her dear sister if she were to confess the wicked deed. Meanwhile, she simply tried to find ways to help lift the domestic burden for Leah—anything to lessen her sense of guilt.

Leah's face shone with delight when she came out of the house, her pleasure evident at not having to face the chore single-handedly. She rushed to Sadie and hugged her but good while Dat grinned and waved and headed back to the barn. "Ach, Sadie . . . and Dat, you didn't have to do this."

Sadie rubbed her hands together. "We wanted to."

Just then Lydiann and Abe came flying out the back door, lunch buckets in hand. "One more day of school till the farm sale,"

Abe hollered over his shoulder, beating Lydiann to the sleigh.

Sadie saw Lydiann pull a face. Then both children laughed and hopped up into the sleigh. Turning to face her, they waved as Leah twitched the reins, pulling out and heading down the long lane to the road.

Sadie, aware of the bitter cold, stood there longer than need be, watching the horse's head rise and fall as the sleigh, soon to be filled with schoolchildren, slipped away from view.

I might've had a sleigh full of my own little ones.

Slowly she made her way toward the house, up the sidewalk shoveled clean of new snow. *'Tis nearly Christmas and I ought to be happy.*

"Oughta be a lot of things," she muttered as she reached for the back door and hurried inside. She didn't move quickly to the wood stove to warm her ice-cold hands and feet. She went and stood at the window, looking out over the side pasture, her gaze drifting all the way to the edge of the woods. Deep in that forest, there were deer hunters probably right now resting and warming themselves in an old, run-down shanty. She wished to goodness the place had fallen down in disrepair, wished Aunt Lizzie might have discovered the flattened shelter on one of her many treks through the woods, its walls of decaying wood lying flat on the snow-glazed ground, just asking to be hauled away.

Sadie recognized anew the one reason she'd ever hesitated to write to Bishop Bontrager telling of her widowhood and of her desire to return home to her father's house: the sordid memories here of the sin she had allowed herself to get caught up in as a teenager, the wickedness she'd shared with the village doctor's younger son. Although she had safely passed the Ohio church Proving and eventually married an upstanding young man, Harvey Hochstetler, there were times when thoughts of Derek Schwartz still haunted her. Did he even know she'd given birth to a stillborn son?

Derry . . . the boy who'd stolen her virtue. No, that was not true and she knew it. She had willingly given up her innocence to a virtual stranger, a heathen, as Dat often said of Englishers. She had known firsthand that Derry was just that, but he had not been a thief those nights in the hunters' shack.

Now, though, having heard that Mary Ruth was seeing Derry's older brother, Robert, Sadie couldn't help but feel squeamish at the wretched possibility of having to meet him one day. This made her tremble, and she hoped such a meeting might be months, even years away. She just felt so helpless at times, missing Harvey something awful, even more so now that she was safely home again, snug in Dat's big farmhouse. Yet the knowledge of that horrid shanty, the place where she had conceived her first child, illegitimate at that, caused her to draw her black shawl around her chin as she looked out toward the dark woods.

If the bishop knew my thoughts, he'd surely be displeased. She knew she ought not to dwell on the past. She ought to think on the good years she'd spent with Harvey, the kind and loving husband the Lord God heavenly Father had granted her . . . for a time. Still, coming home had stirred everything up again. Sometimes she wondered if the almighty One had withheld His favor even though she had turned from her rebellious ways, with the help of the Ohio ministers to begin with . . . and thoughtful Jonas.

She had completed her Proving time in Millersburg well before ever meeting Harvey and moving to Nappanee.

All the babies I carried, she thought. *All of them lost to me . . . to Harvey, too. All the blue-faced wee ones I birthed . . .*

Silently she questioned if the reckless willfulness of her early sin had made divine judgment most severe. Here she was, all this time after, stuck in a mire of doubt and hopelessness, a woman longing for her dead children and husband. The awareness that Bishop Bontrager had set her up as an example to the young people did not make things any easier.

She had long wished for Dat to have known Harvey, for her sisters to have enjoyed her husband's hearty laugh and interesting stories told around the hearth. And yet in spite of the congenial and closely knit family she had shared with Harvey, she had often felt she was marking time clear out there in Indiana, far away from home. There had always been a feeling of waiting to undo what had been already done. She had sometimes cried herself to sleep, longing for Mamma's loving arms and nighttime talks with Leah. All of this unbeknownst to her husband.

I'm home now. Regardless of her initial reservations, she was glad to be living in a big family once again, with Dat and Leah, Aunt Lizzie and Dawdi John, and the eager-faced Lydiann and Abe—finally getting to know her youngest siblings. Most of all, it was fun watching her young sister and brother growing up underfoot, seeing their wide-eyed devotion to Leah. She wouldn't let herself envy Leah for having what she did not—a close bond with children, the memory of having held Lydiann and Abe ever so near as infants, rocking them to sleep in their tiny cotton gowns, rejoicing over their first toddler steps. Constantly, though, Sadie noticed every young one who was the age her children would have been had they lived . . . especially her dead son.

Still, it did seem a bit unfair that Leah was a mother without having given birth, while Sadie had given birth but was not a mother. Yet she wouldn't allow herself to contemplate that too much, not wishing to usurp Leah's position in Lydiann's and Abe's eyes.

Moving away from the window, she trudged to the utility room just off the kitchen. There, she removed her shawl and hung it on the third wooden peg. The first peg belonged to Dat, of course, and she had noticed right away upon her return home last fall that Leah's shawl now hung where Mamma's always had. So, even though there was still a vacant place at the table for Mamma, Leah must have felt no need to leave the wooden peg empty.

Chapter Two

When the nine o'clock auctioneer's chant
began, Abram was ready. He and Abe had
taken plenty of time to scrutinize all the farm
equipment, as well as the field mules up for
sale. Abe followed him around, never leaving his side, and Abram was downright
pleased.

Dozens of men milled about in the snow
and mud, most of them wearing black felt
hats, the telltale sign of an Amishman. They
stood around chewing the fat and telling
jokes, some of them spitting tobacco. Each
potential customer eyed the enormous ar-
ray of farm tools, woodworking implements,
livestock, milking equipment, and odds and
ends of things—old green medicine bottles,
two martin birdhouses, woolen mufflers,
work boots and gloves, and a pile of garden
rakes—all the men hoping for a bargain

price. Their sons and grandsons were off playing cornerball or sitting over on the split-rail fence like black-capped chickadees perched on a wire.

When the time came, Abram raised his head slowly, signaling his first bid on a good-sized box of saws, drills, and sandpaper. The auctioneer scanned the crowd shrewdly, obviously spying another interested farmer. Up another dollar. Abram flickered his eyebrow at the local auctioneer, older than some but known for keeping the crowd loose.

"Who's biddin' against us, Dat?" whispered Abe, jumping up and down, trying to see over the crowd.

Abram put a hand on the lad's shoulder, not wanting to miss his chance at the saws and drills. A few more blinks of the eye and the bidding was done. The other fellow hadn't wanted them as much as Abram had. "Come on, now," he said to Abe. "We got ourselves some right nice handsaws."

He guided his boy through the crowd to claim the goods, saying it was Old Jonathan Lapp who'd dropped out of the bidding when he saw how quickly Abram kept coming back with a higher bid.

"When can I start makin' such bids?" Abe asked as they carried the box of saws and things to the carriage.

"When you're earnin' money." Abram had to smile at Abe's innocent sincerity.

"Just when will *that* be?"

"In due time" was all he said. There was plenty of food to go around, but when it came to cash there was less to speak of these days, what with Sadie living at home now. Leah, on the other hand, put every dime she made from her work at the Schwartz clinic into the family pot. Even so, Abram couldn't afford to pay his young son for his field and barn work before and after school and on weekends. He wouldn't think of doing so until Abe was closer to courting age, a good decade away.

He and his boy spent several more hours at the farm sale following Abram's only purchase. They stood in the barnyard talking with the men, but when Abe's nose and ears began to look mighty red, almost purple, he knew he best be taking this one home to warm up.

———◆———

It was during the buggy ride home that
Abram got to thinking more about the fact
that the gardening work should no longer
fall on Leah's and Lydiann's shoulders as it
had ever since Hannah had married Gid and
moved to Lizzie's former house in the
woods. Sadie and Aunt Lizzie would have to
take up the slack next spring, because Leah
had her hands plenty full, doing a right fine
job caring for the youngsters. He wouldn't
think of asking her to quit her housecleaning
job at the doctor's place. Besides her earn-
ings being such a help, Leah needed a
chance to get away from the confines of
their four walls. He'd heard from the doctor
that his missus felt she couldn't manage
without Leah, so not only had she impressed them with her hard work, Leah had
endeared herself to them, as well.

Thoughts of the Schwartzes led his mind
to Mary Ruth, who was rather taken with
their firstborn, presently studying to be a
preacher. Having not met "honorable"
Robert as of yet, he had only Mary Ruth's
word to go on. Someday, if they continued
to spend time together, he'd have to do the
mannerly thing and meet his daughter's
Mennonite boyfriend.

Lest his thoughts run away with him, he asked Abe, sitting to his left, what he thought of exchanging names in the family this Christmas. He didn't go so far as to say this approach would save some of the family's money, though.

"I'd like to draw Mamma Leah's name, if we put the names in a hat." Abe's blue eyes shone as he turned to look at Abram. "Either Mamma's or Lydiann's."

"Not Gid's, then?" He was taken aback by the serious tone of Abe's remark.

Abe shook his head. "Gid oughta be gotten by Hannah or one of their girls. Ain't so?"

Clicking his tongue, Abram urged the horse onward toward home. Ida's boy was as discerning and devoted as he was youthful. Abram reached down and patted Abe on the knee and nodded, mighty glad to have such fine company this brisk winter day.

◆

The Ohio sun burned bright in Jonas Mast's face, momentarily blinding him, and he moved slightly, trying to avoid its pene-

trating rays, wanting to see clearly the auctioneer's face—the old codger's eyes. After
all, it was the eye contact that he wanted,
having upped his bid this high already.

Dark blue and fluted, the carnival glass
vase was the object of his steady bidding,
and he would not let up, for he knew he had
stumbled upon the best choice of a present
for dear Emma. He could just imagine the
look of sheer joy on her face when he gave
it to her on Christmas Day.

He'd come to the distant farm sale interested in purchasing additional woodworking tools, having heard tell of the auction
through the Amish grapevine. But while
wandering about, he'd discovered antique
dishes, quilts, and other old household
items laid out in the front room of the house,
set just up from the barn on a slope.

If I can just get the final bid, he thought,
raising his eyebrows again to signal the
auctioneer he had not lost interest.

The pretty vase was being held high in the
air just now, and his pulse sped up when he
heard the word "Sold!"

But the auctioneer shielded his eyes from
the sun and, with a mystified look, peered

into the crowd. "I daresay you ain't from round here."

"Name's Jonas Mast," he replied quickly, slightly embarrassed, with the crowd having turned to stare his way. "From up north a ways."

"Well, fine and dandy. Sold to our gut neighbor Jonas."

He had claimed his prize and turned to head back toward his horse and carriage when an old Mennonite farmer came up to him, leaning on his wooden cane. "Couldn't help overhearin', but you're Jonas Mast, ya say?"

Jonas offered a tentative nod.

"Well, if that don't beat all. World's gettin' smaller all the time, 'specially among us Plain folk . . . but with so many Masts and Jonases running round, who's to say if it *was* you, really."

"I'm sorry . . . have we met somewhere?"

"Doubt it," the older man replied, squinting his bleary eyes. "But then again, who knows? Ever live in Millersburg?"

Jonas felt surprise. "Why do ya ask?"

Such a long time ago . . .

With renewed excitement, the old farmer continued. "My cousin and I were reddin' out an old shed yesterday and happened to stumble onto a tattered old letter—unopened, as I recall—with a faded name written prettily on it."

Jonas was downright curious, though unsure if the white-haired man even knew what he was talking about. "Whom was the letter addressed to?"

"*Ach,* to *you,* of course."

"Hmm . . . you don't say." He was altogether befuddled. "Was there a return address?"

The old fellow removed his hat and scratched his head. "Honestly, paid no mind to that."

Jonas found all the talk of a letter puzzling—certainly the man's guess that he had once lived in Millersburg was right, but the rest of the story was downright odd. He stepped closer to the elderly man, noticing a hint of moonshine on his breath. "S'pose I best be headin' on home now," said Jonas, clinging to the antique vase. "Have a gut day!"

———◆———

Having waited near the edge of the school yard in the cold, Lydiann decided she couldn't stand there another minute waiting for Mamma Leah to come fetch her, so she ran and caught up with a group of four other Amish girls walking along the country road. Up ahead, a hard stone's throw away, six boys her age, all from the one-room Georgetown School, walked in the middle of the road, and she watched with interest as they waited till the last minute to step to the side, as if daring a horse and buggy to run them over. Even her little brother, Abe, liked to take part in such boyish stunts, except today he was off with Dat at a farm sale.

She listened as the girls jabbered in Pennsylvania Dutch, not joining in their conversation about the Christmas play, where she was to be Mary, the mother of baby Jesus, come this Monday, Christmas Eve afternoon.

The boys shifted to the right side of the road as a car came toward them, and she noticed the dark-haired Mennonite boy, Carl Nolt, scramble to safety more quickly than either of the three Amish and two English boys. The only child of Dan and Dottie Nolt whistled as he scurried along. The Nolts owned the house where Lydiann's older sister Mary Ruth, a schoolteacher at an all-English school, lived and worked part-time.

"Carl's gonna make *en feiner* Joseph, ain't?" one of the girls said, all smiles.

This brought a round of snickers and "shhs!" but Lydiann pretended not to hear just what a fine Joseph he would be. *Carl has the brownest eyes I've ever seen,* she thought, wondering right then which of his natural parents had passed down the dark eyes to him and why on earth they hadn't kept him.

It was Mary Ruth, who was more like a big sister to Carl than she'd ever been to Lydiann, who'd confided that Carl had been adopted promptly after his birth. Since Mary Ruth was known for sometimes saying too much, Lydiann had never spoken of the matter with Carl. Still, she was pretty sure he had a good heart—at least she thought so from having rehearsed the nativity play during lunchtime recess yesterday and to-day. But pretending to be Mary to a Joseph who was no more Amish than the man in the moon sent a strange chill up her spine. She would never let on as much, though, for the sake of Mary Ruth, who had been bringing Carl with her when she came to the Ebersol

Cottage to visit each week. It seemed Mary Ruth was a little too eager to include Carl in the games played near the wood stove with both Lydiann and Abe. Right peculiar it was, especially since Dat had made it clear he did not approve of Mary Ruth living with folk who had "electric." Such a blight it was, losing one of their own to Mennonites.

Lydiann suspected kindhearted Aunt Lizzie of having something to do with Dat welcoming Mary Ruth, as well as Carl. Aunt Lizzie had a way of poking her nose in and having her say, and Dat didn't seem to mind this much at all. Ever so amazing, really.

Up ahead, riding in a one-horse sleigh, came Mamma Leah. Lydiann quickened her pace, glad to see her. "Come! Have yourself a ride home!" she called to the other children.

The girls responded by hurrying to catch up with her, passing the boys, who lagged behind—all but Carl. "Mind if I come along?" he asked no one in particular.

"Hop on," Mamma said, her cheeks bright pink.

Carl hesitated, looking back toward the boys.

"It's all right," Lydiann said, hoping he

might sit right beside her, though she suspected he would keep his distance.

Carl smiled and climbed aboard, sitting closer to Mamma Leah than to any of the girls.

"When are you comin' with Mary Ruth for a visit again, Carl?" Mamma asked, and Lydiann paid attention to what he might say.

He shrugged his shoulders and said nothing for a moment. Then, when he finally found his voice, he said, "Mary Ruth says we might have all of you over for New Year's Eve . . . if it's agreeable with your father."

"How kind of you, Carl," Mamma replied before Lydiann could speak up.

Carl looked more comfortable now, and Lydiann wondered if he had been bashful before getting on the sleigh because of the boys. Maybe he worried what they might think of him riding with a group of girls.

"Where's Abe today?" he asked. Lydiann nearly missed the question, so caught up she was in her thoughts.

Once again Mamma Leah beat her to a reply. "Oh, he's off to a farm sale with his father."

"Lookin' to buy anything particular?" asked Carl.

Prob'ly some milkin' equipment and whatnot, thought Lydiann. But she didn't say what she was thinking and instead nodded her head and watched the relaxed way Carl sat cross-legged on the hay, wrapped in one of the woolen blankets Mamma Leah had brought along.

"Oh, I 'spect they might just find something worthwhile," Mamma said, looking back over her shoulder. "They usually do."

"I think my uncle went to that sale, too," Carl said. "He used to be Amish, so he likes to go where the Old Order farmers gather."

Lydiann found this interesting. So . . . somewhere in Carl's adopted family there had been at least one Amishman. *Did he leave the church before baptism, or was he shunned like Sadie?* Since Carl said no more, she wasn't about to follow up on the subject. Shunning was much too close to home, what with Sadie going through her Proving time now. Shunnings divided families, turning sisters and brothers into strangers . . . even if the shunned one repented and returned home.

Poor Sadie, pretty as the day was long. What on earth had she done to be treated so?

* * *

The smell of pecan pies baking drifted in from the doorway between the front room and the Dawdi Haus, and the familiar aroma reminded Sadie of Mamma, who had loved the Christmas season more than any other. Drawn by the delicious scent, Sadie headed next door to find Dawdi John napping in his rocking chair—head back, mouth open, and sawing logs rather loudly.

Where's Aunt Lizzie?

Tiptoeing through the small front room to investigate the smaller square of a kitchen, she quickly realized Aunt Lizzie was nowhere to be seen. She glanced at Dawdi, who remained oblivious to her presence, and opened the door leading to the stairs. Instead of calling up to her and risking awakening Dawdi, Sadie stepped lightly, heading upstairs.

She found her aunt sitting in the window of the first bedroom, Lizzie's own, reading the Bible. "Oh, hullo there, Sadie."

"Mind if I sit with you?"

Lizzie nodded. "Make yourself comfortable."

"Couldn't help but smell the pies."

Lizzie smiled. "Thought I'd surprise everyone and serve 'em for supper."

"Abe and Lydiann will like that, for sure and for certain." Sadie grew quiet.

Aunt Lizzie put her finger in the Bible, closing it, and tilted her head just so, looking hard at her now. "Something's on your mind, child. I can nearly hear it from here."

She thought how much better it might be if she didn't give in to the urge to open herself up and instead simply sat there, basking in the love her aunt so effortlessly offered. But Lizzie was altogether correct that there was much on her mind. "I miss talkin' to ya, *Aendi*. And I want to speak about my husband, Harvey, with somebody . . . with you, maybe, if you'd like to hear."

"Well, sure I would," Lizzie insisted.

Sadie related that she wished her family might have had the opportunity to know her husband. "Harvey kept folk in stitches, tellin' one story after 'nother whenever we invited relatives or friends over for meals or whatnot. Among other things, I sorely miss his laughter."

Aunt Lizzie leaned back, relaxing in her chair. "I daresay there is much to miss. I wish to goodness I might've known your Harvey."

Sadie felt suddenly eager to share something of her married years with Lizzie, having kept fairly mum since her return home, her loss having been too recent. She talked of their Christmases together, happily surrounded by Harvey's extended family, as well as the church folk. "Ach, we had the kindest bishop. I often wished he might've met Bishop Bontrager somehow, ya know." She was ever so careful not to step too hard on their bishop's toes here, but there *had* been many times when she felt sorry for Dat and Mamma and other members of the Gobbler's Knob church district, as well as herself. But, lest she show disrespect now for the Lord's anointed, she kept her peace. Aunt Lizzie need not know her private opinion of Bishop Bontrager. Besides, Lizzie had never admitted to having a problem with him.

"I'm glad you had such a fine husband and church in Indiana," Aunt Lizzie said after a while, giving Sadie's knee a pat. "We best be checking on the pies."

Sadie followed her downstairs and helped her set the pies out to cool. They then looked in on Dawdi John, who was still sleeping, before Lizzie motioned Sadie back upstairs. "There's something I've been thinkin' on," her aunt said in hushed tones. "And it's best ya hear it from me."

Sadie wondered if this heart-to-heart talk might involve Leah and her maidel status, or some such sad thing. *Can it be she senses I've kept mum about some of my own meddling in that?*

But Lizzie readily made it clear she had other things on her mind. "When I was but a teenager, I got myself in some terrible trouble, as you already know." She stopped, as if to catch her breath. "I never told you all there was to the story . . . and now I feel you oughta know the daughter I gave birth to is your sister Leah—in all truth, your first cousin." Aunt Lizzie's face was slightly flushed. "Leah has known this since her baptism, and before the Lord took your mamma, she shared this with Mary Ruth and Hannah. I thought it was high time you knew, too."

Aunt Lizzie is Leah's mother? Sadie felt the air go clean out of her. "Leah's your . . . your own daughter?"

Lizzie nodded her head, a tear glistening in her eye.

Struggling to take in this bewildering revelation, Sadie whispered at last, "How does Leah feel 'bout this?"

"Oh, we never speak of it anymore, just as the People do not speak of the shun once a person repents," said Lizzie.

Sadie found this news not only curious but altogether unnerving. Lizzie had given Leah to Mamma and Dat to raise, yet her child had grown up at arm's length, where Lizzie could observe and love her.

A shiver of sadness flew up her back, and Sadie, for a fleeting moment, recalled with dread the days and nights she had frequently heard the cries of a phantom baby, a constant reminder of her first wee one.

"I don't know what to say, really," she confessed, choking down the lump in her throat at the thought of Leah's unexpected bond with the aunt Sadie so admired. "To think you and Leah . . . well, I guess I might've wondered all those years why Leah was the only dark-haired one in the family. But I never would've guessed this."

Aunt Lizzie went on to say that, at the time of Leah's conception, she had been so caught up in her youthful rebellion she hadn't cared what anybody thought. "I just did as I pleased."

Same as I did, Sadie thought ruefully.

"Thankfully, your parents took me in as their own for a time, even as they did Leah when she was born."

"So the young man, Leah's father, never wanted to marry you or care for you?" The question slipped out effortlessly, though as soon as Sadie had voiced it, she felt suddenly sorry. "Uh, that's not at all for me to ask."

"No . . . no, it's to be expected, really 'tis."

But when Lizzie did not offer to say more about Leah's blood father, Sadie knew better than to press the question now burning in her mind.

Just who is Leah's real father?

Chapter Three

"Gid says might just be a gut idea if the hex doctor's on hand for this baby," Hannah told Aunt Lizzie in the privacy of her cozy kitchen on Christmas Eve day. "He thinks we should've had him here for the first two, just to be safe."

She had been pouring tea for herself when who but Lizzie had come knocking at the back door. Having felt awful sluggish all day, Hannah was glad for a chance to sit down and share a nice cup of tea with Lizzie. They'd gotten on to the topic of Hannah's choice of an Amish midwife when Hannah felt she ought to speak up about her fears.

"Dat still feels strongly that Mamma would be alive today if he'd had his way about callin' in the powwow doctor." She watched Aunt Lizzie closely, hoping for some further explanation as to why Lizzie, like Mamma, was so opposed to the sympathy healers.

Lizzie's hazel-brown eyes appeared more earnest now; it was surprising to see her usually cheery aunt turn suddenly solemn. She poured a rounded teaspoon of sugar into her teacup and stirred slowly before looking up at last. "I hesitate to talk much about so-and-so's stubborn stand on this subject, but if I do . . . well, please don't say anything."

"You have my word, Aendi."

Lizzie took several sips of hot tea. Then, setting the pretty floral cup down lightly on its matching saucer, she continued. "This has been a sore point with your father and me for much too long, I must admit. Here lately, though, I think he may be coming round 'bout the things your mamma believed in. I pray so."

Hannah found this admission hard to understand. What was Lizzie saying? That she and Dat had started to see eye to eye on the Amish doctors? If so, what would it mean for her and Gid . . . and the baby soon to be born? Would Dat interfere, try to convince Gid otherwise?

She shuddered to think of risking her baby's life as Mamma had done, only to lose her own. It was a miracle young Abe was as sturdy and smart as he was. Any of the women folk, if they were privy to all that Leah said poor Mamma had gone through to birth Abe, might still be bracing themselves, waiting for something wrong to show up either mentally or physically in her little brother. For Dat's sake and Abe's, too, Hannah sincerely hoped Abe would be healthy his whole life long.

"Are ya sayin' Dat would be opposed to having a hex doctor assist the midwife?"

Aunt Lizzie raised her eyebrows. "Why in heaven's name would you want to do such a thing, Hannah? Your mamma never did. She wanted nothing to do with the powwow doctors."

Sometimes Hannah just wished to goodness she could simply share her opinion without Aunt Lizzie raising a stink, especially when Ida Mae and Katie Ann were napping not so far from the kitchen. Knowing Lizzie as she did, Hannah wouldn't put it past her aunt to speak her mind and then some. Truth was, this minute she didn't feel strong enough to argue her side of

things and regretted bringing up the subject. Sure, Lizzie had her view, but so did
Hannah. And now that she was Gid's wife,
shouldn't she take into account *his* feelings? After all, the growing babe within her
belonged to her and Gid, not to Lizzie.

"I'd rather be safe than sorry, is all," she
whispered, tears springing to her eyes.

Aunt Lizzie placed a soft hand on hers.
"Well, now, Hannah, what's to worry? You
had no trouble birthing Ida and Katie."

Hannah nodded. " 'Tis quite true."

"Why do ya feel the need to invite a spirit
of evil into this house?"

Hannah gasped. *What's Lizzie saying?
Does she actually believe the Amish doctor
is of the devil?*

She'd heard such whispered things from
one of Mamma's Mast cousins—either
Rebekah or Katie—years ago when Dat and
Mamma were still on friendly terms with
Cousins Peter and Fannie, but never before
from Aunt Lizzie.

"I don't think you understand," Hannah
began quietly at first, but she felt the ire rise
in her as she went on. "I want to have a safe
delivery . . . and I want to live to see this

new one grow up—same as Ida and Katie. Why should you want to stand in my way?"

"And why would ya put your trust in someone other than the Lord God? Powwowing is nothing short of white witch-craft. Your mamma said the same." Aunt Lizzie pursed her lips, then stared down at the cup of tea before her, fiddling with the handle.

Hannah shook her head in disagreement but said no more. Something within her wanted to say, *We'll decide for ourselves.* But there was another urging deep inside her, prompting her to think long and hard about this, even suggest that Gid discuss it with Dat himself.

"Death haunts me, Aunt Lizzie," she surprised herself in saying.

Lizzie reached over to pat her hand again. " 'Cause of your mamma?"

"Maybe so . . . and Mary Ruth's first beau, Elias. One just never knows. . . ."

Lizzie fell silent as she stroked Hannah's hand.

Hannah felt the need to fill the stillness, though. "Seems nobody knows for sure and for certain what's waitin' for us on the other side."

Lizzie frowned. "Over Jordan?"

Hannah nodded. "I wish this wasn't so troubling." She continued on, sharing that she'd struggled privately since childhood with the issue of death. "Some days I wish we could simply live forever, the way Adam and Eve were created to."

"Without aging?" Here Aunt Lizzie broke into a winning smile. "Just think, Dawdi John's beard might be dragging on the ground if that's the way the dear Lord intended things to be for us now . . . since Adam fell from grace."

"Guess it was fallin' from grace that turned ev'rything topsy-turvy, ain't? If only Adam and Eve had obeyed God in the first place, things sure would be lots easier."

"Obedience, jah." Aunt Lizzie leaned forward. "Let me tell ya what I think."

For the next half hour or so, Hannah listened as her aunt shared things she'd never heard from an Amishwoman before, except for the one time she'd accidentally stumbled onto Mamma saying late-night prayers. Now she was fairly sure that what Lizzie believed about the Lord Jesus coming to earth to die to offer eternal life was precisely what Mamma had also believed.

Hearing Aunt Lizzie say that we *can* be saved and know it without falling into the sin of pride, that the "Good Book teaches this," Hannah wondered what Gid might think if he knew. And she worried if Gid and the brethren got wind of Lizzie's beliefs, that her newly ordained husband would feel obligated to speak about them to Bishop Bontrager.

Could dear Aunt Lizzie be in danger of the shun? A cold shiver flew up Hannah's back.

◆

Nearly as excited as the children had been at breakfast, Leah rode along in Dat's sleigh to Georgetown School after lunch. Sadie, too, had been invited to attend the Christmas play, but she'd awakened with sniffles and decided to stay home. Aunt Lizzie and Dawdi John had also been given homemade invitations, but the children didn't expect Dawdi to make the effort to venture out on such a blustery day—none of the family did. And Aunt Lizzie had felt she ought to stay put in case Hannah went into early labor, as she had with the first two little ones. Fortunately, she was only a holler away in the little log house.

"Lydiann said she was awful nervous 'bout the play when I took her and Abe to school this morning," Leah said as they rode along.

Dat made his familiar grunt, which meant he'd heard but was somewhat preoccupied.

"There'll be lots of parents on hand, I'm sure." She made yet another attempt to have conversation with her father, since they scarcely ever found themselves alone anymore.

"I hope we won't be expected to sing the *weltlich* carols," Dat said, glancing at her.

"Well, why not the more lighthearted ones?" She found this interesting.

He kept his face forward just now, and Leah thought she saw the corners of his mouth twitch.

"Dat? Did I speak out of turn?"

His chest rose at the question. "No . . . no, that's fine."

She wished he'd talk about whatever was bothering him. Was he missing Mamma still, just as *she* was? Leah wouldn't be so bold as to bring up such a thing. All the same she wondered, though Mamma's home-going seemed a distant memory to her.

"I'm sure Lydiann and Abe are havin' trouble keeping their minds on their school-work right now," she said.

"They're prob'ly getting the schoolhouse ready, I'd guess."

"Jah, puttin' up string across the room to hang up letters spelling out 'Merry Christmas to Everyone!' " she said, glad Dat was talking freely.

He sighed. "Abe said he was mighty happy with the name he drew for Christmas."

"I hope he didn't tell ya who." She had to smile at this. "Abe's quite the little man . . . as thoughtful as any child I've known."

"But he speaks his mind when he wants to."

She knew this was so.

Dat kept the horse going at a steady pace—just right for a quiet talk on a snowy afternoon.

"Sadie seems to be settling in here again, ain't so?" she asked, sticking her neck out a bit.

"I daresay she's missin' her husband something awful." Dat paused, bent his head low, and then continued. "She and I have something in common for the first time."

Leah hadn't thought of it quite like that. But Dat was right. Both he and Sadie shared a great sense of sorrow.

———◆———

Lydiann took her seat as the teacher rang the bell on her desk. She couldn't keep a straight face, because Dat and Leah were right here in this very room, sitting in the back with lots of other folk—parents, grandparents, aunts, uncles, cousins, and babies. It looked to her as if nearly all of Gobbler's Knob had turned out for the school play.

Her first-grade cousin, Essie Ebersol, stood at the front of the room and began to recite a poem. " 'Baby Jesus, meek and mild . . .' "

When Essie returned to her seat, Lydiann knew it was time for a group of older boys to perform their skit. Following that, the boys sang "The First Noel" quite nicely, she thought. *For boys with squeaky voices.*

Soon the teacher started another carol, "Hark! The Herald Angels Sing," and everyone joined in heartily. Lydiann turned quickly and spied Mamma Leah with Dat, both of them singing and smiling.

What a wonderful-gut time of year, she thought. Looking over a few rows, she noticed Abe twiddling his fingers but singing, nonetheless. She couldn't remember ever hearing her little brother's voice in song—at Preaching service, Abe always sat on the side with the menfolk, next to Dat.

She squirmed in her seat a bit, thinking ahead to what was to come. Would Carl remember his lines? *Will I?*

When the final note was sung, the teacher nodded to her and Carl, and to all the angels, shepherds, and wise men. Quickly the angelic host lined up behind Joseph and Mary, and the teacher brought out a wooden manger containing a small sack of potatoes wrapped in a blanket.

"Christ is born!" announced one of the shepherds.

"He is the King of kings," said a wise man.

Carl took a deep breath. "Let us all rejoice with the angels this day."

"Come see the place where the Christ child lay," added Lydiann, feeling a flutter of excitement as she reached down and lifted the holy bundle into her arms. She was thankful their teacher had wrapped the potatoes very tightly. This way, she could hold the "baby" on her lap.

They went on to recite their rhymed verses, and Lydiann was pleased because she—and Carl—remembered every single word.

When the play was over, each student gave a gift of fruit or a candy cane to every other student, and to the teacher. But getting a big hug from Dat and a kiss on the cheek from Mamma Leah was the best gift of all. Both Lydiann and Abe climbed happily into the second seat of Dat's sleigh and called to their friends, "Merry Christmas!"

"Same to you!" their friends called back.

———◆———

When they returned home, it was time for Lydiann to assist Mamma in cooking supper. Sadie was all wrapped up in a blanket, sitting on the rocking chair near the wood stove, so she wasn't feeling well enough to help. If Lydiann wasn't mistaken, it looked to her like her eldest sister had been crying.

She went and offered Sadie a big round orange. *"En hallicher Grischtdaag!*—a merry Christmas to you."

Sadie looked up and smiled, accepting the gift. *"Denki,"* she said softly.

And with that, Lydiann knew for sure and for certain Sadie wasn't only suffering from the sniffles.

Chapter Four

A midnight gale had come up and temperatures plummeted. Upon awakening to the dawn of Christmas, Leah was surprised at the thick layer of frost on the window as she lifted the green shade. Unable to peer out, she stared at the pretty pattern Jack Frost had painted. Once the sun rose over the eastern hills and its rays reached the house, the crust of ice would melt quickly. Then she would be able to see from this upstairs lookout what snowy new shapes the overnight drifting had created in the barnyard and beyond.

For now, though, she was eager to dress and hurry downstairs to make a special breakfast, one that would include baked oatmeal and raisins, baked eggs, and chocolate waffles with a homemade syrup of brown sugar and melted butter.

She lightly touched Sadie's sleeping form. "Merry Christmas to you, sister," she said softly, waiting for Sadie to rouse a bit. When she did, Leah asked if she felt well enough to help with milking, offering to take her place if she was still under the weather. But Sadie shooed her out of the room, saying she was just fine. Leah was surprised that Sadie was so adamant and determined to go out in the cold, especially when she'd felt too ill to attend the school play yesterday.

Making her way down the long stairs, she recalled Dat's remark about Abe and the drawing of names for today's gift exchange. She couldn't help but notice how gleeful her boy had been the past few days, but then he was downright happy most of the time. And, too, she was quite aware that both Lydiann and Abe had been slipping over to the Dawdi Haus a lot recently, and Aunt Lizzie and Dawdi John had been secretive about whatever the children were doing.

Going to the back door, she discovered the same hard coating of frost on the windowpane and knew there was no way to know what she might discover outside unless she yielded to curiosity and opened the

door. When she did so, she was amazed at
the sweeping, arclike hollows beneath the
base of each tree and the odd-shaped
swells of white along the lane that led
around to the bridge of the bank barn,
where Dat and Gid had evenly placed large
stones to rim the way. "Ach, somebody
needs to shovel a path to the barn," she
said to herself, surprised Dat wasn't up yet.

I'll make some coffee right quick, she decided, closing the door to get a fire going in
the wood stove. Reaching for the bundle of
wood Dat had conveniently stacked in the
utility room, probably before heading off to
bed, she realized suddenly just how cold it
was in the house. Why she hadn't noticed
before, she didn't know.

*Lydiann will be shivering . . . and won't be
shy about saying so,* she thought, wondering if Aunt Lizzie was up already next door,
stoking the fire so Dawdi John would
awaken to warmth.

Making haste to get the fire going in the
wood stove now, she smiled at whose name
she had drawn. What delightful surprises
this day held for all. She did wonder,
though, how Hannah, Gid, and the girls
would make it down the long, snow-drifted

hill to join them for the noon feast. More than likely, Dat would have to take the horse and sleigh up there to fetch them. She just hoped Hannah's baby wouldn't decide to come early, what with the main roads nearly impassable. *But no, I daresn't worry. Besides, Hannah's baby isn't due quite yet.*

When Dat still hadn't wandered into the kitchen fifteen minutes later, Leah decided to check on him to see if he had overslept. Making her way through the front room, she noticed his bedroom door was closed.

She hesitated to bother her father, but thinking he might be ill, she put her hand to the door and tapped gently. "Dat?" she called softly.

A slight shuffling sound followed, and then she heard his voice. "That you, Leah?"

"Jah."

"I'll be right out," he said, and she scurried back to the kitchen.

When the oatmeal had been poured into a greased pan and slid into the oven, Dat entered, looking somewhat disheveled. She offered him a cup of hot coffee, and he took it, blowing on it as he stood near the sink.

Abe joined them in the kitchen. "Looks

like I'm not the only late riser," Dat said with a quick smile. "Merry Christmas to ya both."

"And to you, too, Dat," she said, returning his enthusiasm.

Abe's eyes twinkled and he hurried to get his coat.

Sadie came downstairs at that moment, wearing a green choring dress and black apron with a rather bedraggled-looking navy blue sweater. "It'll be right nippy in the barn," she said, glancing down at the buttoned-up sweater, as if to explain the old wrap.

"Want some coffee?" Leah asked. "Or I can make hot cocoa, if you'd rather."

Sadie shook her head. "Coffee's fine."

"Did ya hear the wind howlin' last night?" Leah said as she poured a second cup of coffee, aware of Abe still tinkering around in the utility room.

Sadie nodded, glancing away, but not before Leah noticed a glistening in her sister's eyes. She suddenly felt sad and wondered if this first Christmas as a widow would be as hard on Sadie as Dat's first without Mamma had been.

She set about making hot cocoa for Abe and called to him when the hot drink was ready. He came immediately, face shining. "It's a right special day," he said with mis- chievous eyes. He reached for the cup. "Denki, Mamma."

Mamma . . . The name never ceased to warm her heart.

When they'd drained their cups, Sadie and Dat bundled up and headed outdoors with Abe. Dat shoveled a path as Sadie and Abe came behind with their brooms. Leah watched momentarily from the utility room, having closed the interior door to the kitchen so as not to allow heat to escape. *Please, Lord God, be ever near to my sor- rowing sister this day.*

While the oatmeal baked, she hurried to Dat's room to redd up and make his bed. But before she did, she went to the narrow bookshelf and reached for Mamma's Bible, not the big German family Bible stored in the corner cupboard in the kitchen, but the one Mamma had read repeatedly through the years. Leah noticed the leather wasn't as cold as she might have expected it to be on such a chilly day and wondered if Dat might have been holding this Bible in his strong hands . . . for quite some time, too, maybe.

Heartened at the thought, she moved to the window and read the underlined final verse in chapter fifty-four of the book of the prophet Isaiah: *No weapon that is formed against thee shall prosper; and every tongue that shall rise against thee in judgment thou shalt condemn. This is the heritage of the servants of the Lord, and their righteousness is of me, saith the Lord.*

The verse puzzled her no end, though she had read it repeatedly since first discovering Mamma's pen had marked it. What had this particular underlined passage meant to her mother? Leah was anxious to know.

Closing the Bible, she returned it to its place on the shelf. Then she smoothed out Dat's bedcovers, top quilt and all, and left to return to the kitchen. There she prepared the baked eggs, using Mamma's old muffin tins, placing the round pieces of toast, moistened with milk, inside and then breaking the eggs over the tops.

All the while she pondered the meaning of the verse, finding it peculiar Mamma would have contemplated it in such a way as to take pen to the Holy Bible. Was it possible Mamma had come under some verbal attack, possibly by the church brethren? If so, wouldn't Aunt Lizzie know?

Every tongue that shall rise against thee . . . Those words especially disturbed her. She knew she best cast aside her musings. *'Tis Christmas Day, for pity's sake.*

Sighing, she went to the foot of the stairs to check on Lydiann, only to see her standing at the top, fully dressed, hair combed and pulled back in a bun. "Happy Christmas, dear girl," Leah greeted her.

Lydiann smiled broadly. "Merry Christmas to you, Mamma." Then she added, " 'Twas awful cold when my feet touched the floor."

Leah nodded and had to smile. "Well, speakin' of cold, it might not be a bad idea for you to run out and take Sadie's place after a bit to let her come in and warm up. I'd hate for her to catch an even worse cold."

Lydiann headed down the steps toward her, eyes concerned. "Is Sadie gonna cry again today, do ya think?"

"Well, I hope not. We must be especially considerate toward her on our Lord's birthday," Leah replied, walking with Lydiann to the kitchen. She hurried to prepare the waffle batter, setting the big black waffle iron on the cookstove.

Leah felt at such a loss to explain Sadie's absence for all those years; the People simply did not speak of a shunning after the fact. She hoped Lydiann's curiosity over Sadie might soon subside. *Not just for my sake, but for all of us.*

◆

Leah was pleased when Lydiann willingly headed out to the barn to offer Sadie a rest. But when neither Lydiann nor Sadie came back, Leah bundled up to see what had happened. Reaching the barn, she found Abe and Lydiann looking down at one of the feed troughs—a wooden manger. Sadie, too, was listening with rapt attention as Dat described how the cows' tongues had smoothed the wood over time, making the wood of the manger "nice and smooth . . . fit for baby Jesus."

Surprised at her father's words, Leah stood quietly as she observed the little gathering, which included their three German-shepherd dogs—King, Blackie, and Sassafras—in the nearly balmy atmosphere of the barn's stable area.

"God put the notion in the animals'

heads?" Abe asked, touching the glistening wood with the full palm of his hand, clearly intrigued.

"Jah, I believe so." Dat stooped down, tugging on his long beard.

Lydiann looked up at Sadie just then, and Sadie put her arm around her young sister, who said, "The Lord God must've planned way ahead of time for Jesus to be born in a barn, ain't so?"

Dat nodded, even chuckled. "The Lord doeth all things well, and I daresay this is one of them."

Leah continued to watch silently as Dat spoke openly with the children. *A long time comin'*, she thought, ever so glad.

———◆———

Hours later, after Dat had gone to fetch Gid, Hannah, and their girls in his sleigh, and after Mary Ruth had arrived by Dan Nolt's car, their father had everyone gather in the front room. He seemed almost too eager to read the Christmas story from the Gospel of Luke before the noon meal.

But as intriguing as all this was, Leah was most captivated by the attentive way Aunt

Lizzie watched Dat during his reading of the old Bible. *Can it be she has feelings for Dat, too?*

After the noontime feast, and once all the dishes and utensils were washed, dried, and put away, the family was ready for the gift exchange Lydiann and Abe had been awaiting so patiently.

They assembled in the front room once again, and Abe promptly marched to Dat's side and presented his gift of a handwritten, homemade book. Dat smiled when he turned to the first page and saw the printed names and birth dates of each family member, along with several Scripture verses, all in Abe's own hand. "I learnt them from Aunt Lizzie," the boy explained, looking over at Lizzie and grinning.

Next Lydiann approached Leah. "I drew *your* name, Mamma," she said, holding out her gift.

"Oh, Lyddie, how perty!" Leah accepted the embroidered handkerchief.

"I made it myself," whispered Lydiann, "but with Aendi's help."

Leah hugged her girl close. "Denki, dear one . . . I'll treasure it for always."

"Look at the butterfly," Lydiann said,

pointing to a fanciful green butterfly suspended over a yellow rosebud.

"I see . . . and it's very nicely done." For a moment Leah likened it to the butterfly handkerchief hidden deep in her hope chest, although this one featured a simple embroidery stitch, not the elaborate cutwork style that Hannah had long-ago made for Sadie.

Glancing now at her elder sister, who was seated next to Hannah with eighteen-month-old Katie Ann on her lap, Leah wondered when or if she might return the beautiful hankie to Sadie. But no, the connection to Sadie's stillborn son might easily mar the holy day, and that would be heartless. She dismissed the idea quickly, at least for the time being.

When Aunt Lizzie was not so occupied with Dawdi John, Leah slipped to her side and gave Lizzie the gift she'd purchased. "I had your name," she whispered, handing her a small case filled to the brim with many colored spools of thread and sewing notions.

Lizzie was pleased. "Oh, just what I needed!" she said, giving Leah a kiss on the cheek. "Thank you ever so much."

Hannah and Gid's oldest daughter, three-year-old Ida Mae, giggled as she licked a candy cane. Squirming out of Sadie's lap, Katie Ann toddled to big sister, Ida, for repeated tastes. "That's awful nice of you to share your treat," Hannah said, touching Ida's chubby cheek.

Gid sat with his arm protectively draped behind his wife's chair, looking mighty pleased about the box of saws and other items given him by his father-in-law. Leah suspected Abe wanted to tell—in the worst way—how Dat had "kept at it" to win them at the auction.

"Now, don't be tellin' stories out of school," Dat was heard to say to his exuberant son.

Abe frowned comically and went to sit beside Leah. "My mouth's gonna get me in trouble yet," he told her softly.

She patted his arm. "You're just fine."

The merriment continued on through a good half of the afternoon, till time for milking rolled around again. Gid rose with Abram at four o'clock and told both Sadie and Abe to "stay put."

Not putting up a fuss, Sadie smiled her

thanks, and the two men left the house for the barn.

"I wonder if the manger is even smoother now," Abe whispered to Leah. "For baby Jesus' birthday, ya know."

Leah was touched by her boy's remark, and she pulled him into her arms. "Come here—and don't be sayin' you're too old for a big hug," she said, her heart truly gladdened by the day.

Chapter Five

On the walk to the barn, Abram was suddenly aware of the heavy moisture content
of the recent snow. Every tree branch, every
shrub, and even the roof of the old corncrib
sagged with the weight. Several large limbs
had snapped under the burden, and he
made a mental note to turn them into firewood tomorrow.

Meanwhile, he and Gid had the afternoon
milking to tend to, and feeling the cold
creep through his work jacket and trousers,
Abram quickened his pace toward the barn,
as did his son-in-law.

Inside, they washed down the cows' ud-
ders, pushed tin buckets beneath, and
perched themselves on low wooden stools,
talking in quiet tones as they milked by
hand. The dogs, all three of them, rested in
the hay nearby—Blackie eyed them fondly

and wagged his long tail—while Abram listened without commenting as Gid mentioned their desire to have a hex doctor at
the birthing of their third child. "Not in place
of a midwife, mind you . . . just in case
something goes wrong. What do ya think of
that?"

"Why ya askin' me?"

"Well, 'cause Hannah said she and Aunt
Lizzie had been talkin' it over."

Abram was fairly sure if Lizzie and
Hannah had hashed it out, as Gid said, that
Lizzie would've had her say and then some.
Still, he didn't want to butt in since Gid was
Hannah's husband and the man of his
house. Abram saw no point, really, in speaking his mind, because far as he knew, Gid
had heard through Lizzie what his stand on
powwowing was.

"You don't need my two cents' worth."

"No . . . no, Hannah and I want your opinion."

He toyed with saying straight out they
ought to have as much help with Hannah's
delivery as possible, especially if she was
feeling nervous for any reason. If that meant
having the powwow doctor, then all well and
good. He certainly didn't want to be held re-

sponsible for their making a bad decision, still too mindful of all that had gone wrong when Ida birthed Abe.

He went ahead and told Gid how he'd kicked himself for not having the Amish doctor on hand for Ida that terrible night. "I'd do things completely different now if I could." *Anything to have saved Ida's life. . . .*

Yet his wife's feelings had mattered, too. Ida's opinion had always mattered to him, thus the reason he'd let her have her say now and again, although he had managed to rule his roost, keeping the upper hand for the most part. Sadly that sort of approach had caused great strife and despair for his family, as he had seen all too clearly for some time now. Looking back, he realized how rigid he'd been about Leah's choice of a mate, and he kicked himself every time he thought of her being a maidel. He had been equally harsh with Mary Ruth, insisting on his own way when it appeared Hannah's twin was as content as can be—teaching English schoolchildren, boarding with the Nolts, and attending the Mennonite church. The truth pained him, making it difficult for him to stand by and watch the circum- stances unfold. On the other hand, he believed in the deep of his heart that his daughter had somehow found her intended way, although the path she trod no longer embraced the teachings of the Amish church. It wasn't that she didn't look Plain any longer; she did. But the manner Mary Ruth talked about the Lord God heavenly Father was somewhat foreign to his way of seeing things, though not to his Ida's . . . nor to Lizzie's. More and more, he was making the discovery that Ida's Lord was the same as Mary Ruth and Lizzie's, having spent many early morning hours reading and rereading his wife's well-loved Bible, particularly the passages she'd taken time to underline. Truth be known, he was learning far more than he'd ever expected from such an undertaking.

"Should I take this question up with the bishop?" Gid's voice broke the stillness.

Abram knew better than to encourage Gid to speak with Bishop Bontrager on the matter. Why, the whole thing could blow up in Gid's face . . . in all of their faces, really. The issue of sympathy healers was troublesome amongst the Amish—had the power to divide the church district right down the middle.

"Make up your own mind and stick with it. Do what you think is best for *your* family."

Gid went on to say that his mother was downright opposed and didn't think "white witchcraft" had any business being invited into the sacred places of their home. "*Mamm* has spoken out quite adamantly 'bout keepin' the hex doctors far from our door."

Abram nodded, considerate of Gid's position—stuck between the opinion of his wife and his mother. Not a good place to be for a young man of Gid's character and calling. Abram suggested Gid and Hannah talk further on it.

"Then you must not view powwowing as of the devil, like my mother does."

Gid had him there, and there was no telling how far this conversation might drift from its origins. "What's the Good Book say on it?" Abram surprised himself by asking but felt sure Gid knew him well enough not to hold such a question against him.

"I don't know. Haven't stumbled onto anything just yet."

Abram grunted, wishing he had something pertinent to add, but he didn't.

In the end, Gid would have to decide for

his family. Even so, Abram wondered what difference it made if the blue cohosh herb was used to induce labor when needed, nor did it bother him if a bit of necessary chanting went on. No bother at all. On the other hand, he couldn't get Ida's view on the matter out of his mind.

Mary Ruth sat with Hannah in the front room, near Lydiann and Abe, who were playing with their games at Leah's feet while snacking on the popcorn balls and hard candies they'd received as presents from their neighbors, the Peacheys. Mary Ruth was delighted to hold sweet little Katie Ann on her lap, especially because the toddler's usually bright eyes were looking mighty droopy just now, and Mary Ruth hoped the dear girl might give in to sleep right there in her arms. Oh, how she enjoyed Hannah's little ones, and the joy of being around them stirred up such eagerness as she looked ahead to the day when she might marry and become a mother herself. She wouldn't dare to think too far into the future, though, because she strongly believed the Lord had called her to teach. She was living the life she'd long wished for, sharing her book knowledge with youngsters who had thirsty minds, ever glad to be able to share the love of the Lord Jesus with her students through word and deed.

Holding Katie Ann and listening to Ida Mae's childish chatter helped fill the hours, as did spending the day with her sisters. She was rather relieved to see how well Sadie was doing now that she had been home these two months, and Leah, too, was smiling more genuinely than she had been at past Christmases, at least that Mary Ruth could recall.

" 'Tis awful nice of Gid to help Dat with milkin'," Leah told Sadie.

Sadie nodded, glancing at Abe. "Looks like more than one of us got to stay in where it's warm, ain't?"

To this, Abe looked up from his checkers and grinned. "I wouldn't have minded goin' out in the cold," he said. "I'm a strong one, I am."

This brought a round of "ohs," and Abe put his head down, visibly embarrassed.

"Won't be long and you'll be takin' Sadie's place all the time at milkin'," Lydiann spoke up, pausing in her play with her two faceless dolls.

"Now, Lyddie, that ain't for you to say," Sadie pointed out.

Mary Ruth found the exchange between Abe and Sadie to be amusing and, looking down, discovered Katie Ann had fallen limp in her arms. "Look who's tuckered out." She nudged Hannah.

Hannah smiled. "You've got a tender touch."

Mary Ruth scooted back in her chair, being careful not to relax too much lest the crook of her arm not support her precious niece.

◆

Some time later Lydiann's remark about Carl Nolt made Mary Ruth pay closer attention yet again to the conversation. Lyddie was mentioning Carl's New Year's Eve invitation—"He said his parents want all us Ebersols to have supper with them. Carl told me himself yesterday after the school play," Lydiann happily announced. "I know he meant it, because he's the sort of boy who doesn't fib. You can just tell."

"You're absolutely right about that," Mary

Ruth spoke up, certain Dottie must've shared this with Carl.

"Could ya ask about this, Mary Ruth?" Lydiann pleaded.

Leah stirred, appearing somewhat uncomfortable. "Well, dear one, I think we best wait to see if an invitation comes directly from Carl's parents."

"Jah, I think that's wise," Mary Ruth said, backing Leah up. "Wouldn't be right to just assume it."

"But you don't understand," Lydiann broke in. "Carl was sure . . . I *know* he was!"

Leah reached down and put a hand on Lydiann's shoulder, patting her. "Best not fret. There'll be plenty to do here at home this week while school's out."

"Plenty gut things to eat, too!" Abe piped up a bit too loudly.

Mary Ruth couldn't help but smile. Leah surely had her hands full with these two— that was easy to see—yet her sister seemed as content as ever she'd known her to be. For this, Mary Ruth was most grateful.

Sadie wandered out to the kitchen while the happy gathering continued in the front room. She poured fresh cow's milk into a saucepan and set it on the fire, stirring the milk slowly lest it scald. She would surprise her sisters and the children with hot chocolate.

From where she stood at the wood stove, she could see past the utility room, through the back door window, and out to the white expanse of snow in the barnyard. *When will I see Miriam Peachey again?* Miriam had been so compassionate to her through the scrutiny thus far. Though Sadie was expected to spend time with the older women in the church district whenever she left the house, it was primarily Miriam who had been appointed to oversee her comings and goings. This meant she couldn't go much of anywhere alone, except to visit Hannah and the children, or across the pasture and field to the Peacheys'. She terribly missed her long jaunts on foot, feeling like a caged bird at times.

Presently she stared at the snow weighing down the treetops. The bitter cold would surely visit them again tonight, and she thought of bringing in some wood to stack. Maybe she would tiptoe downstairs in the night to add some logs to the wood stove, like Dat used to before he moved to the downstairs bedroom at the quiet far end of the house. Now he no longer awakened at midnight or after, which meant the upstairs grew cold by morning, and Lydiann's sharp yelps could be plainly heard when she first stepped out of bed. Abe, on the other hand, was all boy—*strong,* as he had declared to all of them this afternoon, and afraid of nothing, least of all ice-cold plank flooring. He climbed jagged tree trunks and rough stone walls, even crawling halfway up the silo one day last October, to Leah's dismay and Dat's forced laughter, though Dat's face had turned ever so pasty. *Some boys are just born tougher than others,* Dat had said with a healthy dose of pride, but Sadie decided, then and there, that Dat viewed Abe's daring from the standpoint of previously having raised only girls.

All that aside, both Lydiann and Abe were the happiest of children, and their cheerful faces reminded her of earlier days growing up in this old farmhouse, when she and Mamma had been ever so close, spending all day together cooking and baking, cleaning and talking . . . as fond of each other as Lydiann and Abe were of Leah now.

"Anybody for hot chocolate?" She sang

the question as she carried the tray into the front room.

"Ach, we'll come to you," Leah said, meeting her halfway. "No need to risk spills with youngsters."

That was Leah, always thinking on the practical side. No wonder Mamma had chosen her to raise Abe and Lydiann. No wonder Aunt Lizzie looked ever so kindly on Leah; each time Sadie happened to glance at her aunt, she was aware of that deep admiration.

———————◆———————

Tuesday, December 25, 1956
Dear Diary,

I feel sure it won't be long now and our new baby will make his or her entrance into this world. Goodness, it would be awful nice if we'd have a boy to help Gid and Dat and young Abe with the outdoor work. Leah encourages Lydiann to be out in the barn and whatnot more than I see necessary. But, more and more, Leah and Dat are having equal say in the raising of Lydiann and Abe, seems to me. I sup-

pose that is both good and bad, although I'd have to agree with Gid that Leah dotes on Abe rather too much. She's awful protective of him, even saying he isn't old enough to go ice fishing with Dat, Gid, and Smitty come this Saturday, but Abe begged and pleaded and got Dat to intervene but quick. So they're all planning to go over to Blackbird Pond early that morning, more than likely as soon as milking's through. I hope I have this baby before then. Most uncomfortable I'm becoming!

Gid and I have together decided there's nothing whatsoever wrong with having the Hexedokder wait in the front room when I go into labor with this one. Just knowing that, I'm already feeling much better . . . whether or not my mother-in-law's in favor of this. She's beginning to irk me some, what with all the say-so she's been given— by the bishop, no less—in overseeing Sadie's Proving. Give some folk a bit of authority and they crave even more. I hope Sadie behaves herself, truly I do, but it's hard to know what's going on in her head, let alone her heart. She seems more brooding than I remember her to be . . . and no wonder, given what she's gone through.

Last night I had a troubling dream, one I don't know what to make of. All of us were gathered, sniffling, in a small, dark room, surrounded by un- recognizable sounds. Dat's face was drained of color, and he was struck dumb, unable to speak. Leah, though I recognized only her form, stood tall, like a beacon of light in the dimness. Since I don't normally have such dreams, I wonder if this was a result of all the sweets I've been nibbling on this week. Then again, I hope it's not a bad omen. For sure and for certain, we've had our share of heartache round here.

Respectfully,
Hannah

Chapter Six

Midmorning Thursday Abram and Gid cut down the dead branches left dangling by the heavy snows, spending a good part of the sunny but cold morning dragging chopped limbs into the woodshed to dry. Abram enjoyed working with his son-in-law and he told him so. "You just don't know how lonely an old man I'd be without ya workin' by my side."

Gid looked at him cockeyed, as if to indicate he wasn't used to hearing such soft words from a man. "You ain't old, Abram."

"Oh, but I feel my age ev'ry morning when I rise. Besides that, my baby boy is seven today."

Gid went about stacking the branches, remaining silent, as if waiting for him to continue.

"Next farm auction, you and I oughta go

together. Abe will prob'ly jump at the chance to miss a day of school, too, 'cept Leah will frown on that." He rambled on, saying how well both Abe and Lydiann were doing in their studies. "I can only hope they don't get the notion to seek after higher education like Mary Ruth did."

Abram wouldn't admit to worrying like an old hen some days about losing more of his family to the fancy English world. No way, nohow, did it look like Mary Ruth would ever give up her new life, with its electricity, fast cars, and Bible studies. Fact was, she was getting herself in deeper all the time, what with spending nearly all her free time with the doctor's elder son, Robert. Well, he had no intention of letting his mind wander in that direction, so he straightened himself and asked Gid what he thought about asking Gid's brother-in-law Sam Ebersol to join them for ice fishing on Saturday.

Gid nodded his assent.

"I'll ride over there and talk to Sam this afternoon, then," Abram said. "We'll have us some tasty fish to fry up for supper this weekend." The thought of the catch and the time of fellowship sent his spirits soaring.

◆

Following the noon meal, Sadie dried and put away the dishes and utensils, then headed to the front room, where she sat to finish stitching a floral design on a set of pillowcases that had arrived a month ago in the trunk containing her wedding gifts and small household linens from Indiana. When the sudden sound of knocking came at the front door, she was surprised to see the mailman standing on the porch.

"Good afternoon," the man wearing the familiar postal hat said. "Sorry to bother you on this cold day, but I thought it best to be extra careful with *this* letter delivery." He held out to her a stained envelope with the words *Return to sender* stamped across the front. "Looks like this here got lost somehow or other," he said, pointing out the October 1947 postmark, "nine years ago now."

Sadie nodded her astonished thanks and stood at the door holding the letter marred and frayed by the years. Upon careful examination of its terribly faded writing, she was stunned to realize it was an unopened letter from Leah to Jonas Mast. Somehow it had found its way to the Ebersol Cottage.

Could this be the letter I threw away?

Turning it over, she saw the envelope was soiled, as if it had, indeed, been in a pile of rubbish at one time. Yet how on earth had it resurfaced after nearly a decade?

Impossible, she thought, noticing the letter was still sealed shut.

Having attempted to bury the shameful deed deep within her forgetfulness, she felt convicted as she stared at the envelope, evidence of her wrongdoing.

What should I do now?

She and Leah had forged a new relationship these months since Sadie's return, and she was far too hesitant to open up an old and hurtful wound. Besides, there'd been many letters flying back and forth between Leah and Jonas when this letter was written.

She'd thrown it away once in the heat of anger; why not discard it again? Better yet . . . burn it. Coming clean about this dreadful thing would serve no purpose now. Best to leave things be, let the truth remain concealed and her sin covered up once and for all.

Or, better still, she could simply slip the letter into the mailbox for Leah to discover on her own. No confession required. Even though Leah might wonder why Jonas had never opened the letter, or why it was being returned all these years later, Sadie's part in its disappearance would remain undiscovered. Besides, wasn't she already paying for past sins? The imposed Proving was proof, and she could never ever go back and right all the wrongs.

Nagging thoughts tormented her as she paced the floor. After all, this letter was by no means her property. Leah deserved to have it returned to her with a full apology.

What will good-hearted Leah think of me? Will she despise me? She cringed at the prospect of the confession Leah surely deserved.

Yet the fact Leah seemed so jovial, what with today being Abe's birthday and all, made Sadie feel her sister might take the news of the long-lost letter awful hard.

Not today, she thought. Nothing good would come of the truth this day. Heart pounding, she slipped the letter into her dress pocket and hurried upstairs, where she deposited it between several layers of clothing in her own drawer in the tall bureau.

Feeling justified in her choice to ignore this for the time being, with Leah's best interest at heart, Sadie hurried back downstairs and picked up her sewing with trembling hands.

———◆———

Leah was glad to get out and breathe some fresh air that afternoon. Abe and Lydiann were filled with chatter during the buggy ride to visit Uncle Jesse Ebersol and his family, and Leah was hoping her dearest friend, Adah, might be on hand, as well. Sadie had also agreed to come along, though not as eagerly as Leah would have thought, seeing as they'd all been rather cooped up in the house. For her part, Aunt Lizzie had looked a bit droopy in the face when Leah announced they were heading over to Jesse's for an afternoon visit. Lizzie felt she ought to stay home with Dawdi John—something it seemed to Leah was becoming her lot in life. Leah felt a twinge of sadness at the thought of Aunt Lizzie once again missing out on an opportunity to do the kind of visiting she so thoroughly enjoyed, and Leah promptly decided she would offer to stay behind next outing.

"Too bad Lizzie couldn't join us," Dat said when they were about halfway there.

"She's such a kindhearted soul, never complains 'bout tending to Dawdi's needs," Leah agreed.

Dat turned and smiled at her full in the face. "Sounds like someone else I know." He clicked his tongue and the horse sped up some.

"Oh, for goodness' sake," Leah said, catching on.

Sadie, sitting to Leah's left, patted her sister's shoulder. "Jah, 'tis for goodness' sake!"

Dat said no more, and Leah was suddenly conscious of Lydiann's voice in the seat behind her. "You daresn't tell nobody," Lydiann was saying, soft and low, to her brother.

"I won't promise not to tell," Abe said. "That's girl talk."

"No . . . no, now you listen to me," Lydiann's voice grew louder for a moment, then softer.

From that, Leah assumed Lydiann was cupping her hand around Abe's ear.

Evidently she was not to be privy to the rest
of this furtive conversation, and she wasn't
so sure she cared to be, especially when the
name of Carl Nolt was mentioned several
times in the space of the next few seconds.

Leah remembered what she had been
thinking and doing as a girl Lydiann's age.
Nearly all her waking hours had been spent
working around the animals—feeding and
watering them, cleaning the stalls, working
with Dat in the fields, too. Thankfully
Mamma had birthed Abe, which meant
Lydiann could learn to cook and sew at a
young age, unlike Leah, who had never attended a quilting frolic till she was nearly
sixteen. She smiled, recalling that first quilting, how she'd pulled up a chair to the enormous frame where the colorful Diamond-in-
the-Square pattern was to be stitched. So
much water had passed under the bridge
since that September day. Truly now she
was her own person, with the Lord God's
help, and mighty glad of it, too. Gone were
the days of longing for what she didn't have,
and she was as content as when she had
been growing up under Dat's and Mamma's
watchful eyes on their peaceful farm.

Sadie startled her out of her reverie. "Oh, lookee there, Leah. Adah's come."

Sure enough, dear Adah was getting down out of the family carriage, her two young sons already scurrying about as she turned to wave.

She looks so happy, thought Leah. Adah's husband, Sam, Leah's first cousin, was a hardworking and kind man, and as Sam and Adah picked their way through the snow toward the big clapboard farmhouse, Leah recognized again how nice it was that Adah was now her cousin, as well as her closest friend.

"If Adah and Sam are here, don't ya think Smitty and Miriam might just show up, too?" Leah asked, hoping so for Sadie's sake, since heavy snow had kept any of them from tromping through the drifts to visit the Peachey farm the past few days. Smitty had driven over in his sleigh to deliver pretty bags of hard candy and nuts for Lydiann and Abe on Christmas Eve, but none of them had ventured out on foot to take baked goods to Miriam Peachey, who, she'd heard, was looking ahead to vacating the main farmhouse and moving into the Dawdi Haus come spring. Dorcas, their youngest, and her husband, Sam Ebersol's best friend, Joseph Zook, and little ones planned to take over the Peachey farm. From what Dat had told Leah, Smitty wasn't quite ready to throw in the towel and fully retire; he would keep a hand in shoeing horses, gradually turning over more of his customers to Gid as time went by.

As Dat brought the horse to a stop, Lydiann broke the stillness, telling Abe what Carl had recently told her at school. "A two-year-old Amish neighbor boy named Johnnie Weaver drank some kerosene and had to be rushed to the emergency room last week," she said.

"No foolin'?" Abe replied.

"I guess he was okay once he got some oxygen."

"Why'd he want to drink something so awful?" asked Abe.

To this Leah said nothing, enjoying the innocent exchange as she hopped down from the buggy and fell in step with Sadie.

"It's beyond me why," said Lydiann. "But you can ask Carl 'bout it when we see him on New Year's Eve."

Lydiann may be sadly disappointed, thought Leah, fairly sure that even if they were invited to the Nolts' place for a meal, Dat would decline.

Sadie noticed Uncle Jesse's face light up when he came to the back door and saw who was there. Her uncle grabbed Dat and slapped him on the back, mighty glad indeed to see his younger brother. And right away she spotted Miriam Peachey over at the table, whispering to Aunt Mary Ebersol, pointing their way. *Perhaps they've come to celebrate Abe's birthday, too,* thought Sadie.

Sadie's guess turned out to be true when Aunt Mary brought out a bowl of butterscotch pudding, as well as a rich chocolate pie, hermits, and pecan drops. Sadie helped Aunt Mary and Miriam set out a stack of plates and the necessary utensils, but when it came time to serve the desserts, only Lydiann, Abe, and Adah's boys, along with the women folk, sat down to eat. The men—Uncle Jesse, Dat, Smitty, and Sam— all stood around the wood stove talking Dutch. Sadie didn't wish to eavesdrop, but she couldn't help but hear Dat inviting Uncle Jesse and Cousin Sam to join in Saturday's ice-fishing outing.

Sadie couldn't see what was so appealing about that. *What's the point of sitting outside and freezing yourself for a couple of fish?*

Miriam slid in next to her on the wooden bench, reaching for the butterscotch pudding. "Your mamma loved her puddings," Miriam said, glancing at Sadie but then looking over at Lydiann and Abe, across the table.

"Did she have a favorite?" asked Abe.

Miriam paused and frowned a moment. "Well, now, I'll bet your big sister Sadie might know that."

Sadie smiled, recalling many happy hours making a variety of custards and puddings in Mamma's big kitchen. "She loved the smell of chocolate pudding, that's for sure. But a favorite? I guess I'd have to say either graham-cracker or date pudding."

"Oh jah," added Miriam. "Your mamma loved her date pudding, she did."

Lydiann had both her elbows on the table now as she stared across at Miriam. "Our first mamma was your best friend, ain't so?" she said.

Miriam blushed all shades of red. "Well,

I'd have to say I thought of her as my closest friend, jah."

"And I'd have to say my best friend's a boy," Lydiann piped up in response. "A Mennonite boy!"

Abe clapped his hand over his mouth, looking at Lydiann, who must have realized how she'd sounded. "Best be eatin' more and talkin' less," he said, repeating one of Dawdi's sayings as he poked her in the ribs.

Adah's little boys were busy with their bowls of pudding and too small to have caught the embarrassing banter between Abe and Lydiann. But Miriam hadn't missed it, not one iota; Sadie knew this because she'd heard a gasp escape Miriam's lips.

"Are ya havin' a happy birthday, Abe?" Miriam asked, her voice pitched higher than usual.

Sadie felt as though she might lose her composure and start laughing, although she was ever so sure such an outburst might not be the wisest thing for a widow in mourning. Besides that, Miriam was sitting only a few inches away from her. What would she say if she also knew of Sadie's reluctance to return Leah's letter and make a heartfelt apology?

Thoughts of the rigid period, penance for her sins, calmed her quickly, and she sat back and became an observer, immersing herself in the cheerful chatter, especially between the birthday boy and his next-oldest sister. Sadie's gaze drifted to Leah. To think she had, all those long, sad years, assumed Sadie had been married to Jonas, yet she showed Sadie not a hint of past bitterness now. Today especially, Sadie found herself wishing for a tongue-lashing from her sister, if not worse. Truly, Leah exemplified a forgiving spirit, just as Mamma had all her days, but surely there were limits even for someone like Leah.

There, in the midst of the laughter and the celebrating, Sadie felt as sad as could be, missing both her husband and mother. She'd thought she would have a lifetime with Harvey, and here she was a widow. Had she taken their wedded happiness for granted? She felt torn between longing for Harvey and believing she'd squandered Mamma's final years, yet had she stayed put in Gobbler's Knob with Mamma, she never would have met and fallen in love with her Harvey. Oh, sometimes there was just

no sorting through emotions so raw and unnerving.

When the dishes were cleared away,
washed, and dried, Sadie sat in the front
room with Miriam, glad to be alone with
Mamma's bosom friend. "How are ya feelin'
this week, it bein' Christmas and all?" asked
Miriam, touching the back of Sadie's hand.

"Well, it's not the happiest Christmas I've
ever had," she admitted. "But it's *wunder-
baar*-gut being back home in Gobbler's
Knob. I've been enjoying the fun with
Lydiann and Abe."

Miriam nodded, her eyes intent on Sadie.
"But ya must be thinking 'bout your loss,
too."

Sadie looked down at her black apron, so
much a part of her daily attire. It was cut
from the same bolt of fabric as her mourning dress, making it difficult to tell where
one began and the other ended. "Some
days I think I might wear black the rest of
my life." *For all the deaths . . .* She didn't
say what she was really thinking, because
she'd confided only in Leah regarding the
many stillbirths.

" 'Course you'd be thinkin' thataway,"

Miriam said, sighing. "Harvey's passing is still fresh in your mind."

"He was a good man," Sadie said. "He never lost his temper that I know of, not once. He spoke kindly of everyone, and he got along famously with all his siblings."

Miriam listened, her gaze not straying from Sadie's. "How many brothers and sisters?"

"Five brothers and three sisters." Lest Miriam wonder why Harvey's siblings hadn't invited her to live with one of them, Sadie explained that, after his death, she had felt the Lord God was calling her home to Lancaster County.

"Oh, such a blessed thing to hear, Sadie! Does our bishop know of this?"

"No . . . I said not a word." She wouldn't reveal she cared not one whit for Bishop Bontrager, not as far as she was into the Proving now. If he knew the full truth about her, would he consider even this punishment too slight? Surely he would, but Sadie couldn't bear much more, most days wishing she could simply blend into the mopboards.

"I'm thinkin' he oughta know," Miriam was saying. " 'Tis high time."

"Please, no. . . . Let's just keep that between us . . . and my family. No need to tell
the bishop." She felt so strongly about this,
tears sprang up.

"Ach, Sadie, I'm ever so sorry I said a
word." Miriam leaned forward. "I'm just awful glad you're back with us, and I'm sure
your father feels the same."

All Sadie could do was nod, her heart
heavy under a weight of her own making.

Chapter Seven

There was a special quietude at the midafternoon hour Lorraine Schwartz had always taken pleasure in, especially in summertime when the heat of the day required a catnap or, at least, a rest from the fierce sun. This Friday, though, was not to be compared in the slightest with the dog days of late July or August. The old year was dying fast, and she had drawn the curtains and curled up by the roaring fire Henry had kindly built for her in the handsome tiled fireplace not too many feet from her easy chair. With a cup of chamomile tea in hand, she had been reading the Scriptures until the telephone's ringing prompted her to rise and pick up the black receiver.

"Schwartz residence. Lorraine speaking."

"Hello, Lorraine. It's Dottie Nolt."

"Oh, how are you today?"

"We're just fine, thanks. How was your Christmas?"

"Quiet . . . but very nice. You?"

Dottie shared how she and Dan had enjoyed watching Carl unwrap his presents and that their son had been especially pleased at receiving a new sled. "But the reason I'm calling is to invite you and Henry for supper on New Year's Eve."

"Well, how thoughtful of you." Lorraine knew they had no plans whatsoever. "I'll check with my husband, but I think it's safe to say we'll accept. Thank you, Dottie. What can I bring?"

"Just yourselves. This is Dan's and my treat. We're inviting several neighbors, and Mary Ruth will be here, as well, so please extend the invitation to your son Robert."

"I will indeed."

"We also plan to invite Mary Ruth's family."

"That'll be nice to get better acquainted," said Lorraine.

Minutes later, when Henry came in from the clinic, she shared with him Dottie's kind invitation.

He stiffened visibly. "You didn't accept, did you?"

"Well, yes, I did." She was puzzled by his response.

Henry shook his head. "Call back and decline . . . say we have other plans."

"But we don't, dear. We would simply be alone on New Year's Eve, unless, of course, Robert should decide to stay home and not spend the evening with Mary Ruth. But I hardly think he'll want to do that."

Again Henry shook his head, frowning deeply. "Please call Dottie back, Lorraine."

His words reached her ears, but it was her memory that served her best. Henry was resistant, most likely, because the Nolts were mainly responsible for her renewed interest in church.

It was Robert's arrival at the front door that brought the conversation to a quick end, for which Lorraine was grateful. And when the first thing out of his mouth was "Dottie Nolt's having a New Year's Eve dinner party, and we're all invited," she was secretly relieved.

That said, Henry dropped his opposition. *Good,* she thought, *no need for me to embarrass myself with a return phone call to Dottie.* Robert obviously had more influence over Henry than she ever would.

◆

Gid paced the floor in the front room of the log house, stopping now and then to keep Ida Mae and Katie Ann occupied with their toys. He was nearly tempted to stand with his ear to the door of the birthing room, where he felt sure Hannah was in the final throes of labor. Against his mother's wishes, he had summoned one of the men hex doctors, who sat not but a few yards from him on a rocking chair, watching the girls play. Hannah had been disappointed to discover that Old Lady Henner, the most powerful Amish doctor in the area, no longer made house visits, so they'd had to settle for this solemn-looking man.

At least he's someone to talk to, he thought, carrying *The Budget* over and offering a section of the newspaper to the older man. "Got any relatives out in Ohio?" he asked, hoping to make small talk.

"Two cousins."

"Ever go 'n' visit?"

"Nope."

Not so keen on conversing with a brick wall, Gid wandered to the kitchen, poured himself a tall glass of water, and stood at

the back door, staring out at the open
woods, deprived now of leaves. The sky
had opened up some, and he was grateful
for the light, conscious as he was at this
moment of the seasonal rhythms of his own
life.

This waiting was difficult, a good test of
his patience, and he contemplated the Old
Ways: the father-to-be hiding behind a
newspaper, uninvolved, or pacing the floor
somewhere in the house. Hannah had once
told him there were some women who simply slipped behind a bush of a summer and
had their wee babes unattended. He
flinched at the thought of darling Hannah
having to birth *her* babies that way. Not as
long as he could ride for a midwife—and, in
this case, the hex doctor, too—would his
wife give birth alone. Leah had planned on
being on hand, as well, but hearing of
Hannah's insistence on having the hex doctor come, Leah had hastily changed her
mind, to Hannah's disappointment.

When the cries of a newborn pierced the
air, he felt strangely relieved that the midwife had managed to deliver his son or
daughter without the help of the man in the
sitting room.

Hurrying to the bedroom door, Gid waited for word to come from the midwife. When it did, he was told he and Hannah had a third daughter. "She's a rosy one," the midwife said, motioning for him to enter the room.

He made a beeline for his wife, leaning down to kiss Hannah's brow, then cupping her chin in his hand. "*Ich lieb dich,* Hannah." He pushed back a wispy strand of her strawberry-blond hair.

"Oh, Gid, I love *you.*" She held up his new daughter, now wrapped in a thin blanket. "Awful perty, she is."

"Have ya thought of a name?"

Hannah smiled up at him sweetly from the bed. "I think it's your turn."

He had been pondering this and asked what Hannah thought of Miriam, after his mother. "We could call her Mimi for short."

Nodding, Hannah said it was a wonderful-good name. "I like it."

So it was settled, and although he'd hoped for a son this time around—with the name Mathias all picked out to honor Dawdi Byler—Gid was most grateful Hannah and the baby were all right. Truth be told, he was altogether ready to thank the hex doctor for his time and send him on his way.

———◆———

Leah was overjoyed at the news, her-
alded by Gid himself, of the birth of little
Mimi Peachey, and by Saturday morning
Leah had held Hannah's darling baby several times already. Now she sat in the
kitchen near the wood stove with Aunt
Lizzie while Dat, Abe, and a group of men
headed over to Blackbird Pond for a morning of ice fishing. She had cautioned Dat,
privately, to keep his eye on adventuresome
Abe, this being the boy's first such winter-
time experience.

"Oh, he'll be just fine," Aunt Lizzie had
said when Leah told her of her concern.

"I s'pose I worry too much."

"Jah, but then all mothers do," Lizzie
replied with a knowing smile.

She had noticed for some time now that
Aunt Lizzie no longer called her "honey-
girl," as she had all her growing-up years
and beyond. Did she think Leah too old for
the nickname? She didn't know and dismissed the thought as they settled into their
study of Scripture, reading aloud the entire
fifty-fourth chapter of the book of Isaiah.
When Leah came to the final verse, the one

she'd found underlined in Mamma's old Bible, she asked Aunt Lizzie about it. "Do you have any idea why Mamma would have marked this one?"

Lizzie looked down for a time, then, raising her face, she said slowly, "My sister Ida—your dear mamma—was rebuked harshly by Preacher Yoder, a good many years back." She paused and sighed, her hand at her throat, and then continued. "Your mamma went to speak with Deacon Stoltzfus one day, unbeknownst to any of us—"

"Not even Dat?"

"Abram would've put a quick stop to it had he known."

"Why'd Mamma go to speak to the brethren?"

Lizzie put her finger in the Bible to mark the page. "Well, she had oodles of questions . . . passages in the Good Book puzzled her no end."

"Did she share this with you?"

Lizzie nodded. "Oh, we had our talks, just the two of us."

Leah held back a bit, not wanting to push too much. "I hope Mamma got her answers."

Lizzie straightened in her chair and slowly opened the Bible yet again. "That she did . . . and then some."

Leah inhaled deeply and reread the underlined passage. *No weapon that is formed against thee shall prosper; and every tongue that shall rise against thee in judgment thou shalt condemn.*

According to Aunt Lizzie, Mamma had gone over Dat's head, taking her issues to the preacher, of all things, who apparently admonished her to remain silent. Mamma had been judged for her curiosity . . . no, for her intense hunger for the Lord Jesus, a hunger Leah now shared for "the living Bread" as she read through Mamma's cherished Bible.

"The worst of it," Lizzie added, "was that Ida lost her peace."

"She spoke up?"

"Talked back . . . kept askin' even more questions, trying to defend herself when she was to be silent," Lizzie explained. "Not a gut idea, I should say. And for this she was threatened with the shun."

The air went out of Leah and she began to understand more fully Mamma's tremendous pain during Sadie's seemingly endless shunning. When she had composed herself, she noticed a tear roll down Aunt Lizzie's face.

"Sometimes it's ever so hard. . . ."

Leah reached out a hand to comfort Lizzie. "Did the preachers succeed in putting the *Bann* on Mamma?"

"They came close . . . but Abram managed to get the upper hand with her, at least till all the dust had settled and the bishop wasn't keeping such a close eye on them." Lizzie attempted to blink back more tears but failed.

Leah offered her a handkerchief from beneath her own sleeve, feeling sorry for bringing up such a painful topic.

———◆———

Leah listened as Lydiann excitedly repeated herself about "goin' to eat supper at Carl's house tonight." The family was all bundled up, and both buggy seats were rather full and spilling over, what with Abe on Leah's lap and Lydiann and Sadie bunched up together so Dat, Aunt Lizzie, and Dawdi John could squeeze into the front seat.

Quite surprisingly, a handwritten invitation had arrived in the mail from Dan and Dottie Nolt on Friday. To Leah's further amazement, Dat had instructed her to accept. How all this had come about, she was unsure, although they had been sufficiently warned by Lydiann, hadn't they? Still, Leah found it interesting that Carl had managed to get his parents to invite Amish folk for a New Year's Eve supper, even with Mary Ruth's help. Leah could only hope they as a family weren't sitting ducks to be influenced toward Mennonite ways. That would not go over whatsoever with Dat.

Suddenly feeling playful, she bounced her knees, and Abe laughed. "Mamma's got awful bony knees," he said as she jostled him.

Dawdi John craned his neck in their direction. "Ya best be thankful you ain't sittin' on *my* knees, young man."

To this Lydiann let out a giggle. "Oh, Abe . . . I say you oughta be glad ya have a place to sit at all. Or maybe you'd rather walk."

"Well, it ain't so far to the Nolts' place," Abe shot back.

"Remember when Abe was a little tyke?"

Dat said more to Lizzie than to the rest of them. "I used to balance him and Lydiann both on my knees."

"Oh, I remember," Lydiann said.

Leah had to smile. "I don't think that's quite possible, dear."

"But I *do*!" Lydiann insisted.

Dawdi John chimed in, "Well, now, ya must be a mighty *schmaert* one to recall what happened when you was hardly out of diapers."

"Ach, Dawdi!" Lydiann said a bit too loudly.

"Now, Lyddie," Dat scolded over his shoulder.

"Shh," whispered Leah, patting the heavy woolen robe on top of Lydiann's lap.

Lydiann continued muttering but did not say anything more, and Leah was grateful. It wouldn't do to have a lippy Lydiann on board, not this night. With Dat's word of rebuke, silence reigned but for the muted, yet heavy *thud* of the horses' hooves against encrusted snow. Sleigh bells sounded in the distance, joined, as they passed another Amish farmhouse, by the familiar peal of a supper bell.

When they arrived at the Nolts', Leah noticed Carl was leaning up against the front room window, peering out. For a fleeting moment she recalled her excitement as a girl going to visit young Jonas and her other Mast cousins; then she got out of the enclosed buggy and turned to offer her hand to Lydiann and Sadie as they stepped down and onto the snow.

It took no time at all for Lydiann to also spot Carl. "Lookee there, Mamma," she said, tugging on Leah's arm. "My best friend's waitin' for us." With this, she took off running, embarrassing Leah thoroughly and, no doubt, Aunt Lizzie, as well.

Dat, meanwhile, tied the horse to a boulder as Lizzie helped Dawdi John up the shoveled walkway, both moving nearly as slowly as cold blackstrap molasses.

Chapter Eight

His smile contagious, Carl Nolt told each person where to sit at the long trestle table, which reminded Lydiann of their own at home. When it was her turn, he led her to the place beside Aunt Lizzie. "Denki," she said, and he grinned the way he had when he was Joseph in the Christmas play, leaning near baby Jesus as their teacher had prompted him. She couldn't help but think Carl had a kind face. *Like the real Joseph must've had.*

When Carl seated himself across the table from Lydiann, she was ever so glad, because this way she could observe him without much effort. Her curiosity about his adoption was going to get the best of her sooner or later, though she didn't quite know how to bring up the topic. What *was* it like to be an orphan, anyway? She couldn't

imagine it, really, except, of course, she herself could be considered a half orphan, having her sister Leah as a substitute mamma.
So, in a way, maybe she did understand
Carl's family situation better than she realized. Maybe that was why she liked him as
a school chum, although Abe and Carl were
also good pals, since the boys played together at recess and ate lunch together at
noon.

She wondered if Mary Ruth had taught
Carl to read some Pennsylvania Dutch,
or . . . was it possible his uncle, the one
who enjoyed attending Amish farm sales,
had instructed him? If so, maybe *that* was
something she could ask Carl about here
before too long.

Jah, I will, once school starts up again,
she decided.

———————◆———————

Leah, who had been awake since four-
thirty that morning, was beginning to tire of
table talk come nearly eight o'clock. Dottie
Nolt had served supper much later than the
Ebersols were used to, though Leah hoped
no one suspected how weary she felt. She

sat straight as she listened intently to the talk between Dat, Dawdi John, Dr. Schwartz, and Dan Nolt, with occasional remarks from the women, especially Aunt Lizzie and Dottie. Leah had not been surprised to see the doctor and Lorraine arrive ten minutes after Dat reined the horse into the driveway, although the fact that the Schwartzes and Robert were also invited— something Lorraine had shared with her Saturday—had completely slipped Leah's mind, and she had failed to mention it to Dat prior to their coming. Still, Dat seemed to be faring well, and he appeared to try to include Lizzie, seated next to him, in the conversation with the Nolts, whom he seemed more relaxed talking to than Robert Schwartz, not surprisingly. Aunt Lizzie, for her part, was not at all shy about entering in, seemingly comfortable talking about everything from the snowy weather to Dottie's delicious recipe for chicken with mushrooms.

Dr. Schwartz and Dan discussed something they'd read in the newspaper about a professional baseball team called the Dodgers and a proposed new stadium for downtown Brooklyn, New York. Leah could merely guess what such an enormous place might look like, having witnessed only their Amish young folk playing baseball or cornerball in meadows at one gathering or another. Meanwhile, she noticed how Sadie's face became drawn, her lips tense, whenever the doctor spoke, and Leah's heart felt especially tender toward her suffering sister.

The talk that most interested her, though, came from Mary Ruth's lips—here lately, she and Dottie had spent an entire day making cottage cheese. "And, not to boast, but Dottie caught on real quick," Mary Ruth said, eyes shining with the telling.

"We made butter, too." Dottie nodded, apparently pleased with the end result of their labor.

Aunt Lizzie's face broke into an even wider smile. And Leah thought Lizzie's heart must surely be gladdened by the news that Mary Ruth was passing along some of the Old Ways to Dottie. *What a nice thing,* Leah thought, wondering if Dat might also be heartened at this domestic talk. But one look at her father made it clear he was now caught up in conversation with Robert, despite Dat's seeming reluctance to approach him at the start of the evening.

How odd for Dat to meet Mary Ruth's beau this way, contemplated Leah. But as the evening wore on, she felt it hadn't been such a bad idea, seeing that Dat and the doctor's elder son were getting along quite well.

She dared not think too hard on that herself, however—each time she pondered how truly odd it was for Derek's brother to be sweet on one of Sadie's sisters, she felt a bit ill. To think the same union that had given life to thoughtless Derry had also produced well-mannered Robert. She knew firsthand what an upstanding young man Robert was, for she'd had ample opportunity to encounter him while cleaning his mother's house.

Amidst the comfortable talk of the adults, Leah noticed Lydiann smiling at Carl across from her. But, by the time dessert was served, Lydiann's face had become serious, a sharp contrast to her earlier high spirits.

Leah sighed, wondering what might be bothering her dear girl. Was it possible she was dreading the end of a wonderful-good evening? After all, the two youngsters were close friends, although she sometimes wondered how Dat felt about Carl's weekly

visits with Lydiann and Abe and, occasion-
ally, Sadie, as well, who had been known to
join the children on the floor near the wood
stove, playing games. Surely Dat wouldn't
want to risk a Mennonite youngster as a
close playmate to Lydiann and Abe, and
she had recently considered recommending
to him that the children not continue attending the one-room Georgetown School,
which met the needs of the growing rural
population of Plain and fancy children alike.
Besides, there had been talk amongst the
People of building an Amish one-room
school in Gobbler's Knob, following the recent consolidation of public schools. But so
far nothing had been done to make this
happen, although with the divine appointment falling upon Gid, there might be more
interest now, especially if Leah took it upon
herself to voice Dat's concern about Carl,
Lydiann, and Abe becoming too friendly.

Sadie's first reaction upon laying nervous
eyes on Robert Schwartz was of absolute
surprise, not because he reminded her of
Derry, but because in every way he did not.
Mary Ruth's beau was nothing at all like the
brother she remembered—even his man-

nerisms were unlike those of the dark-haired, dark-eyed boy who'd captured her heart, only to smash it to pieces. Robert's thoughtful demeanor and the way his eyes genuinely admired her sister were a marked contrast to the almost leering way Derry had always looked at her.

Recalling her youth, she realized anew what a tease she had been, seeking out fancy English boys to flirt with nearly every Friday night. It was no surprise she'd attracted the unwholesome advances of a young man such as Derry.

All that's behind me, Sadie thought, wishing she might have done things differently, yet recognizing her weakness for male attention. She still found it difficult to live without a man, no matter that she was a widow and drawing close to thirty years old.

———◆———

"It was nice you could finally meet my father," remarked Mary Ruth as she and Robert sat together in the formal parlor. Such a pleasant room it was, with several windows facing north, toward the vast woods, which could readily be seen during daylight hours. Framing the wide doorway, gleaming wood reflected the light of two reading lamps mounted on the wall behind the settee.

All the good-byes had been said, and Mary Ruth had enjoyed the evening immensely, except that her twin and her newly expanded family had stayed snug at home, which was understandable with a newborn in the house.

"Your dad's quite a talker," said Robert. "I wasn't sure what to expect."

"Once you get acquainted with him, Dat's not one to shy from speaking his mind, that's for sure."

Going to the window, Robert stood silently.

"Everything all right?" she asked, getting up to stand near him.

"Sure," he said, not convincing her.

"There's something on your mind."

As he turned, Robert's eyes seemed to search hers. "I'm falling in love with you, Mary Ruth."

Her heart leaped up at his words, but she felt torn, as well. Robert had yet to learn the terrible truth regarding Sadie and Derek, and she felt compelled to reveal the past and the resulting apprehensions that troubled her at the prospect of an engagement. She must find the courage to share what she had held so close all this time.

"I care deeply for you, too, Robert," she replied softly. "But there is something you must know, if you don't already."

"Dear, what is it?" He reached for her hands. "Have I done something to offend you . . . said something out of turn?"

She assured him that was not the case and let unfold the story of the day she had seen his younger brother running down Georgetown Road. "He was fit to be tied."

"You met Derek?"

She nodded and then continued. "More than once. Your brother and my sister . . . poor Sadie, were . . ." She couldn't bring herself to say the word *lovers.*

Robert was frowning, evidently puzzled. "What is it?"

"Sadie had a baby . . . with Derek."

Robert flinched suddenly and shook his head, as if unable to believe his ears.

"My sister had a wild *rumschpringe,* and she met your brother somehow, somewhere—I don't know much about that." She sighed, sickened at the thought of being the one to inform him, for it was obvious he was not aware of this shocking news. "Their baby . . . was stillborn, and Sadie was unrepentant about her relationship with Derek, which, I was told, was the reason she left to go to Ohio. And why she was eventually shunned."

He looked at her as if astounded. "Oh, Mary Ruth, I had no idea."

She was sorry to upset him, yet relieved he apparently believed her.

He squeezed her hand and held it for a moment, staring down. When at last he looked at her, his eyes were intense. "At the very least, I must apologize for Derek's behavior toward Sadie."

She felt grateful for his words. "Please . . . can we keep this private . . . just between us?" She had almost hesitated to ask this, but he immediately agreed, and she was rather surprised he didn't inquire of her further, asking if there might have been some misunderstanding . . . if another young man might have been the father of her sister's child. But nothing of the kind was mentioned, and Mary Ruth felt he trusted her implicitly.

Still, neither knew how to handle the fact

that a marriage between them would have the unintended consequence of also uniting Derek and Sadie once more, if only as in-laws, serving as a lifetime reminder of their regrettable past.

The evening had taken a much different turn than the romantic moment Robert must surely have had in mind for them. Heart heavy, Mary Ruth accompanied him to the front door. He kissed her cheek before he slipped out into the cold night. "I'll call you soon, dear."

"Good night," she said, the softly spoken word *dear* lingering in her mind long after midnight.

Chapter Nine

Jonas settled back into his favorite chair by the fire with a copy of *The Budget,* enjoying the many accounts of Christmas from various towns around Ohio, sometimes even chuckling aloud in the stillness of the kitchen. He read till his eyes were tired, then stood up to put out the gas lamp.

Sitting back down, he took pleasure in the silence as his eyes slowly became accustomed to the darkness. Emma had long since turned in for the night, having suffered a head cold for a second day. He delighted in recalling the happiness on her sweet face at his gift on Christmas morning—the antique vase.

His mind wandered back to the encounter with the aging fellow he'd met at the recent auction, where he had seen and bid on the colorful vase. He found himself wondering

if, indeed, he was the person—the particular Jonas Mast—meant for the old letter, as
the elderly gentleman had seemed to indicate. And the more he pondered this, the
more he wished he'd spoken up, offered to
ride to wherever it was the man was living
and see for himself the letter in question.

Not usually curious, he surprised himself
by repeating the event in his mind. Tired as
he was, Jonas did not wish to see the new
year in, as groups of young people were
sure to be doing this night—one group, in
fact, just down the long dirt lane that
passed the farmhouse. He knew there were
couples building a bonfire on the frozen
lake, probably making ready to roast marsh-
mallows. He and Emma had seen a good
many youth gathering there on previous
New Year's Eves, and if by chance some of
the boys drank too much moonshine, the
immature noises of glee carried well over
the lake and down this way.

Tonight, however, he didn't care to know
how many were shivering in the cold or
showing off for their sweethearts—if indeed
they were. He wondered if most were in the
middle of rumschpringe and if they would

end up joining church sooner rather than later.

For a moment he contemplated the Bann put on him by the Gobbler's Knob church. It was peculiar that a revered minister would impose such a ruthless punishment, shunning those who did not stay put in the church of their baptism . . . not to mention those pursuing a livelihood other than farming. All the same, Jonas knew of several other like-minded brethren here locally, some being ultraconservative Swartzentruber Amish.

Inhaling deeply, he was grateful that Emma scarcely ever sought to explore the landscape of his past, though he had responded through the years to any number of questions she'd had about Lancaster County and his family.

Growing weary, Jonas rose to his feet and headed upstairs.

———◆———

Leah noticed how bright-eyed Abe was as he sat himself down at the breakfast table New Year's Day, after having helped Dat and Sadie with the milking. Lydiann had remained indoors again to help Leah make cornmeal mush, fried eggs, and bacon, something she was doing more and more at both Dat's and Leah's bidding.

"We oughta have some hot cocoa for breakfast, too," Lydiann said, a mischievous smile on her face. " 'Tis better tasting than coffee."

"But hot chocolate doesn't go well with fresh-squeezed orange juice, do ya think?" Leah asked, standing at the cookstove.

Lydiann shrugged and continued to set the table. "I don't give a care, really."

"Something botherin' my girl?"

"Jah." Lydiann wandered over and stood next to Leah.

Leah was eager to listen, and by not saying more, she got Lyddie to open up and share her heart.

" 'Tween you and me, Mamma, Mary Ruth really annoys me, 'cause she lives over there with the Nolts and not here with us. And she dotes on Carl something awful."

So that's what was troubling her last night. She's jealous of her sister's affection for Carl, Leah decided.

"I thought you and Carl were pals."

"Maybe so, but . . . it's just that . . ." Lydiann hesitated; then she shrugged.

Leah patted Lydiann's arm. "I daresay things'll change as time goes by." She was thinking of how likely it was that Mary Ruth would settle down and marry, and once that happened, their sister wouldn't be so connected to the Nolts—especially to Carl, which was apparently the crux of Lydiann's complaint.

"What if Mary Ruth likes Carl better than me?" Lydiann suddenly burst out, tears pooling in her eyes.

"Ach, Lyddie, come here." She held out her arms to hold her girl and drew her near. "There, there . . . you mustn't fret now. You've got Abe and me . . . and Dat, too." She named off Aunt Lizzie and Dawdi John, as well. "And you've got Sadie," Leah added. "You and your eldest sister have become quite close in a short time."

Lydiann dried her eyes and sat on the long bench on the near side of the table. "But what if Sadie leaves again?" she asked. "Why'd she live somewhere else anyway . . . all those years?"

"Her husband lived in Indiana—you know that."

"No . . . I mean before she was married. How come she ended up out west, 'stead of livin' here in Gobbler's Knob?"

"Perhaps someday you'll know . . . when you're older."

A strained silence fell over the kitchen and was abruptly broken when Dat pushed in through the back door, clunking inside wearing his work boots. Sadie was right behind him, cheeks as red as cherry tomatoes.

Leah rose to welcome them. "Come wash up . . . breakfast is nice 'n' hot." She motioned for Lydiann to scoot over and sit at her usual place, aware of the brooding look on the girl's face. *Lyddie's sullenness mustn't get the best of her,* thought Leah, hoping to find a way to nip it in the bud.

———◆———

Leah felt in the pit of her stomach that something was amiss, even before Dat and Gid came in the house mid-morning to warm up awhile, eager for some hot coffee and freshly baked chocolate-chip cookies. Her dread deepened when Dat and Gid both said they hadn't seen hide nor hair of Abe.

"Not since immediately following break-fast," Dat said.

"We thought he'd run an errand for you—over to my mamma, maybe," Gid said.

Upon hearing this, Leah headed straight for her woolen shawl.

Dat's hand on her arm interrupted her. "I'll go 'n' look for him," he said. "You stay here with the family . . . in case he comes home a-hankerin' for some hot cocoa and cook-ies."

She let go of her shawl and stood with her back against the hard wall, watching her father shove his big feet into mud-caked work boots. With not a sigh or a word of good-bye, he reached for his heavy coat and scarf and stepped out the back door.

He's worried now, because I am, she thought. Dat could read her, so to speak, from all the years they'd worked side by side in the barn and the fields, no doubt. He knew how she thought, and when moments like this arose, he trusted her instincts. Something was terribly wrong, and now Dat knew it, too.

Chapter Ten

Abram inhaled deeply through his nose lest he chill his lungs as he tramped through the frozen pastureland toward the barren cornfield and eventually Smitty's wide meadow. The path he cut through the ice and snow made a direct line from his house to the Peacheys' back door, where he chose to stop, since Miriam somehow observed most everything that went on from the many windows in her kitchen. When she came to the door and welcomed him inside, she asked right away if he was looking for Abe. He assured her that he was.

"Well, I saw him head out to the pond," and here she pointed and raised her chin a bit, staring hard in the direction of Blackbird Pond, where they'd gone ice fishing three days ago.

"How long ago?"

"Oh, it's been some time." Miriam wore a sudden frown. "A good two hours or more, I'd have to say."

A tremor of foreboding caught Abram off guard, and he turned and swiftly headed down the steps, waving his hand in farewell without looking back.

Two hours . . . in this cold?

He could not imagine what Abe might be doing out in this frigid weather, and he quickened his pace.

———————◆———————

Lorraine Schwartz had been rather astonished at how much her husband had seemingly enjoyed himself at the Nolts' house last evening. When Henry had first met the Ebersols there, she'd noticed that he was somewhat standoffish, yet as the ice was broken and people began passing the food, eating and talking, he relaxed and entered into conversation with Abram, who was quite an interesting fellow, Lorraine thought. She had also noticed her husband discreetly studying Sadie, whom Lorraine had recognized with a jolt, to be sure, recalling the urgent look on Sadie's young face when she had unexpectedly come calling for Derek years ago.

Something else had caught Lorraine's interest last evening. It was the way Henry spoke to young Carl Nolt—his gestures, the softness in his voice. She couldn't help but notice the camaraderie between them and wondered how it was that Carl, healthy as he had always been, would have connected so well with Henry on so few clinic visits. Yet Henry was undeniably playful and easily succeeded in drawing out the young boy. *Henry will be a wonderful grandfather someday,* she thought with a smile.

Presently making her way to the kitchen, the recollection of the supper next door caused her to wish the whole group of them might enjoy yet another opportunity to dine together. *Perhaps at Robert's wedding . . . if Robert can indeed win Mary Ruth's heart.*

She would not hold her breath on that matter, however, because Mary Ruth gave the distinct impression she was holding back. Lorraine didn't mind if Robert took his time wooing the former Amish girl, for she was fond of both Mary Ruth and her older sister Leah. Each of the Ebersol girls was sweet in her own unique way, although the pained, sad eyes of their eldest sister, Sadie, caused Lorraine to wonder just what the beautiful girl had ever wanted with Derek that distant night, waiting for hours on their front steps for his return home.

———————◆———————

"Abe . . . no!" Abram gasped, sucking cold air into his lungs as he stooped down. There before him lay his son facedown on the ice of Blackbird Pond. He called to him and rolled him over, patting his face at first, and then slapped him one quick smack, becoming even more alarmed when Abe did not respond. Not even an eyelid flickered.

"Abe!" he hollered.

Still no response.

Abram panicked and, not wasting another moment, he scooped his limp child into his arms and carried him back to the Peacheys' house. Somehow or other Abe had been knocked out cold, and the fierceness of the winter weather distressed Abram as he pounded his fist on Smitty's storm door.

This time the blacksmith himself came and opened the door, his eyes growing round when he spied unconscious Abe. "*Himmel,* come in, Abram, come in."

"He was all sprawled out on the ice," Abram said, a catch in his voice as both Smitty and Miriam gathered near.

"Lay him out on the rug here, close to the wood stove," Smitty offered.

Miriam knelt beside Abe, touching his hair and face. "Ach, he's ice-cold."

Abram's heart caught in his throat and he realized he was petrified with fear. As gently as he could, he removed the boy's shoes and socks to check for frostbite, noticing immediately the telltale signs of hard and shiny grayish skin.

"We best not be warmin' him too quickly," advised Miriam, hovering near Abe and wearing a worried frown.

Abram made an attempt to keep his emotions in check, but the strange chalky pallor of his boy's face caused him grave concern. He shook Abe and called to him, "Can ya hear me, son? Wake up!" but to no avail.

"I best be ridin' for the hex doctor," Smitty said, resting his big hand on Abram's shoulder.

The smithy turned and was heading toward the back door to begin the process of hitching up when Miriam let out a moan. She shook her head and was weeping, which brought the smithy back into the kitchen. "Why must ya first think of pow-wowin'?" she asked. "Why not call for a *real* doctor—Dr. Schwartz, not but a mile down the way? He's ever so much closer, ain't so?"

"Ach, Miriam, can't ya see Abe's in trouble here? There's no sense callin' for Dr. Schwartz when what the boy needs is the *Amish* doctor," Smitty replied, his brow creased with a deep frown.

Abram struggled greatly, going back and forth in his mind, knowing full well the time might be short. *My boy could be dying,* he thought. *My only son . . . I can't let what happened to dear Ida befall my Abe.*

Always before he'd decided for the pow-wow doctor—it was the best way, the method that made the most sense to him.

But what would Ida want me to do? She sacrificed her life giving birth to our boy. He labored over this, feeling the burden as seconds ticked away. He must hurry and do something . . . think on it later.

Yet he knew the answer—knew it in his innards—for not only had his devout wife made her wishes known in her whole-hearted disapproval of the powwow doctors, she'd also left her legacy of beliefs in the form of her own Bible, marked up almost to the point of irreverence. Abram knew this as well as anybody, because, for the past several months, he had been reading every New Testament Scripture Ida had underlined on healing and other issues.

Smitty stepped out to the utility room within Abram's sight and pulled an additional woolen scarf off the wooden peg. "Well, who's it gonna be? Dr. Schwartz or the hex doctor? By the looks of Abe—all conked out like that . . ." Smitty's voice faded.

Abram could just imagine Lizzie having her say if word got to her ears about this, and even though he had always put his trust in the sympathy healers, all of a sudden he experienced a strong desire to please Lizzie, as well as his beloved Ida.

With a conviction that surprised him, he made his choice. "Ride to Dr. Schwartz, and make it quick!"

Miriam sighed, obviously relieved. Then, as if in prayer, she closed her eyes while Smitty rushed out the back door.

Watching Miriam kneeling there beside Abe, he wished Lizzie were here with him, too, for though she had a regular tendency to share her opinions a bit too freely, she might know what to do for Abe's frostbite— at least that. And she was as encouraging as the day was long, which would be of help to Abram at this terrible moment.

Now that Smitty was gone, he hoped against hope he had done the right thing. This being New Year's Day, what chance was there of the doctor being home? A niggling fear crept in at the back of his mind.

He continued to sit cross-legged on the floor next to Abe as worrisome thoughts nagged him. When he thought he might lose the ability to keep his chin from quivering, Leah startled him by flying in the back door.

"Dat . . . what on earth!" Immediately she slid to her knees beside Miriam, close to her little brother lying on the floor . . . in truth, her *son.* "Oh, Abe . . . Abe." Then to Abram she asked, "Whatever happened? Where did ya find him?"

"He must've gone walking out on the pond and tripped . . . fell forward, hitting his head. When I found him, he was knocked clean out . . . near frozen, too." Abram could hardly manage that much.

"Splash some water on him, maybe," Leah suggested, and they tried that, but Abe lay still as death, his breath mighty shallow.

Will he ever open his eyes again? Abram held his own breath, steeling himself against the worst.

Leah was now holding Abe's small hand in her own, cradling it as she took his pulse, glancing up at the round day clock, high on the kitchen wall. "Seems a mite too slow," she whispered, eyes locking on Abram. "Where's Smitty?"

"Gone for Dr. Schwartz," Miriam answered quickly as she reached an arm around Leah and pulled her near.

Ida's death weighed heavily on Abram's mind—after seven long years, images of that night were still vivid: the hushed, sad tone of the midwife; Leah's ashen face and the way she had held Ida's wrist so gently, taking her pulse just as she was this minute lovingly caring for Abe. "Dr. Schwartz'll be here in no time," he heard himself say for Leah's benefit. "We can't lose hope."

"Oh, my sweet, precious Abe," cried

Leah, putting her face next to his now. "I love ya so . . ." Her soft crying shook her shoulders.

Placing his hand on Abe's ankle, too aware of the stiffness, Abram wrestled to bring to memory one or two Scripture verses that dealt with troublesome times— so many there were—but why couldn't he recall a single one? And why was it Ida always seemed to have had a fitting verse on the tip of her tongue for nearly every occasion?

Ida had ignored the brethren in all of that, he thought. *She outright disobeyed by studying the Bible, even memorized certain verses, because she couldn't keep herself from it, as she'd always said.* Her yearning had caused her grief—for Abram, too—but somehow or other she'd managed to keep from having the Bann put on her by the bishop, maybe because Ida agreed to keep her opinions on Scripture to herself. Although, in the end, his wife had felt comfortable enough to keep sharing her views on the Bible with him, for she had known him all too well. Never, ever would he have turned her in to the bishop or any of the brethren. His love for Ida had been stronger than his devotion to Bontrager or to the church.

At last the words of the psalmist David crept into his mind: *He shall call upon me, and I will answer him: I will be with him in trouble; I will deliver him, and honour him.*

Reaching now for Abe's other hand, Abram clutched it between his own rough and callused hand and closed his eyes right along with Miriam and Leah.

O Lord God and heavenly Father, hear my desperate prayer. . . .

Leah was astonished to see her father's head bowed as they waited for Smitty to return. Silently, she joined him with a prayer of her own. *Lord, please allow Abe, our dear boy, to live . . . let him open his eyes and suffer no lingering ill effects from this nasty fall,* she prayed. *I trust your grace and mercy, Lord, your many kindnesses to us.*

The prayer was the best she knew to offer, and she wished either Aunt Lizzie—who'd remained at home with Dawdi John—or Mary Ruth were on hand to offer a spoken prayer of faith. She certainly didn't feel comfortable beseeching the Lord almighty out loud herself, and her heart fell as she again looked at Abe's stony white face.

Sighing deeply, she felt as if her own heart might stop beating if Abe did not soon blink his shining eyes open or twitch one of his childish fingers. Anything at all.

Chapter Eleven

"Abe Ebersol, seven years old," the young nurse repeated, writing Abe's vital information on her clipboard. "Date of birth?"

Leah replied quickly, "December 27, 1949."

"Does he have any allergies?"

"None that I know of." Leah glanced over at Dat, who was sitting, slumped in a heap, on one of only two chairs in the semiprivate hospital room. Her father was unable to be of much help after his ride in Dr. Schwartz's front seat, where he'd stiffly braced himself for dear life while Leah and Aunt Lizzie sat in the backseat with unresponsive Abe stretched out between them. Drawn by her growing concern, Lizzie had shown up at the Peacheys' just before Dr. Schwartz's arrival, and by the look on Dat's face, he was ever so grateful to have her here.

Dat was distraught beyond anything Leah could recall in recent years, and she felt terribly sorry for him. Goodness, he hadn't ridden in the front seat of an automobile much at all, and never at such a high speed.

As soon as the nurse left the room, having tended to a doctor-ordered oxygen tent for Abe, Aunt Lizzie said, "He'll be comin' to . . . here 'fore long." But her voice trembled, and Leah noticed Dat glance up at Lizzie, his eyes softening.

"Jah, I daresay he will." Leah retuned her gaze to poor Abe, lying as quiet and motionless as can be. Oh, how small a boy he was, even though he'd grown out of nearly all his school pants lately. She'd teased him just last week that he was shooting up like a weed, "and much too fast at that." At this moment, as unchecked tears rolled down her cheeks, she promised herself she would never, ever again grumble about such things, even in jest.

"Let's talk in Dutch," Dat said suddenly, getting up and leaning on the bed rail closer to Abe.

"A wonderful-gut idea." Lizzie rose to join him.

Softly they reminded Abe of their love for

him. Aunt Lizzie even spoke of the day the men had all gone ice fishing and what fun he'd had—and of the fish fry they'd enjoyed that evening. All the while the nurse came in and out of the room to check the boy's vital signs.

———◆———

Not long after Dat and Aunt Lizzie had slipped out to the waiting room for some water, Leah turned to see Gid and Hannah coming in the door, babe in arms. "Oh, Hannah . . . Gid!" She ran to her sister and buried her face in Hannah's neck.

"We came as soon as we could get Ida Mae and Katie Ann settled in with my folks," Gid explained, saying Sadie had remained with both Lydiann and Dawdi John.

When Leah had composed herself, she took Mimi from Hannah and saw Gid reach for Hannah's hand. Together, they went and stood at Abe's bedside; he had been wrapped in several warm blankets in an attempt to slowly raise his body temperature, which was low due to prolonged exposure to the elements. The hospital staff had also surrounded his head with an oxygen tent and was watching him closely for signs of a brain concussion.

"Does anybody know what happened?" Hannah whispered. "Did he slip and fall?"

Gid reached around her and drew her near as Hannah began to sob in his arms. "Dear . . . dear," he said.

"Ach, this is just what I saw in my dream," she cried, and Gid, trying his best to soothe her, suggested they join Dat and Lizzie in the waiting area.

This left Leah alone with Abe and the tiny infant asleep in her arms. Her heart went out to Hannah, who seemed terribly fragile today, both physically and emotionally, likely from having given birth so recently. The shock of Abe's accident had no doubt set her back even more.

Slipping quietly to Abe's side, Leah began to sing the song Mamma had taught her so long ago: " 'Jesus loves me, this I know . . . for the Bible tells me so.' "

The baby in her arms stirred slightly, and she leaned her face near to sing to sweet and tiny Mimi, too. " 'Little ones to Him belong . . .' " With each precious word, she realized that these dear ones did, in fact, belong to God, and she was suddenly too overcome to continue singing.

Instead, she found Abe's hand and touched it lightly, hoping she might feel a hint of a stir. Anything to give her hope.

◆

After a while Hannah and Gid returned to the hospital room to get Mimi. They visited with Leah a bit longer, although Leah could see in Hannah's eyes that she wasn't ready to come to town just yet, especially under such distressing circumstances.

Soon Gid looked tenderly at Hannah before nodding his good-bye. "God be with you, Leah," he said, and they turned and waved, leaving the room again nearly as fast as they'd returned.

There was little time between clusters of visits, and Dan and Dottie Nolt arrived soon after with Mary Ruth. Dottie told Leah that Carl had wanted desperately to come, but they'd asked Lorraine Schwartz to look after him because he was under twelve and wouldn't be allowed upstairs to the room anyway. "It was Lorraine who came running over to our house to announce the sad news, asking us to pray for Abe."

Leah clung to Mary Ruth's hand as she listened, ever so glad to see her. "I was hopin' you'd hear somehow and come."

"All during the ride here . . . we were praying," Mary Ruth said of the three of them.

"Denki, oh, thank you," Leah told Dottie, accepting a concerned embrace.

Meanwhile, Dan excused himself to go in search of Dat and Aunt Lizzie, after Leah explained how distressed her father had been earlier. "He's having the hardest time seein' Abe like this. We all are, truly." She stopped, not wanting to go on so for fear Abe in his stupor might hear them talking.

Mary Ruth nodded. "Dan will do Dat some good," she said, offering a brave smile even in the midst of her tears.

A hush fell over the room, apart from the periodic *swoosh* of the oxygen tent, and Leah and Mary Ruth moved to the foot of Abe's bed. "Let's pray for him together," her sister whispered.

Leah could not speak for the lump in her throat as she gratefully nodded.

Mary Ruth began as if she were humbly addressing a dear and close friend, and as her sister raised her petition to the Throne of Grace, Leah whispered her own prayer. "Dear Lord, thank you for sending Mary Ruth here today. . . ."

Repeatedly Sadie had tried to console Lydiann, who was still crying upstairs in her bedroom. She *had* managed to get Lydiann to lie down—the poor girl was emotionally worn out over Abe's accident.

Downstairs, Sadie paced from the kitchen all the way to the front room and back again, wishing for some word on their brother. Anything at all would help to alleviate her pent-up feelings. She was all too familiar with such frustration, having suffered similarly for hours on the day the startling report of Harvey's fatal accident had come, unable to get to the hospital until too late to say her good-byes to her darling.

The Indiana bishop had been on hand during that dark, sad time, and she wondered again why the bishop here couldn't be more compassionate to her . . . or even encouraging. Clenching her jaw, she recalled how she'd felt upon receiving the harsh letter Bishop Bontrager had sent in response to her request to return home. He had pointedly stated she was a "most vile woman in need of repentance," and he even hinted that he doubted she would have contacted him if not for her widowhood. He had also dared to suggest her husband's untimely death showed she was most likely under God's judgment.

Sadie wondered if she could ever truly forgive the bishop for those words and what he'd forced upon her, yet she had no choice but to walk in obedience to the *Ordnung* lest she fail her second Proving time and be cast out of her father's house.

Truly, she wanted to be found worthy to live amongst the People, and she didn't see herself remaining under Dat's covering for the rest of her life. Although it was much too early for her to think about such things, she hoped to have the chance to marry again someday, perhaps to a widower, once she was past her grieving for Harvey. After all, she had been happiest when married, and happiness was her ambition in life, regardless of Bishop Bontrager's frequent insistence in his sermons that obedience to the church is the highest calling for God's children. "Obey or die"—the words had both discouraged her and, at times, kept her on the straight and narrow, even finding their way into the core of her late-night dreams. And she couldn't help but recall the teachings of the upstanding Ohio bishop she had known back when she was staying with the Mellingers. *Oh, the remarkable wisdom of the ministers of Millersburg!* She knew she ought not let the encouragement of Scripture go unheeded.

Aware of a voice in the Dawdi Haus, she headed through the adjoining door and found her grandfather alone, talking to himself. "Dawdi?" she said so as not to startle him, bending low beside his chair. "Are you all right?"

He lifted his tear-streaked face. "I can hardly stand to think 'bout what happened to that young'un," he said, voice breaking. "Abe's a right fine boy, he is. Just don't understand what he thought he was doin' going to Blackbird Pond like that."

She rose and pulled up a chair to sit near her grandfather. "Jah, I know it's awful hard on all of us, but we daresn't give up hope."

He nodded slowly, though it seemed with great effort. "That there boy's the apple of your father's eye. He's everything to Abram."

"A son is ever so precious to his father." *And to his mother,* she pondered, having to look away and collect herself a bit.

"I daresay the family will still be away at the hospital come suppertime." He was obviously anxious for some word, just as she was.

Sadie offered to make him some coffee, but Dawdi shook his head.

Making an effort to help him get his mind off young Abe, she picked up *The Budget* and began to read from its pages. Two humorous stories from Sugarcreek, Ohio, got Dawdi quieted down. After all, it wouldn't do to have both Lydiann and Dawdi crying buckets of tears over Abe. What good would it do? Sadie herself had shed too many fruitless tears over things she could not change.

But there were some things that *could* be altered, and she thought again of the letter that had come out of nowhere, as if the Lord God had dropped it into her lap to see if she might actually do the right thing at long last. Of course, she still had no idea how poor Leah would react.

It was after she finished reading to Dawdi that Sadie decided she could no longer wait to fess up to Leah. She must come clean once and for all as soon as Abe was home and feeling better.

It was decided Leah would stay the night in the hospital with Abe, and both she and Aunt Lizzie were now talking this over in the family waiting area while Dat went into Abe's room to sit with him. Her father was still berating himself for having introduced Abe to ice fishing not but a few days ago. "Dat needs his own bed and a nice hot meal besides," Leah said, to which Lizzie agreed.

"I daresay word'll get out quickly enough," Aunt Lizzie said, "and you'll have plenty of visitors here with ya tonight, dear one."

Leah knew this to be true, for Plain relatives and friends often gathered around a family during such times of crisis. She wasn't hesitant to be here alone, though. No, she worried more about what she would do if Abe should take a turn for the worse.

"Lydiann will be awful glad to see you and Dat come home." Leah rose. "Dawdi will be, too."

"And Sadie will have supper on by now." Aunt Lizzie looked up at the clock. "I best be gettin' Abram thinking 'bout headin' home." She went to Leah and slipped her arm through hers. "Are ya sure you'll be all right here?"

She couldn't say outright that she would be, but then again she couldn't openly speak of her fears. "Don't worry over me. Look after Dat . . . get him home for now."

Lizzie nodded, smiling sweetly. "All right, then." And they walked arm in arm down the hall to Abe's room.

Dat was coming out, a look of sadness on his face as they approached him. "Abe's still passed out."

"We must leave him in God's hands," offered Lizzie.

"Easier said than done," Dat replied. "I just hope I did the right thing. . . ." His voice trailed off.

"Whatever do you mean, Dat?"

"By having Smitty get Dr. Schwartz . . . bringing Abe here."

"You did just what Mamma would've wanted," Leah replied.

"Lizzie here would've chewed me out but gut, otherwise," Abram admitted with a fleeting smile. "But that's all right, I guess. She's had her say-so in the past, just as Ida often did."

Dat's acceptance of Lizzie's aversion to hex doctors seemed related in some way to his possible romantic interest. Leah had noticed Lizzie patting Dat's hand today, and just now she felt strongly that if Dat *was* falling for Lizzie after being a widower for this long, then so be it. Leah found the prospects quite interesting, even promising, since Aunt Lizzie had most likely given up on ever being married.

Grateful for the help and heartening Lizzie had offered this day, she hugged her good-bye and waved to Dat as they made their way down the hallway together. Thoughtfully she watched them for a moment before heading back to spend the rest of the night with Abe.

Settling into a chair, she suddenly felt alone and downright melancholy. With Dat and Aunt Lizzie gone, she was the sole caretaker of Mamma's son, who was presently sleeping so soundly inside his oxygen tent, he scarcely moved.

———◆———

She must have dozed off, although for how long Leah didn't know, till she became

aware of a sound in the room and assumed
it was the night nurse. She blinked her eyes
open to see Abe's eyes opening, too.

"Mamma . . ." he said faintly.

Her heart sped up and she rushed to his
side. "Oh, Abe . . . you're awake!"

"Mamma," he whispered again, smiling
weakly now.

"Jah, I'm here, dearest boy."

He lifted his hand to meet hers.

"You're better, ain't so?" She wished Dat
and Aunt Lizzie were here for this wonderful
moment.

Abe tried to sit up but began to moan,
putting his free hand to his forehead. "Ach,
my head hurts somethin' awful."

"Well, now, sure it does," she said, encouraging him to lie still. "Ya smacked it a
gut one on the ice."

He frowned. "I don't remember any such
thing. When was this?"

She was quick to tell him he'd conked his
head hard, knocking out the memory of his
being at Blackbird Pond earlier today.

"No . . . no, I was never there today . . .
not since Dat and all went ice fishin'. Why
would I be goin' over there alone, any-
ways?"

Leah's throat went dry and she became anxious, afraid Abe's accident might have caused mental damage. "Try to rest quiet-like while I go 'n' get the nurse. I'll be right back."

She returned alone and hovered near him, eager for the nurse to observe him and to help her understand what was causing Abe to talk so.

Promptly her dear boy closed his eyes again, and for a moment he lay there as still as he had before awakening minutes ago. She felt a strange sensation in the pit of her stomach—something akin to fear.

She stood there beside Abe's bed, help-less to do anything but watch him breathe, when at last the nurse hurried in the door. Leah told of Abe's having come to, and the nurse seemed quite pleased, then touched his arm to awaken him again to take his temperature, pulse, and blood pressure.

When Abe complained more loudly about his headache and a ringing in his ears, the nurse said she would get him some pain medication. She rushed out of the room and returned quickly with a pill and a glass of cold water. "This will make you feel much better."

"Denki," said Abe softly.

Leah got the courage to speak up and say that Abe did not seem to remember having fallen, and the nurse explained that it was normal following a grade-three concussion. "A grade three is determined by a loss of consciousness, and symptoms can continue for a full month or longer," the nurse clarified.

"Do ya mean to say Abe might have to miss school for that long?" Leah asked.

"He'll need bed rest for several weeks, at least. I wouldn't rush him back to school, no." The nurse listed a number of other possible symptoms—memory loss, severe headaches, nausea, slurred speech, vision disturbance, fatigue, and more. She went on to mention that Abe would probably require a follow-up exam in two weeks.

When the sound of the nurse's footsteps faded, Leah sat back in the chair. For now her mind was more at ease.

"You'll stay with me tonight, Mamma?" Abe asked.

She moved her chair next to his bed. "I'll sit beside you all the night through."

In the dim light, she silently began to count her blessings, as well as Abe's. Her boy was alive, able to talk, hear, and see. *Thank you, dear Lord,* she prayed, keeping a watchful eye on her sleeping little brother—the son of her heart.

Chapter Twelve

Hannah finished nursing tiny Mimi and placed her gently on her shoulder till several soft burps escaped the infant's rosy mouth. Then she wrapped Mimi securely in soft blankets and placed her snugly in the cradle handmade by Dawdi Mathias back when Hannah was expecting Ida Mae. Just as dear Mamma had often done, Hannah looked in on the older girls, both soundly sleeping, before tiptoeing to the window of the bedroom she and her husband shared.

This room, which she had enjoyed setting up when she and Gid had first moved into Aunt Lizzie's former home as newlyweds, was altogether comforting in the partial light. Aware of the stillness, she watched as the moon ascended gradually over the far-away hills to the east, wishing Gid would hurry back home. He'd gone down to the

Ebersol Cottage on foot after they'd stopped to retrieve Ida Mae and Katie Ann from his parents' house, following the brief hospital visit.

Longingly she watched the candle-lit windows on the main floor of her father's house, particularly the golden light from the kitchen, which shone most brightly. *They're all gathered near the wood stove. . . .* She could just imagine her family together, Dat and Aunt Lizzie having arrived home a short while before, and Dawdi John, Sadie, and Lydiann hungry for word about Abe. Gid, too, was keenly interested in hearing how young Abe was doing, as well as finding out why Abram hadn't called for the hex doctor, as he'd heard his father had suggested.

She recalled Aunt Lizzie telling her that such practices had the power to hinder one's walk with the Lord God, thus hampering the hope of salvation. Truth be known, she didn't so much care for her aunt's take on spiritual things and knew she'd never embrace Lizzie's outspoken faith, nor Mary Ruth's, for that matter. Such boldness went against the Old Ways, she was sure, but she dared not discuss such a touchy subject with her husband, instead writing down her thoughts in her journal as she had been doing for a good many years.

Tonight, however, she had scarcely the energy to stand at the window, feeling dismal and left out here at home with her little ones, missing the current news from Dat and Aunt Lizzie.

Is Abe going to live?

She fought back the tears, fairly certain Leah had stayed behind at the hospital, knowing her sister as she did. Ever so strong . . . and altogether calm in the midst of such a trying time, that was Leah. It had also been so after Mamma's death.

Hannah sighed, recognizing again her lack of similar fortitude. She couldn't have done what Leah had done . . . or what she continued to do, giving up all opportunities to wed. But now, thinking on that, Hannah was altogether happy Leah *had* broken up with Gid, so to speak, although she knew from his mouth that, when all was said and done, *he* had been the cause of their breakup. And rightly so, since he longed for his own household and flesh-and-blood children, which he was certainly having with Hannah—one after another. Yet, thus far, she had failed to give him a son.

Maybe next time the Lord God will see fit to give us a boy, she thought, moving away from the window and heading to bed. Her ears would have to wait till morning for some word on Abe. She was just too tired, and not long from now, in a few hours, Mimi would be crying yet again for nourishment.

A familiar dread of darkness over-whelmed her as it seemed to nearly every night, and Hannah went again to check on her children, ever worried that they might sleep too soundly, never to awaken. Even with her baby safely born, the gnawing fear of death seemed to shadow her every move.

◆

The evening progressed, bringing with it a steady trickle of visitors to the waiting area—Uncle Jesse Ebersol and nearly all his family—and Leah was especially glad to see Adah among those who had come to keep her company through the sunless hours.

"Ya mustn't wear yourself out," Adah advised sweetly, her big eyes revealing the concern of a best friend. "Will ya promise you'll rest when ya can?"

Leah's lip quivered and she said she would.

"This too shall pass," Adah offered, sitting beside her. "A concussion is a worrisome thing, but I have a feelin' you'll see him up and goin' about his work and school in no time."

Leah opened her heart and shared what the nurses had told her to expect about Abe's condition if things went normally. To this Adah frowned, yet she stood her ground. "Trust the Lord God for healing," she whispered, glancing around her lest she be heard and misunderstood.

A bit surprised at this, Leah kept her voice low, saying she had been doing just that, but she was awful glad for Adah's encouragement. "I felt I nearly lost my own son this day," she admitted. "And Dat, oh goodness, you best be prayin' for him, too. He needs it as much as Abe, I'm thinkin'."

Saying she would remember the whole family in her prayers, Adah gripped Leah's hand and added, "Nothin's impossible with the Lord God. Ya have to hold on to that."

When all of this recent faith had sprung

up in Adah, Leah didn't know. But she wasn't too surprised to hear such things from Miriam Peachey's daughter, knowing what she did about Mamma's good friend and the way she believed, though quite secretly, in the saving grace of the Lord Jesus. Like Miriam and Adah, a growing number of the People seemed to be embracing the blessing of prayer.

———◆———

Come ten o'clock, the family waiting room grew empty and quiet, and soon Leah was alone with Abe once again. She was distressed that he seemed disoriented at times, as though he had lost his way in his mind and could not get back to where he belonged. The nurse had talked about accident-related amnesia, something that should fade with time, and hopefully that would be the case with Abe. For now, though, Abe continued to complain about a growing list of symptoms. At first light tomorrow some tests would be done, the nurses assured her.

Leah settled into the oversized leather chair, aware of Abe's steady breathing.

Tomorrow we'll know more. She wrestled with the thought, hoping the doctor would indeed have more for her to go on, something to help her grasp all the strange things happening with Abe.

———◆———

A horrendous thirst awakened Abram in the night—a powerful urge to get out of bed and go to the kitchen for some water. Along with the intense craving was the lingering memory of a nightmare. In his dream, Abram had made repeated attempts to reach Abe, yet he had slipped on the ice himself, his arms stretched out before him, unable to save his son.

Attempting to recover from the dreadful sense of helplessness, Abram drank the glass dry in one continuous gulp. The events of the day played in his mind as he padded back to his bedroom, and all he could think of now was that Abe and Leah were far removed from him this night . . . nearly an hour away by horse and carriage. He was beholden to Henry Schwartz, the kindhearted doctor who had probably saved Abe's life. Once Dr. Schwartz had ar-

rived and Abram had carried his unconscious son out to the doctor's car, he'd
clung to a measure of hope that Abe was
going to be all right in the long run—and
without the help of the hex doctor.

But presently, in the dimness of his room,
he prayed silently that he'd made the right
decision for his son . . . for Leah, too, who
was tending to Abe with her heart, no doubt
getting precious little sleep herself. Time
would tell, Abram knew.

Such a day it's been, he thought.

In time Abram yielded to slumber and
was disturbed by yet another dream. Abe
had slipped into a hole in a pond created for
ice fishing, his small hands thrashing about,
his weak voice calling for help as he slipped
farther and farther from the opening, at last
bumping his head against the frozen pond
above him and drowning in the frigid wa-
ters.

Breaking out in a cold sweat, Abram
awakened, wishing for the dawn. He arose
again and sat on the edge of his bed, struggling to control his yearning to see with his
own eyes that Abe still lived.

I should've stayed at the hospital. . . .

Going to get another drink, he stood at

the kitchen window and looked out across
the snowy pastureland, this plot of land
owned by his own father and grandfather
before him. Had either of them ever spoken
to the Almighty the way Lizzie did . . . the
way Ida had always done? The way *he'd*
silently prayed at his injured son's side?

Again he felt a nudging within to call on
the name of the almighty One, if only in a
whisper. Inhaling deeply, he began. "O Lord
God and heavenly Father, will you hear and
honor this prayer I make? Will you look after
young Abe this night . . . and Leah, too? Will
you shine your light of love kindly upon
them while they are so far away from my
care? Amen."

He felt altogether odd about the act, yet
there was something truly strengthening
about speaking this way in prayer. He had
never done so before in his life, having been
instructed against it, and the actual doing
was such an eye-opener, he wondered why
on earth Bishop Bontrager was so opposed
to something so powerful—something as
potent as some of the People viewed a hex
doctor's chanting.

But even more than the sense of power in

the room was the prevailing peace, an assurance that Abe would indeed survive.

"Father in heaven, hear my prayers for young Abe," whispered Mary Ruth as she walked the length of her bedroom, with only the light of the moon to guide her way. "Touch my father and Sadie and Lydiann . . . and Dawdi John, too, with your saving grace. Minister your abiding strength to Aunt Lizzie and Leah, and call Hannah, my dear twin, and her husband, Gid, and their little ones to the eternal truth of your Word. These things I pray in the name of the Lord Jesus. Amen."

"O Lord God, let Abe live," Sadie prayed silently beneath the coverlet of the bed she normally shared with Leah. "Let young Abe live a long and healthy life."

She wondered if Leah was able to rest at the hospital. But no, more than likely she was keeping watch over Abe. *If I'd raised him as my own, I'd be doing the same,* she contemplated, sighing into the darkness. *If I'd stayed put, I would have been here for*

Mamma to ask for my *promise on her deathbed.*

Too often she let her mind wander to this: that had she been living at home, Leah never would have been anywhere near the birthing room with Mamma, Aunt Lizzie, and the midwife. For Sadie had always been Mamma's right-hand girl, and prior to the years of her rumschpringe, they had scarcely ever been apart. She had worked alongside Mamma in most every respect.

She pictured Abe lying still as a stone in a hospital of many strangers—Englishers mostly—and was startled at a keen sense of not wanting to lose him to death. *Just as I lost my only son.*

Weeping now, she felt compelled to continue her prayer to the almighty One.

"Dear God, let my brother live so that I might know him . . . so that he might come to love me in part as he does Leah." Only after praying this would Sadie allow herself to rest.

What's to become of us if Abe dies? Lydiann wondered, lying wide-awake, having cried her eyes dry. *Am I to grow up alone?*

She thought she heard Sadie down the hall and raised herself up in the darkness to listen. The graceful, beautiful sister she'd missed knowing for nearly her whole life was sniffling in her bed, crying over Abe, too, probably. Getting up, she pushed her slippers on and tiptoed to the room her mamma Leah and Sadie shared. She tapped gently on the door. "Sadie, it's me . . . Lyddie."

She was told to come in, which she did gladly, especially thankful when Sadie held open the heavy quilt to welcome her to climb in.

"I could use some company tonight, too," said Sadie, her voice raspy.

"That's gut, 'cause I'm awful sad." Lydiann slipped into bed and felt the warmth of Sadie's arm around her. She nestled down like a kitten in a wicker basket.

"No need for both of us to be lonely tonight," Sadie whispered.

Lydiann smiled through her tears. "Were you ever, well, lonely before . . . ?"

"Before I moved home, ya mean?"

"Jah."

"I'd have to say I was always missing my family . . . especially Mamma . . . the mother

who birthed both you and me. We were always ever so close."

Lydiann wondered if she dare ask the
question burning within her. Was this the
right time to bring up such a thing? She
sighed and tried to go to sleep, but rest
would not come. Turning over, she lay facing the ceiling.

"What are ya thinkin' now?" Sadie asked.

"Not sure if I oughta say."

"You can ask me whatever ya like. How's
that?"

She could just imagine Mamma Leah saying this wasn't a good idea—not tonight,
not now, not ever. But Lydiann didn't so
much care at the moment what anybody
thought. So she asked, "Why were ya
treated so, Sadie? Why'd ya have to go
away?"

Chapter Thirteen

Two days following New Year's Day, along about midday, Abe was released from the Lancaster hospital. Evidently Dr. Schwartz had been keeping in touch with the attending physician by phone, for he kindly offered to drive both Leah and Abe home—"to avoid further jostling in a buggy" was precisely the way the doctor had put it to Leah. She realized anew what wonderful-good friends and neighbors the Schwartzes were, and she'd gotten up the nerve to tell Dr. Schwartz as much during the ride back to Gobbler's Knob. Together, she and Abe had sat in the backseat, Abe leaning against her and quietly complaining of dizziness the length of the trip.

Once she resumed her work at the clinic, Leah intended to ask Dr. Schwartz privately about Abe's continuing symptoms, including his insistence that he had not returned to the frozen pond. The rest of the family would, no doubt, be just as concerned as she once Abe got settled back at home.

Meanwhile, they—*all* of them—had much to be grateful for, because their boy's injuries could have been far worse.

◆

Lydiann tried to keep herself from bawling as she greeted Abe, she was so happy to see him. "What was it like at the hospital? Did the nurses take gut care of ya? Did they let you eat ice cream?"

"I think we best let your brother rest up before ya ask *too* many questions," Mamma Leah said, to which Dat agreed, nodding his head.

The entire family, including Dawdi John, who'd hobbled over from next door, stood in Mamma's kitchen, awful happy to see Abe again. But it wasn't long before Mamma Leah and Dat were taking him upstairs to lie down.

"Isn't he all better?" Lydiann followed them to the bottom of the stairs and looked up with longing as her brother leaned hard on Dat's arm.

Briefly turning around, Dat chided her, "Hush now."

Lydiann hurried to Sadie's side at the cookstove, where she had cooked up her best corn chowder. "What do ya make of that?" she whispered. "Abe comes home and he can hardly walk. I saw him, Sadie. His balance is off-kilter!"

"Don't ya worry none," Sadie replied. "He'll be as gut as new . . . you'll see."

But Abe wasn't better that evening or the next morning, neither one. And Lydiann worried something truly terrible had happened to him over on Blackbird Pond, something Abe might never recover from.

Then and there, she decided it best not to tell her school friends what she'd seen with her own eyes, even though they were all asking about Abe. Dat had already gone to the school and informed the teacher that Abe would be missing some days—just how many, no one could say.

———◆———

The day following Leah's return with Abe, Sadie found her in the kitchen sweeping the floor. Silently, she set about cleaning up the wood stove, wondering how to raise the subject of the letter she'd hidden in her bureau drawer. She considered yet again the new barrier it was bound to create between the two of them as she continued her work, rubbing hard at the cookstove's surface. Maybe this still wasn't the best time, but Sadie couldn't wait another minute. Ever since her decision to come clean, the letter had begun to bore a hole in her bureau drawer, as well as in her heart.

So when Leah stopped sweeping to fetch the dustpan, Sadie straightened and inhaled deeply. The second she reappeared, Sadie blurted, "It's time I talk to ya 'bout something, sister."

"Oh?" Leah was obviously innocent to what Sadie had in mind, for she continued with her work, bending low to sweep the floor debris onto the dustpan.

"I hate to upset ya, really I do . . . but I've been wanting to make something right. And for a gut long time now."

At once Leah ceased her work, her eyes red and her face still pale from lack of sleep, most likely. "What's on your mind?" she asked.

Momentarily Sadie reconsidered. *How*

selfish of me. Sighing, she knew she must not turn back. "When I was livin' in Millersburg years ago, I did something I must ask your forgiveness for." She pressed on. "It was a horrid thing I did. Unforgivable, truly."

Blinking her eyes, Leah frowned and stood tall with the broom upright in her hand. "I have no idea what you're talking 'bout."

" 'Course, you don't." Scarcely could she go on, but she admitted how vexed she had been at the time over what she felt had been an outright betrayal on Leah's part. "I was awful angry you upped and spilled the beans to Mamma and Dat 'bout my wild days . . . me gettin' myself in the family way 'n' all. So one day, when one of your letters to Jonas arrived in the mail, I dropped it in the rubbish as a way to get back at you—it wasn't till it was too late that I realized what a dreadful thing I'd done. By then it was beyond possibility to retrieve the letter."

Leah's face flushed red with unmistakable ire, but as quickly as she allowed her wrath to show, she stepped back and breathed a great sigh. "I don't care to rehash my resentment during those disturbing days"—

she wiped her brow with the back of her hand—"but it does wonder me if that letter might not be the one explainin' some needful things to Jonas."

Meekly Sadie whispered, "You can know that for sure and for certain."

"What do ya mean?"

"It's upstairs . . . tucked away." Sadie quivered. "The mailman delivered it here recently. . . . It must've fallen out of the trash truck all that time ago, although who can be sure just what happened for it to find its way back here now."

Leah's eyes flickered. "Jah, go 'n' get the letter for me."

Hurrying upstairs, Sadie found the concealed letter, her pulse racing as she hoped against hope her sister might find it in her heart to forgive.

Taking short, quick breaths, Leah placed her hand on her chest. *Why, O Lord, must this be happening now . . . when my thoughts of Jonas are few and far between?*

Faithfully she had been reading Mamma's old Bible, and with her heart wide open, the Scriptures were filling the void left there by her tenderness for Jonas. God's Word offered her strength and even solace for her loneliness.

Yet now she couldn't help but recall how she'd felt so terribly heartbroken, assuming her sister had stolen her dear beau when Sadie had lived near Jonas during the time of his Millersburg cabinetmaking apprenticeship. In her desperation at the perceived deception, Leah had fully given herself up to the mercy of almighty God, drawing courage for her life from the love of her heavenly Father.

Sadie returned, holding out the letter. "It's soiled but unopened all the same."

Leah nodded, unable to speak as she inspected the discolored postmark.

Sadie's voice was soft yet strained. "Can you ever forgive me?"

Intently examining the envelope, Leah could not reply. She could discern the month and year—not the actual day—and went quickly to the utensil drawer and pulled out a table knife, slicing through the top of the envelope . . . and into the long-ago past. Suddenly it all felt so recent.

Opening the letter, she recognized the handwriting as her own and read the first few lines. Immediately she knew this surely *was* the most important letter she'd ever written. To think Jonas had never known . . . never even laid eyes on it!

She glanced up and noticed Sadie turning to leave the kitchen, heading slowly, if not forlornly, toward the stairs. *Can you ever forgive me?* Her request echoed in Leah's ears.

How many secrets must we bear? Leah clutched the letter, grateful for the privacy, and wandered to the window, struggling not to shake as she read through to the end.

When she finished, she refolded it gently and slipped it back into the safety of its envelope. *He never read my answers to his pointed questions about my friendship with Gid. Jonas never knew my heart on this. . . .*

She held it close to her and bowed her head under the burden of her pain. *No wonder his letters stopped,* Leah thought tearfully. *No wonder he never returned home to marry me.*

Chapter Fourteen

"Something's awful wrong with Abe," Hannah confided in Mary Ruth, who'd come for a late afternoon visit nearly a week after their brother's discharge from the hospital. "He ain't nearly the same, and I've seen firsthand that it's true." She had to swallow hard as she tried not to cry, still wishing Dat would come to his senses and have the hex doctor work his magic on the boy.

Mary Ruth held little Mimi in her arms, rocking her slowly while Ida Mae and Katie Ann stacked small towers of wooden blocks near the cookstove. "Lorraine told Dottie head injuries of this nature take time to heal . . . and that came from Dr. Schwartz, naturally. Funny how the grapevine works on the outside, too."

Hannah didn't find talk of the grapevine at all amusing. Truth was, Mary Ruth's frequent visits were beginning to annoy Gid, being themselves the subject of tittle-tattle amongst the People. He'd told Hannah before Abe's accident, "Not such a gut idea for an Amishwoman-turned-Mennonite to be comin' round here and fillin' the preacher's wife's head with all kinds of nonsense." He'd also confided the bishop had put him on the spot, questioning Hannah's close ongoing relationship with a Mennonite.

Mary Ruth's my sister, for pity's sake, Hannah had thought at the time, not daring to speak up. After all, having received the divine ordination, Gid was always right— God's choice of a shepherd to this flock. There was to be no questioning the man of God, even though there were times when she did secretly wonder how the Lord God could look on Bishop Bontrager's heart and be pleased. Was it possible for a divine appointment to go off beam . . . for a man reckoned to be the messenger of God to become blind and puffed up with pride?

She could only hope such a thing would always be far from true of her handsome husband, although she had always known him to have an opinion about most everything, just as both of their fathers staunchly

did. The two older men had been quite similar in their thinking on most things, except
here lately Dat hadn't heeded his friend's
advice to call the hex doctor—Gid had said
as much. This puzzled her no end, and she
was relieved Abe had managed to survive
the blow to his head despite what *might've*
happened with Dat disregarding the importance, even the sway, of a sympathy healer.

"When did you last see Abe?" she asked
Mary Ruth, getting up to take Mimi from her
to nurse her.

"Just yesterday, when I took Carl for a
visit after school." Mary Ruth said that Carl
had been worried to the point of an upset
stomach over his friend.

Hannah smiled faintly. "Well, it's mighty
sure Carl's become nearly part of the family,
seems to me." She wondered what her sister might say to that.

"Dat hasn't always been so keen on
Carl's visits, but it seems to me that recently
he's been a little more easygoing." Mary
Ruth paused, giving Hannah a small smile.
"He's surely got a new spring in his step."
Mary Ruth rose and went to rescue several
blocks the girls had allowed to roll under the
corner cupboard. She got down on all fours,

laughing as she did, because Ida Mae had come running over and hopped on her back as if Mary Ruth were a horse.

Hannah admitted she'd observed the same thing. "I suspect Dat won't always be a widower . . . though it ain't our place to speculate on his business," Hannah said, lifting baby Mimi onto her shoulder for burping. She wondered if now was the right time to tell Mary Ruth what Gid had said about her visits here, though it pained her to think of doing so. Instead she again brought up the subject of her concern for Abe.

"Leah says our brother has been talkin' nonsense. His balance is off-kilter, too. It's got her mighty anxious."

Mary Ruth sat back down in the chair near the window, the light coming in and resting on her slender shoulders, making her hair look even blonder. "He must've hit his head awful hard."

Hearing Gid's footsteps outside, Hannah felt awful nervous now. *What'll my husband say if he finds Mary Ruth here again?*

She immediately rose and headed to her bedroom to put Mimi in her cradle, hearing Gid's voice as he greeted Mary Ruth out in the front room. Standing behind the bedroom door, she was hesitant to return, so she waited there, eavesdropping.

"Is Hannah here?" Gid asked.

"She's tucking Mimi in" came Mary Ruth's reply.

There was a lull, but soon Gid said, "This ain't easy to say, but I've been thinkin', Mary Ruth, 'bout the People and all. Seems it might be better if ya didn't speak your mind to Hannah so much."

Mary Ruth remained silent.

"Might just be best, too, if ya didn't come round here so often," Gid said flatly. "Hannah bein' the preacher's wife now and you bein' . . . well, Mennonite. Just doesn't set so gut with some folk."

Ach, Gid! Hannah clutched her heart, because she'd never heard her husband talk so, not in that severe tone of voice . . . not even to a stubborn horse. She felt she might burst out crying.

———◆———

As Mary Ruth walked down the mule road toward her father's house, she could think only of her brother-in-law's stern admonishment. The formerly pleasant Gid had surely changed since his divine appointment. Fact was, Hannah needed loving encouragement—she'd sunk into near despair over Abe's accident, and even life's small concerns seemed to pull hard at her. And now was Mary Ruth to obey Gid's warning and be cut off from her own twin sister? A more intimate friend she'd never known.

She breathed in the wintry air as she made her way out toward the main road, bypassing a visit with Leah and Abe, although her heart longed to stop in for a short while. She wouldn't give in to worry over Abe, though, because she had made up her mind she was going to trust the Lord for her brother's healing. She must stand on the promises of God, let Him be at work in young Abe. "In all of us," she said aloud.

Soon her thoughts turned to Robert. While they had continued seeing each other since their frank discussion about Derek and Sadie, there had been no marriage proposal. Without a doubt, Robert was an upstanding man, one kind and good in every respect. She had every reason to love him. Robert had all the qualities a good preacher should possess—and all those of a good husband, too.

She found it curious that both she and Hannah were connected to ministers. One who humbly taught the full truth of God's Word, and one who, having been raised a smithy's son, was much more skilled at shoeing horses than at helping folk shod their feet with the preparation of the Gospel of peace. After all Gid Peachey had never had a speck of training. When the lot fell on a man, there were often days and weeks of actual mourning as the newly appointed man accepted the responsibility, even the burden, of the People resting soundly on his shoulders. Mary Ruth could just imagine that weight on Gid now, which might have been the reason for his harsh remarks to her today. Yet she would not allow her encounter with him to bring her discouragement, for a dispirited person was open to even more opposition from the enemy of the soul.

So Mary Ruth marched along the road with head high, ever so confident in the Lord. She was sure that in God's time, He could turn even this for good.

◆

Days had passed since Sadie's revelation, and since then Leah had seemed distracted, encumbered by her continued care of Abe. Or perhaps it was newfound resentment toward Sadie that made Leah so distant, although it seemed unlike her sister to hold a grudge. Still, one thing was altogether sure: no offer of forgiveness had come. *Maybe she's had enough,* thought Sadie.

Meanwhile the original peace she'd experienced at her confession had faded, and old thoughts had returned to haunt her— memories of dear Harvey and her blue babies. Memories, too, of her shunning, Leah's seeming betrayal of her, and of Derry and the terrible sin with him that had set things in motion. *If only dwelling on the past could make things different for me.*

The afternoon weather had turned blustery and cold when Sadie spotted Mary Ruth out on the road. *Maybe Mary Ruth knows something of Derry . . . if he happens to know the fate of our baby,* Sadie thought. But she decided she best not take off running after her, though she surely wanted to. She simply stood there at the front room window, gazing after her sister, wondering just what Mary Ruth might know about Derry Schwartz. *Will she say what she knows?*

Finally, having tried her best to stay calm and not give in to impulsiveness, she told Leah she was going for a short walk and donned her wool coat, black outer bonnet, and snow boots.

"Where are ya headed?" Leah looked a bit surprised at the amount of outer clothing she was piling on.

"Need some air, is all."

"Goin' up to see Hannah, maybe?" Leah pressed, eyes revealing more disquiet as Sadie reached for her muffler and mittens.

"Haven't decided just where," Sadie fibbed, feeling a sting of guilt, yet not changing her plan as she turned and walked out the back door. A strong wind nearly blew her back into the house, but stubbornly she pushed ahead.

When at last she caught up with Mary Ruth, she was more than a half mile from home, farther away than she had been since the outset of her present Proving. Farther, too, than was allowed on her own, really, but Sadie felt she was safe from Miriam's eyes on such a cold and snowy day. Besides, if she kept her face forward, who'd know it was she beneath the big black winter bonnet?

"I saw you from the window," she told Mary Ruth, matching her stride as they went. "Need to talk to you privately."

Mary Ruth's face was red with the cold, but she didn't mince words. "Shouldn't you head back, what with the rules of your Proving and all?"

Sadie shook her head. "I'll risk that for now."

"Well . . . what's on your mind, then?"

Inhaling, she held in the frigid air before breathing out. "I've been wantin' to ask ya something for the longest time," she began. "It's about your beau's brother."

"Derek?"

"Do ya happen to know him at all?"

Mary Ruth hesitated, as if pondering her response. "I've seen him only twice. Once long ago at the vegetable stand and, later, out on the road at Christmastime some years ago now. Why do you ask?"

Pausing, Sadie worried how her questions might sound, but she persisted. "Do you know he was the father of my first baby?"

Mary Ruth nodded. "In fact, he wasn't shy about telling me who he was that Christmas Day. I must say, I was mighty surprised."

"Did he ask about the baby . . . or me?"

Mary Ruth said she recalled that afternoon quite clearly. "He seemed to be in a big hurry . . . headed down this same road, toward the house."

"Our house, ya mean?"

"That's right. He was out of sorts, swinging his arms like he was lookin' for a fight."

Sadie didn't care to reflect on the way Derry had behaved when he was irritated; he'd displayed his bad temper too many times for her to forget. "Did you tell him I wasn't livin' at home any longer?"

"Since we'd heard you were married to Jonas Mast back then, I said you were out in Ohio somewhere and married. That was all."

Sadie slowed her pace now. "Anything else?"

"He asked if you'd had a boy or a girl, and I told him your baby son had died at birth. That was pretty much the end of the conversation. He turned and left, headed back toward his parents' house."

Sadie breathed more deeply, taking all this in. *Derry had been heading toward Dat's house. Why was that?*

They fell silent for some time, walking more briskly to keep warm.

When they grew closer to the Nolts' place, Sadie asked if ever Robert talked about his brother.

"Last I heard, Derek's stationed somewhere out in Washington state. He hasn't been home in seven years . . . not since that Christmas." Mary Ruth was frowning. "I'm worried that you're asking all these questions, Sadie. You never should have met him in the first place. Why would you want to know about him now?"

Abruptly, Sadie stopped walking. "I wondered what he knew. I guess I thought it might help me to put the whole thing to rest and forget the past."

"This happened a long time ago. And since I've told you everything you need to know, why not head on home?" Mary Ruth urged. "I'm nervous for you."

Sadie felt she was walking on dangerous ground, too, having wandered this far already. "Jah, s'pose you're right."

Mary Ruth turned and hugged her. "So long for now."

Waving, Sadie turned and started back down the lonely road. She shivered against the fierce cold and, when the weather turned even more blustery, she wished she'd stayed put at home in the kitchen near the wood stove. What did it matter, anyway, that Derry had asked about her or their baby? *So cruel he was,* she thought.

Less than halfway home, a squall of snow came up. She tugged on her coat and drew the muffler around her neck more securely, bracing herself against an afternoon storm that had in short order become a full-blown blizzard.

Sadie tried in vain to see her way, unsure if she was wandering toward the shoulder or out into the middle of the road. But she kept going, hoping she might make it home before Dat or Leah began to worry. Her hands, feet, and face were so cold they were beginning to sting with pain, yet she must not focus on that. Reminded of young Abe's struggles with frostbite, she happened to notice automobile headlights creeping toward her. Moving out of the way, she was surprised to see Robert Schwartz waving at her through the snowy windshield.

Mary Ruth's beau stopped, opened the car door, and insisted she get inside. "What are you doing out in this?" he asked.

She didn't think twice about accepting his invitation, even though the mandate on her Proving was once again breached the minute she climbed inside the warm car. "Thank you," she said, shivering uncontrollably. "I thought I could make it home. . . ."

"Thank the Lord I saw you."

"Jah." She was grateful indeed and kept her face forward, sitting stiff as can be as he turned the car around and headed toward her father's house. "I'm much obliged," she said, not knowing what else to say now that she was alone with Derry's elder brother.

"Your family will be glad to see you safe," Robert said.

She mentioned she'd just spent some time walking with Mary Ruth. "She sent me on home."

"I'll get word to her by phone that you're safe and sound, once I arrive home."

By phone . . .

Truly, Mary Ruth had all the conveniences of the world—a handsome boyfriend with a fast, warm car; a pretty house to live in with heat, electric, and a telephone.

She was glad for the offer. "I might've lost my way in the storm if you hadn't come along."

"If not that, at least I may have spared your hands and feet from frostbite."

She smiled at that, though her face was so numb she could scarcely feel the muscles move. "There's the lane to the house," she said, pointing to the left.

"Thanks, I would have missed it," he acknowledged with a chuckle. Making the turn, he stopped the car without a warning and set the brake. "Uh, Sadie." He turned to face her. "Mary Ruth shared with me what happened between you and my brother some years ago." His face was solemn, even sad. "I'd like to offer an apology on behalf of Derek."

Sadie was both stunned and moved. "That's kind of you, but it's not for you to say." Still, she greatly appreciated the courteous gesture.

"It's best, I believe, that my brother's long gone. Otherwise, you might be tortured by running into him from time to time."

"Jah" was all she could manage to utter, looking away now.

Without saying more, Robert released the brake and inched the car forward. The tense conversation was behind them, yet she marveled at the timing of her encounter with Mary Ruth's beau. Who would have thought, when she'd set out to catch up with Mary Ruth earlier, she would be hearing apologetic words from no less than Derry's own brother?

However, when they arrived near the back door, she was completely aghast. Bishop Bontrager was walking to his carriage, leaning hard into the wind. But just before he moved to step in, he looked straight at her. Their eyes met and held.

"Oh," she groaned with deepest despair. "I'm surely ruined."

"Beg your pardon?" Robert said.

She shook her head, again muttered a feeble thanks for the ride, and headed out into the elements, toward the house and her certain *Schicksaal*—her fate.

Chapter Fifteen

The bishop motioned for Sadie to follow him back into the house, where she stood, unmoving, in the utility room as the man of God announced to both her father and herself that she was to be sent away for her disobedience.

Sent away? She hung her head not so much in shame as resentment. Surely Bishop Bontrager knew she would never have accepted a ride with a man had it not been for the severe weather. Still, she knew she'd ignored the rules of the Proving and for that deserved what she was getting.

Dat spoke up. "But the blizzard . . ." he said, attempting to defend her. "Sadie wouldn't have—"

"Such has no bearing on the matter at hand," the bishop said, cutting him off. At once the older man turned and pushed out the door, leaving Sadie standing alone with Dat, scarcely able to raise her eyes to his. When she did so at last, she caught his look of both disappointment and aggravation. With a low groan, Dat walked toward the kitchen.

Bishop would've sooner I froze to death, Sadie decided, going to the window to watch his horse and buggy head down the lane toward the main road. The back of the buggy whisked out of sight as it quickly became shrouded in the whiteout of dense, wind-driven snow. Moving from the doorway, she hung her coat on the wooden peg and, feeling dreary, removed her mittens, muffler, and boots. From the kitchen came the low hum of voices—no doubt the rest of the family was talking about the bishop's visit.

Why'd he come on such a dismal, stormy day, anyway?

Suddenly she knew: The bishop had come to see how poor Abe was faring.

She could have kicked herself for having chosen this day to display such open disobedience. The lie she'd told Leah earlier hung on her conscience like a yoke; she'd drifted much too far from the house, not to mention accepted a ride in an automobile with a man. All were clear violations of the Proving.

Sadie sighed deeply. *How foolish I am to have tempted fate so. . . .*

Leah had suspected all along where Sadie had gone, because not but a few minutes before her departure, Mary Ruth had walked past the house, probably coming from a visit with Hannah. *If Sadie didn't flat out lie, saying she didn't know where she was going!* Now her untruthful sister was coming into the kitchen, her cheeks mighty red from the cold in spite of her ride home in Robert Schwartz's car, of all things. What on earth was she thinking?

Sadie didn't stop to say hello or to join in their conversation, all of them having hot cocoa at the table—she simply forced a smile and made her way to the stairs. Leah could hear the quickness of her sister's footsteps as Sadie nearly flew upstairs.

She's been caught again, Leah thought, feeling both sad and worried about what additional church discipline might do to Sadie's emotional state. She found herself tuning out the talk around her, anxious about how the bishop would ultimately handle this transgression, with Sadie already nearly three months into her Proving.

———————◆———————

The afternoon after the bishop's visit, while Abram and Leah were out in the barn amidst the cows and the milk buckets, Abram brought up his great frustration, for possibly the third time. "Sadie needs to be livin' with us, not somewhere else. 'Tis not for widows to live apart from family."

Leah was sitting in Sadie's usual place under Ol' Rosie, squeezing the cow's teats for all she was worth, evidently irritated no end. "This could push Sadie into deepest grief yet again. Seems to me she just got home."

"Jah, I was surprised she held up as well as she did yesterday. The bishop talked mighty straight to her. His face was downright purple."

"So . . . do ya think Bishop will hold a firm stand?" Leah asked.

Abram considered this. "Hard to say. I'm hopin' he comes to his senses, and right quick."

Abram went on to mention he'd spoken with Dawdi John about the bishop's harsh stance toward Sadie, and Dawdi agreed they must go along with it, whether they liked it or not. "What about Mary Ruth— could she make room at the Nolts' for Sadie?" he asked.

Leah sighed softly. "How would that set with the brethren, her livin' with Englishers and all?"

"The Nolts are less fancy than, say, the doctor and his wife. I don't know where else she could go right now." His heart sank as he worried about losing another daughter to the world. He wanted Sadie under *his* roof, or within close riding distance at least, in hopes the bishop might allow them to visit her on occasion. Most folk under church discipline benefited greatly from words of kindness and admonition.

Truth be known, Abram wished he'd spoken up even more to the bishop yesterday when Sadie returned home—the elderly minister was taking this much too far. *Sure, she's broken specific requirements of the Proving, but the discipline doesn't seem to match the offense.* If Robert hadn't come along in his car when he did, who knows where they might've found his eldest daughter. Abram's heart was torn between the Ordnung and his love for Sadie, and there was no getting around it.

———◆———

Leah's good-byes to Sadie were not nearly as emotional as Lydiann's tearful farewell. Poor Lyddie followed her all the way out to the sleigh, crying her name. Now she stood with nose pressed to the front window, watching Dat take Sadie up to the Nolts'. Dottie herself had surprised them by coming over, once the roads were plowed, to drop Mary Ruth and Carl by to visit Abe, who was still suffering headaches and frequent dizzy spells. Leah had made it a point to follow Dottie out the back door, where she had quickly shared the family's dilemma, taking care not to point fingers at the bishop. Surprisingly Dottie had taken to the idea with enthusiasm, and the arrangements had been made just that quickly. Sadie had crossly gone to pack her bags when Dat had okayed the plan.

Lydiann burst out sobbing to high heavens when she could no longer see the horse and sleigh moving down Georgetown Road. "Dat's takin' my big sister away from me!"

"Ach, don't cry so, Lyddie," said Leah, going and wrapping her arms around her. "Surely the bishop will let us visit Sadie now and then . . . help her get back on the straight and narrow. Surely he will."

"But you don't know that for sure . . . and she's goin' to Mary Ruth now . . . and Carl, too." Lydiann wept in Leah's arms. "Just when I was gettin' to know her. Just when . . ." She cried as if her heart might break.

Leah let Lydiann cling to her. "We can pray this will all work out for the best."

Lydiann leaned back and looked up at her with tear-filled eyes. "What do ya mean?"

"I 'spect I'll be talkin' to God 'bout all this," she whispered to her dear girl. "And you can, too."

Lydiann blinked her eyes and a slight frown crossed her brow. "I don't understand."

"There are times—like right now—when the Lord God wouldn't mind hearin' a prayer from our hearts. One we make up on our own, so to speak."

"Not the prayers we usually say in our

heads, then? The ones we think of at dinnertime and before bed?"

"That's just what I'm tellin' you. There are times when, if ya feel as if your heart's breaking, 'tis best to call on the Lord and say what's on your mind."

Lydiann burst into a smile just then and pressed against her, hugging her hard. "I'll just do that, Mamma. I will!"

And deep within herself, Leah knew she, too, must be offering similar prayers more often.

◆

Mary Ruth cried when she saw Sadie standing at the front door. She hurried to greet her sister, and the two fell into each other's arms. "Oh, Sadie, I'm so sorry."

"Ain't your fault," Sadie whimpered. " 'Tis all my doin'. I deserve this . . . I know I do."

Mary Ruth led her upstairs and showed her where she could put her clothes for the time being, saying that Dottie had offered more storage space in a seasonal closet down the hall. "You'll be ever so comfortable here," she said. "You'll see."

Sadie sat on the bed, looking all around.

"Mercy sakes, I've never seen such a perty bedroom." Then she smiled a little. "Well, now, how could I, since I've never been inside an Englisher's bedroom before now?"

Mary Ruth didn't want to tell Sadie that it wouldn't take too long and she'd become adjusted to the warmth of the rooms each morning, not to mention the indoor bathroom and other luxuries. But such modern conveniences were not good enough reason to leave Amish life behind. "I'm glad you'll be stayin' here," she said, going to sit next to Sadie on the bed. "Maybe we'll get caught up some now."

Sadie nodded sadly. "Denki, Mary Ruth, for sharin' your room and all."

"I'm glad to do it." She hoped to share more than just the room. Given the time, Mary Ruth was eager to share the Lord Jesus with Sadie, as well.

———◆———

Dat was a late riser that Saturday, so Leah went to his door and knocked lightly. "Dat? It's Leah . . . are you awake yet?"

"Jah, come in" was his reply.

Feeling right peculiar at his response, she

did as she was told. She saw him sitting in
the corner of the room near the gas lamp,
Mamma's open Bible on his lap. "Leah," he
said, "do you happen to know, by chance,
when your mamma started markin' up this
here Bible?"

A breath caught in her throat, and she
saw then that tears filled his eyes. "It was
some years ago . . . long before Lydiann
was born."

A nearly reverent hush passed between
them.

"Are ya certain?" Dat asked.

She nodded her head. "Mamma loved to
read God's Word." She hoped she wasn't
speaking out of turn, recalling the quiet
tones in which Mamma had spoken on the
several occasions she and Leah had discussed such matters.

"I awakened at midnight," Dat said. "The
wind . . . or maybe it was the Lord God,
woke me out of a deep sleep. I've been sittin' here reading near every underlined passage in this here *Biewel* . . . two or three
times each."

Leah stood silently, staring at her father.

Dat placed one hand gently on the open
pages. "I have to admit that I think I know

why your mamma walked the floor nearly ev'ry night, prayin' over her children . . . and me. Jah, believe I do. . . ." His voice faltered.

Leah knew, as well, but she yearned to hear Dat say it, wanting to know if he truly understood just what it was that put a near-holy smile on Mamma's face each and every day.

"Ida grasped the most important things about God. She understood them . . . and she lived them, ain't so?"

Leah nodded. "Oh, Dat, she did that."

He closed the Bible and placed both hands on top. "I want what my precious Ida had. How should I go 'bout getting it?"

Leah glanced over her shoulder, wondering if either Lydiann or Abe had come downstairs yet. "The best I know to tell ya is to do what I did . . . open your heart wide to the Lord Jesus." She wouldn't reveal at this moment that she'd nearly memorized some of the passages in Mamma's Bible.

"The Good Book says to come to Him as a little child," Dat said, wiping his eyes.

Leah felt a lump rise in her throat. "I should say so" was all she could whisper for her joy.

———————◆———————

Once the milking and breakfast were finished, Abram wasted no time. He found Lizzie in the small kitchen of the Dawdi Haus.

" 'Tis a brisk mornin', but I'd like to take ya out for some fresh air and maybe a sticky bun," he said quietly, lest her father overhear their conversation from the front room. "How'd that be?"

Her pretty hazel eyes lit up like it was Christmas all over again. "Can ya first spare me a half hour?"

Too eagerly, he bobbed his head. "I'll get the horse hitched up and come for ya right quick."

She beamed her interest, and he headed back through the tiny front room, where John was starting to snore—or pretending to.

———————◆———————

This was no time to give in to his emotions, yet Abram longed to reach for Lizzie's hand as they rode along in the privacy of the family buggy. His heart pounded at the idea, and it was all he could do to redirect his thoughts. Yet the woman he had come to love was sitting next to him, and they were alone, under heaven's canopy.

They talked of Sadie's pitiless ousting by the bishop, and Lizzie pointed out that Sadie had seemed to purposely go beyond the boundaries of the Proving. "Wouldn't ya say so, Abram?"

"Jah, I agree on that, though I don't see it as out-and-out rebellion." He went on to share how troubled he was by their bishop. "It's one thing after 'nother, seems. I almost wonder if Bontrager has it in for me and my household."

Lizzie nodded, stirring as she sat next to him in the carriage. "Dear Sadie's bound to be doubly dejected about now, still mournin' her dead husband and all."

If Abram didn't control himself, he might simply allow the horse to trot along, let go the reins, and take this outspoken but dear woman in his arms right now in broad daylight. And, goodness, wouldn't that be a telling picture if someone came riding along in the opposite direction?

For a fleeting second, he wished he were a young fellow once again and he and his sweetheart-girl were out riding under the covering of night. No wonder young folk courted after sundown. Made plenty of good sense to him, now that the tables were turned and he was the one falling in love . . . for the second time.

But first things first. "Lizzie?" His voice cracked as he held tight the reins.

"Jah, Abram?"

"I want to tell ya 'bout what happened to me this morning while I was readin' Ida's Bible." He found it mighty easy to pour out his heart to his deceased wife's devout younger sister. "I believe I've seen the light . . . a long time comin', I daresay."

He knew Lizzie understood what he meant when she gave him the sweetest smile he'd seen in recent memory. "Ach, 'tis true. I see Jesus in your eyes."

He nodded, eyes filling quickly with tears. "I've resisted much too long, sorry to say. I 'spect heaven's pursuit of me has the Lord himself near tuckered out."

Her soft laugh encouraged him greatly. "I guess you can say you've joined the ranks of the silent believers, ain't so?"

"There ain't a doubtful bone in my body."

"Thank the Lord above," she said.

"Jah, the Lord sought me out, indeed." He drew in a long breath, because what he planned to say next was definitely going to be more difficult. "I've been thinking 'bout something else, too, for quite some time."

Will she welcome this *news?* he wondered, becoming more hesitant now that he realized how far out he was about to stick his neck. No question, the thought of her rejecting him would do him in. Should he forge ahead?

It was then she surprised him and reached over and placed her hand on his. " 'Tis all right, Abram. Say what's on your mind."

Caressing her hand, he turned to face her. "Lizzie, my dear, I'm head over heels in love with ya."

Her smile was even brighter than before.

He didn't waste any time. "Oh, ya just don't know how awful much. . . ."

They rode along for another good half hour, but before they came to the turnoff to the Ebersol Cottage, Abram asked with confidence, "Will ya accept me as your husband?"

" 'Course I will, Abram. I'd be right happy

to." Lizzie didn't shilly-shally one bit. By the look on her face, it was evident Lizzie knew, just as he did, that they were meant to be together as husband and wife as soon as possible.

He lifted her small hand to his lips and planted a kiss there, not caring at all now who spied them.

———◆———

Glory be! Lizzie felt as if she might take off flying, so happy she was as she headed into the Dawdi Haus. "Dat, I've got somethin' to tell ya," she called to her father, who was still snoozing in his favorite chair.

He roused momentarily, eyebrows raising, then eyelids flitting shut.

"No, no, now—stay awake to listen to your maidel daughter," she said, crouching near his knee. "I've got me a beau, Dat: Abram Ebersol, your own son-in-law. Now, what do ya think of that?" She watched his expression closely. How would he take his Ida's being replaced by her sister?

Hearing Abram's name must have awakened him, for now her father was all eyes. "Well, now, what did you say?"

"You heard me, didn't ya? And you're the first to know something else . . . I'm gettin' married here 'fore too long." She could scarcely keep her voice at a whisper, where it needed to be, at least for now.

An endearing smile spread across her father's craggy face. "Ah, Lizzie . . . my dear girl. I'm mighty glad to hear it." He paused before saying, "I guess I'm not too surprised, really. I've been wonderin' if the old fella wasn't sweet on you."

"So, then, you're all right with it? You can give us your blessing?"

He chuckled—it was a quick little cackle, almost gleeful. "Aw, go on. You's don't need my approval. You're old enough to make up your own minds, for goodness' sake!"

Leaning over, she kissed his rough cheek. "I'm ever so happy . . . really I am."

"Happiness is short-lived, I daresay, so make the most of it while ya can." He was grinning now, and he reached for her hand and squeezed it.

"I just wish my mother had lived to see this day."

He nodded. "It's natural you'd be thinkin' thataway."

She rose and headed for the kitchen,

where she set to brewing a nice big kettle of tea—a kind of celebratory pot to be shared between her elderly Dat and herself. *Truly, I've never been so happy!*

Chapter Sixteen

Time dragged. Lydiann watched the minute hand move toward the numeral twelve, ever so anxious for ten-o'clock recess to come this bright and snowy Monday. She knew Carl had some seatwork to complete before he would be allowed to play, so she'd volunteered to help redd up the cloakroom while he worked at his desk and the teacher was outdoors supervising the rest of the children.

At last it was time, and the teacher reminded some of the younger pupils to sharpen pencils and visit the outhouse. When Lydiann got the go-ahead to sweep the cloakroom, she was glad. Once all the children had filed out to recess, she took the broom from the hook and hurriedly swept the dirt from the floor, scooped it up into the dustpan, and dumped it into the trash can near the teacher's desk. That done, she tiptoed over to Carl's desk, where he was dawdling with his pencil, not working his problems.

"Did ya get behind in arithmetic?" she asked.

"A little."

"But you ain't doin' what you're s'posed to, are ya?"

He pulled a face and then put down his pencil. "What're *you* doing inside during recess, anyway?"

"Got somethin' to ask, that's all." She glanced toward the door, hoping none of the other pupils would come bursting in just then. "I've been wonderin'. Can you read Amish even though you don't speak it?"

His face turned red but he nodded. "I know it from my uncle Paul, the one who used to be Amish. He taught me to read Pennsylvania Dutch, which isn't, by the way, called Amish."

"Sure it is."

"No, that's only what Amish folk call it." He looked so determined, she decided to let him have the last word.

"Did your uncle ever join church?" she asked, more softly now.

"Nope. He bought himself a tractor instead."

"Oh." She thought on that. "Seems he must not have thought much of the Old Ways, then."

Carl shrugged. "Not when it comes to farming. Why waste all that time plowing, planting, and harvesting with horse-drawn wagons and whatnot when you can be done with it in short order with a tractor? Seems right silly to me."

"But tractors have inflatable tires, and that's a no-no."

Again he shook his head. "Rubber tires or steel tires, tractors or horses or mules. Isn't it all about getting the job done?"

"You'd have to talk to our bishop 'bout that."

"So you can't think for yourself?" Carl smiled faintly.

She pouted at that. "I've been wonderin' something else."

"What now?"

She didn't like his tone but pressed on. "What's it like bein' adopted?"

"You oughta know that."

"What do ya mean?"

"I don't want to speak out of turn, but

aren't you and Abe adopted in a way? Mary Ruth says your real mamma died when Abe was born, so your sister Leah has raised you like you're her own."

Mary Ruth says . . .

Why was her sister's name so quick out of his mouth? Still, she thought on what he'd said till she got up the nerve to ask, "Do you know your true family at all?"

He stared at her. "That's a silly question and you know it, Lyddie. I'm living with my true family. It doesn't matter to me who my birth parents were."

"*Were?* Do ya mean your parents died?"

"I didn't say that."

She could see he was upset, even angry. "I'm sorry, Carl."

"No, I don't think you are." He got up and went to the cloakroom, where he threw on his coat and scarf and hurried outside, slamming the door behind him.

Now what have I done?

Not only had she poked her nose in Carl's life, but he would surely catch what-for since she'd kept him from completing his seatwork.

He's got every right to tattle on me, Lydiann thought, returning to the cloakroom to make sure there was not a speck of dirt on the floor.

———— ◆ ————

The coffee shop in Apple Creek, Ohio, was jam-packed with customers, especially the back room, which was solely populated by Amishmen. Jonas made his way through the maze of tables toward his friend Lester Schlabach, who nodded his head when he caught sight of Jonas.

"Sounds like a crowded hen house in here," Jonas commented amidst the chatter.

Lester laughed. "You oughta come out for coffee more often . . . you'd get used to the racket mighty quick."

"S'pose so, but orders for hope chests keep me downright busy these days—almost more work than I can handle on my own. Must be plenty-a girls turnin' sixteen this year."

"Awful gut for the pocketbook, I'll bet."

Jonas agreed and motioned for the waitress. He ordered a pot of coffee and a raspberry sticky bun for each of them—his and

Lester's favorite pastry—insisting today was his treat.

When the waitress had gone, Lester stroked his beard, pulling it into a point. "I saw in *The Budget* that Eli Gingerich is goin' out of the plumbing business and is havin' himself a big sale here 'fore too long."

"I saw that, too. He wants to tear down some of his old shop and rebuild it to make a woodworking one."

"Some competition for ya?"

"Not a problem, really. Ain't enough woodworkers to go round here."

"That old bishop of yours back in Pennsylvania prob'ly wouldn't see eye to eye with ya though, ain't?"

Jonas looked hard at Lester and solemnly nodded his head. The mention of Bishop Bontrager reminded him again why he'd ended up living here in Ohio all these years, estranged from his parents and brothers and sisters. "Doubt I'd agree with much of what Bishop Bontrager thinks anymore."

"Seems to me I recall you sayin' he didn't take too kindly to fellas who shunned farming."

Shunned. He supposed Lester had completely forgotten that he lived under the

Bann himself, although it did not affect Jonas in his daily routine here. Nevertheless, he did have a family in Pennsylvania he missed terribly.

"My old bishop felt it was a fella's duty to follow in his father's footsteps and work the land. He took a mighty strong stand on that." *Among other things,* he thought. Shunning folk for leaving behind the church of their baptism was unheard of in Wayne County, far as he knew. "I wish my people back home could have a chance to sit under the teaching of the Apple Creek bishop. There was a wonderful-gut bishop like that in Millersburg, too," he said, recalling the short time he'd spent with the Mellinger family. It had been David Mellinger who had given him such a strong start in cabinet-making with a valuable apprenticeship. "Those two Ohio bishops and my former bishop are the difference 'tween night and day, for sure and for certain."

Lester perked up his ears. "You mean to say your Pennsylvania family doesn't hear sermons like ours?"

"Well, it would be awful hard to know that anymore, really." It felt to him as if many decades had come and gone since his last visit to Lancaster County, back when he and Leah Ebersol were engaged and looking ahead to a happy and bright future together. He could only assume that Bishop Bontrager still kept the clamps on the People of Gobbler's Knob and Georgetown, but there was no way to be sure, since all communication had been cut off to him— and *from* him. He cared not to cause trouble for his parents and siblings, or his extended family and former friends, by attempting to make forbidden contact. *What's done is done.*

He hadn't planned to, but he began to tell his new friend how he had a whole batch of siblings, some of whom were grown and probably married by now. "My youngest brother and sister will be ten years old come this April."

"Twins?"

"Jah, and I haven't seen them since they were babies."

"How odd . . . them havin' a big brother they've never known."

Sadly he agreed. But there was nothing he could do about any of that. With the blessing of the heavenly Father and the People here, he'd put his roots down deeply and joyfully in Apple Creek. What more could a man want?

———◆———

It was a brutally cold afternoon when Mary Ruth suggested she and Sadie go and sit near the fireplace in the Nolts' well-decorated front room. Sadie politely accepted the cup of hot peppermint tea her sister offered, her sad eyes brightening when Carl came to kneel beside her, showing a drawing he'd made at school.

"That's awful perty," Sadie said.

Carl handed the picture to her. "It's for you . . . to keep."

"Well, how nice." Sadie stared down at the crayoned picture of a big brown horse and a small gray buggy. "This looks like the bishop's horse," Sadie said, holding it up for Mary Ruth to see.

"Well, I'm not so sure about that. Seems to me it might just be Dat's horse," Mary Ruth replied, studying the drawing.

Carl frowned. "How can you tell the difference when there are so many horses and buggies?"

"Oh, believe me, we know," Sadie laughed.

Mary Ruth nodded. "Same way an Amishman knows which straw hat belongs to him, even though dozens of hats might be lined up on a bench."

Carl asked about Amish farm life, and Sadie seemed eager to tell him about milking a cow by hand, feeding chickens, and pitching hay to the mules and horses. "Sometime you should talk to Leah 'bout all that," she said. "She knows all there is to know about farm animals."

Mary Ruth found herself daydreaming about next Friday evening, when Robert planned to drive her to Honey Brook, where they would dine at a "very fine restaurant." A tingle of excitement ran up her spine as she wondered if he would again say he loved her. If so, she wondered if it was the right time to say it back to him. Handsome as he was kind, Robert would make any girl's heart glad, yet he had chosen her, and the passage of time had proven that neither of them wanted to let anything prevent their hopes for the future—not even the past foolishness of her sister and Robert's younger brother. In any event, the likelihood of Sadie and Derek ever crossing paths again was quite slim.

She turned her attention back to Sadie and Carl, who were now sitting side by side on the hearth looking at a storybook. Sadie's voice was gentle and low, but the expression she gave to the phrases on the page impressed Mary Ruth so much she wondered if she might invite Sadie to come with her to school as a volunteer tomorrow. She could certainly put someone to work part-time helping with a few struggling pupils. *It might keep Sadie's mind off herself,* Mary Ruth thought. But then she worried that such a thing might put Sadie even more at risk with the Amish brethren, so she decided against it.

What's to become of her?

Sadie had confided to her just today she wouldn't be staying on at the Nolts', wanting to find work outside the Amish community, but Mary Ruth hoped that wouldn't happen, not when it would break the hearts anew of everyone in the Ebersol Cottage to see her leave them once more. If her time here lasted long enough, maybe Sadie might begin to understand more of God's plan for her life, perhaps through the simple

Bible stories she was even now reading aloud.

———————◆———————

Leah picked her way through the ice and snow to the barn to speak with Gid and Dat, leaving Abe alone at the table with his schoolwork. "I won't be long," she'd told him, rushing out the back door into the dusk.

In the stillness of the stable, she cautiously asked Dat's and Gid's permission to pay a short visit to Sadie tomorrow at the Nolts', telling them she wanted to encourage her to repent to the bishop for her misconduct. Leah also had something else on her mind, but she didn't go so far as to reveal that.

Dat looked at Gid and asked, "Have ya given any more thought to what we discussed?"

Gid shook his head. "Haven't talked to the bishop just yet, no." He paused, glancing at Leah. "I'm the youngest preacher in the district and . . . well . . ." He didn't finish the thought, but Leah knew he must be hesitant to make waves with Bishop Bontrager.

Dat continued. "Well, I can see your point, but it's important we get our girl back home."

Gid nodded thoughtfully, but it was fairly obvious to Leah that he wasn't so keen on the idea, what with the bishop's tough stand on breaking the requirements of a Proving.

But Gid seemed to catch Leah's sense of urgency when she said she'd heard tell from Mary Ruth that Sadie was thinking of getting a job and moving closer to Strasburg.

"Sadie isn't *that* stubborn, is she?" he asked.

"Jah," Leah replied. "But I daresay she's not thinkin' clearly yet . . . still distraught over losin' her husband so awful young."

Gid put down his pitchfork. "I'll go 'n' talk things over with the bishop and see what can be done."

"You're headin' over there *now*?" Dat sounded mighty surprised.

"Time's a-wastin'." Gid looked right at Leah and smiled. "Wouldn't it be mighty nice if this family came together once and for all?"

Leah felt joy in her heart at his words. But would he actually succeed in getting the bishop to change his mind?

———◆———

After enjoying Dottie's delicious crumb cake with applesauce, Mary Ruth and Sadie slipped away upstairs to the bedroom they now shared, where Mary Ruth offered to brush her sister's hair.

"Aw, you don't have to do that," Sadie said, seemingly touched by the gesture.

"But I want to." She coaxed Sadie to sit on the chair while she stood behind her, whispering a silent prayer.

"Ya know, Leah and I used to take turns brushin' each other's hair of an evening," Sadie said softly, even sadly.

"We both have happy memories of growing up in Dat and Mamma's big house." Mary Ruth began making long sweeps down Sadie's golden locks with the brush.

Sadie nodded. "Ain't that the truth."

They talked about the endless winter, how cold it was, and how much Mary Ruth loved teaching school.

Out of the blue, Sadie asked, "When will Carl turn ten?"

"This spring."

She was silent for a moment, then— "Same age as my first little one . . ."

Mary Ruth's heart went out to her, and she wondered if being around Carl was an emotional hardship. "Do you find it difficult to be around Carl for that reason?"

"Oh no . . . not at all," she promptly reassured her. "My stay here has been delightful—hardly the punishment the bishop had planned for me. But even so, I need to find my own place and land myself a job."

"You'd really leave the Amish life behind?" Mary Ruth asked. "Is that what your heart's telling you?"

"Oh, I don't know what I want anymore. I can hardly abide the bishop and his rules— I just felt so locked up in Dat's house. There were plenty of days I wished I could hop in the buggy and drive off to Georgetown to run errands or whatnot. And now look where I am. Like a person without a home."

Mary Ruth felt now was the moment to share one of her favorite Scripture passages with Sadie. "I've been wanting to tell you something that's helped me a lot during some of my darkest hours," she said, not waiting for her sister to respond. "It's from the Proverbs: 'Trust in the Lord with all thine heart; and lean not unto thine own understanding. In all thy ways acknowledge him, and he shall direct thy paths.' "

Sadie turned to face her, chin quivering. "I've heard those verses before."

"Do you remember where?"

Sadie nodded. "From Mamma. She used to recite Scripture while we cooked and baked together. I always wondered, though, why some of her favorite Bible verses weren't ever read at Preachin' service."

"I wondered that, too."

"Out in the Ohio church—and later in Indiana—the preachers stressed different verses than they do here at home."

Mary Ruth listened with interest and then told how terribly she'd struggled at Elias Stoltzfus's funeral and how she'd finally found what she had longed for her whole life at a Mennonite church, not so many days following his death.

"If it's divine guidance you're looking for, Sadie, it can be found in God's holy book." She went to her dresser and picked up the black leather Bible Dottie had given her as a gift. "Everything I need to live my life each day is right here." She held the Bible close. "Sometimes I think I could simply read it instead of eating. That's how dear it is to me."

"Oh, Mary Ruth, bless your heart, you're cryin'." Sadie reached out her hand.

"They're joyful tears," Mary Ruth confessed with a warm smile. *Sadie's opening her heart,* she thought, full of thanksgiving.

Chapter Seventeen

Leah awakened in the morning to the sound of fussing coming from Abe's bedroom. Quickly she scurried into her slippers and made her way down the hallway. When she looked in on Abe, he was all tangled up in his bedclothes, struggling to get loose. "Mamma, Mamma!" he was crying. "The room's spinnin' round and I'm stuck. I have to get out of bed."

Panic seized her heart and she sat down with him. "There, now, lie back, Abe. I'm here . . . just rest." She stroked his forehead gently, her other hand on his chest. His heart was pounding nearly out of his rib cage, and he was breathing ever so fast. "You'll be all right now. Take longer breaths . . . that's right. Jah."

Whatever had caused him so much turmoil this morning? She couldn't imagine, nevertheless she stayed right there with him till he quieted down enough to fall back to sleep.

He's exhausted, she thought, straightening the sheet and blankets, taking care not to awaken him. Dr. Schwartz had kindly suggested she bring Abe in for yet another checkup, and now she was determined to do so . . . as soon as she felt comfortable taking him out in this cold weather.

She hurried back to her bedroom to dress, setting forth on her daily routine. Once her hair was twisted tightly on both sides and the low bun at her neck was secure, she put on her head covering and went to her hope chest at the foot of her bed. There she located Sadie's delicate butterfly handkerchief.

She truly hoped she wasn't making a mistake in taking it to her sister today. Ever since Sadie's confession, Leah had pondered the past—Sadie's and her secret keeping. The whole kettle of secrets had brought a world of hurt. Yet looking fondly now at the pretty handkerchief, she couldn't be sure how Sadie would respond to receiving this physical memory of her first dear baby's birth.

Is this the right time, Lord?

◆

Two hours before she was to arrive at the clinic for work, Leah could hardly wait to head off on foot to see Sadie. A growing urgency to forgive compelled her along as her boots plodded through the snow. She felt she was carrying an unnecessary burden, and it was time to do what she knew she must—what she longed to do.

When Sadie flung wide the front door, Leah blurted, "Ach, sister, I just had to come see ya."

Sadie's eyes narrowed and a brief frown creased her brow. "Come in, come in," she said after a moment, nearly pulling Leah inside. "Here, let me take your wraps and mittens."

"Denki, but I shouldn't be long." She sighed, hurrying into the front room, following Sadie. "I miss ya so much," she said.

Sadie's pretty eyes shimmered with tears. "Oh, Leah . . ." Sadie reached for her hand.

"I've come to say something else, too"— Leah struggled to continue—"something that has been brewin' in my heart."

Sitting next to her on the settee, Sadie said, with trembling lower lip. "I'm awful sorry for what I did against you and Jonas, honestly I am. I don't deserve your forgiveness, Leah. It was plain awful to hurt you the way I did. The letter I took belonged to Jonas. . . ." Her apology trailed away into a sniffle.

When at last Leah was able to speak, her voice sounded thin to her own ears. "Oh, Sadie, I *do* forgive you . . . I do. I came here to set things right 'tween us."

At this Sadie seemed overwhelmed, her eyes welling up with tears. Leah drew her near, and they embraced with fond sisterly affection.

When they broke free, Leah was at a loss to know what to say. Second-guessing her plans to show Sadie the butterfly hankie, she wondered, *Is this really the best time? Will it open new wounds for her?*

Still searching for words, Leah said quickly, "Lydiann wanted me to tell ya hullo."

Sadie sighed. "And you say the same back for me, won't ya?"

" 'Course I will." Leah sat tall and straight—uncomfortably so. "And I'm hopin' you'll think of askin' the bishop to forgive ya . . . soon, maybe?"

Sadie hesitated, and Leah feared she'd perhaps spoken out of turn. "I know 'tis an awful trying thing," Leah said.

Sadie nodded, and her words were soft and labored as she spoke. "I've heard tell— best not say from whom—that the brethren may be payin' me a visit."

Leah's heart rose at the thought. Gid's meeting with the bishop had accomplished *something.*

Sadie folded her hands. "Not so sure what I'll do 'bout it."

"What do ya mean?"

"I daresay I don't deserve a second chance . . . if that's what the ministers are thinkin'."

Leah faced her. "Well, you surely didn't mean to get yourself in such a pickle, did ya?"

"Frankly, I don't know what came over me, wantin' to meander away from the house like that." Sadie paused. "I never should've lied to you."

"This has all been so hard on you," Leah replied. "It'll be all right. You'll see."

Sadie drew in a deep breath. "I thought comin' home would be easy somehow, but . . . oh, Leah, the memories are everywhere for me. I thought they were buried in the past, but . . ." She nearly gasped. "Being here, I still think of my first baby ever so often. Is that so wrong?" Sadie wept softly now, but her gaze held Leah's, as if a newfound trust was developing between them.

It is *time,* Leah thought hopefully. Touching Sadie's hand gently, Leah reached under her black apron. "I'm hopin' what I have here might help make ya feel some better." She took from her dress pocket a handkerchief. "I thought you might want to have this back," she whispered, holding it up.

"Goodness me," said Sadie, obviously recognizing the cutwork embroidered butterfly. "Isn't this . . . ?"

Leah nodded.

Raising the white cotton hankie to her face, Sadie brushed it against her cheek. "Where on earth did ya find it?"

"On the sidewalk leading to Dr. Schwartz's clinic."

"How'd it get *there*?" Sadie asked, appearing startled.

"I wondered that, too, but it looks as if Dr. Schwartz simply forgot to return it followin' the night of your baby's . . ." There was no need to go on.

Sadie fingered the handkerchief lovingly. "Thank you ever so much, Leah. 'Tis the closest thing on earth to my wee son."

Leah was moved by Sadie's response, and she wished she'd returned the hankie sooner—perhaps upon Sadie's return home last fall. *Still, she's happy to have it now, and that's what matters.*

Minutes later Dottie came in carrying a tray of goodies and hot cocoa. Leah rose and offered to help serve her sister. "No, that's all right. This is what I love to do," said Dottie, setting the large tray on a table near the settee.

"Thank you," Leah said.

"Jah, this'll hit the spot," Sadie added, the handkerchief laid out on her lap.

Dottie pointed to the hankie, a bright look of recognition in her eyes. "Well, now, that looks exactly like the embroidered hankie an acquaintance of mine had and lost."

Leah felt herself frown, but it was Sadie who spoke up. "Here, have a careful look-see," she offered, holding the handkerchief up for Dottie to inspect. "I have a feelin' you must be mistaken, 'cause if you'll look closely you'll see that this is one of a kind. Hannah made it especially for my sixteenth birthday."

Dottie touched the edges of the emerald green butterfly. "No, I'm quite sure I've seen this before today . . . or one exactly like it."

Dottie was so unyielding that for a moment Leah wanted to ask where she thought she'd seen it, but then they got to talking about the stitching and how Hannah must have a very steady hand to create such beauty.

"Fannie Mast pointed out some of the same lovely features on the butterfly hankie she had. A gift to her," Dottie said matter-of-factly.

Leah's eyes locked with hers. "Fannie, ya say?"

Dottie nodded. "She's an Amishwoman with a set of boy-girl twins the same age as our Carl. Fannie had a hankie like this with her one day. I couldn't help noticing it when she was sitting in the waiting room at Dr. Schwartz's clinic with her twins, just as I was with Carl. We talked quite a lot, exchanged names, and got along famously, I must say." Here she laughed a little, and then she told how she and Fannie had seen each other several other times since. "I purchased a bushel of apples from the Mast orchard this past fall. Real nice folk, they are."

Leah felt slightly queasy hearing talk of her former beau's family.

"Did you say Fannie lost the handkerchief she had like this?" Sadie's question disturbed Leah's thoughts.

Dottie nodded, returning the handkerchief to Sadie. "Quite some time back."

"Well, there's only one like this, that's for sure," Sadie said pointedly.

For a fleeting moment, Leah wondered if this hankie *was* in fact Fannie's, especially since she'd found it lying on the sidewalk just outside the clinic door. Was it possible Cousin Fannie had dropped it on her way to a doctor visit? *How could that be?*

Yet the way Sadie was going on now with Dottie about this absolutely being Hannah's handiwork, Leah dismissed the notion that there could be two identical hankies.

———◆———

"God be with you, sister," Leah whispered as she hugged Sadie good-bye. She was relieved to note her sister's spirits had greatly improved.

Outside, though, Leah was unable to forget Dottie's self-assured remarks about the butterfly hankie. *No, I'm quite sure I've seen this before today,* Dottie had said.

Impossible, thought Leah as she headed around the corner to Dr. Schwartz's clinic.

There she began by sweeping and cleaning the floors, and then moved on to dusting the furniture in the waiting area.

After a time she stopped her work and went to see if Dr. Schwartz was in his office. Along with Dottie's supposed memory of that same handkerchief, Leah had also been struck by Sadie's renewed grief for her first baby, born in Aunt Lizzie's former log house on the hill.

Till now Leah had rejected the notion of approaching Dr. Schwartz again on the subject, but today's visit had made her certain it might help Sadie if she knew her baby was buried in the vacant lot below the Peacheys' farmland. Why else would Dr. Schwartz tend the tiny grave?

Another recent storm had blown piles of snow against the north side of the clinic, and she could see the tops of drifts at eye level out the doctor's lone office window as she waited in the doorway. "Mind if I come in?" she asked.

"You certainly may, Leah." He pushed up his glasses and studied her for a moment. "How's Abe feeling now? Back to school?"

"Not just yet, but Lydiann brings home plenty of schoolwork to keep him out of mischief."

"And the dizzy spells, have they lessened some?"

"Not much just yet and it does worry me. He still has a bit of confusion when he gets to talkin', too."

The doctor's eyes narrowed and he removed his glasses. "Bring him in and I'll check him over for you. No charge." He went on to ask about the follow-up tests made at the hospital. "Anything show up there?"

"Nothin' alarming," she told him. "But he doesn't yet remember a stitch of what happened that day, and it clearly annoys him. His mind used to be ever so sharp."

Dr. Schwartz assured her that the symptoms should diminish over time. "I know it's difficult, but try to be patient and keep Abe as calm as you can."

Leah had to laugh. "Well, he's all boy, so that ain't an easy task." They exchanged small talk for a bit; then Leah decided to ask the thing plaguing her.

"I hesitate to bring this up, really," she began. "It's just that Sadie's strugglin' these days." She quickly explained as best she could something of the Proving requirements and the burden they placed on her sister. When she revealed that Sadie had temporarily moved in with the Nolts, he admitted to having already heard this news from his wife, Lorraine and Dottie having become good friends over the years.

"I hate to ask, but I wondered if it might not help Sadie somehow to know . . . well, ever since I stumbled onto a little grave on your property, I've wondered if, by chance, you might've buried Sadie's baby there."

He started at her words and his eyes squinted nearly shut. "What do you mean to imply?"

"I saw you clipping the grass in one small spot, tending to it, last spring."

The doctor rose suddenly. "You surely recall that your sister's baby was quite premature. You saw him yourself. There was simply no need for a burial."

"But . . . your car was parked nearby, and Lydiann and I saw you while we were walkin' back from Mamma's grave at the Amish cemetery."

His eyes avoided hers for a moment, and then he turned to face her. "What you saw was my attempt at dowsing for water." He indicated there was a small spring-fed pond on the same sweep of meadow—not to mention Blackbird Pond behind the smithy's property, not so far away—and he assumed there might be a well on his land. "And there is."

"But there *was* a grave . . . I know it, for sure and for certain," she insisted.

The telephone rang just then, jolting her nerves, and the doctor excused himself, wasting no time rushing off to the receptionist's desk.

Alone now, Leah thought again about what she had seen that warm day, but she was fairly sure the doctor had not been carrying a forked water-witching stick. No, he had been down on all fours, working close to the ground. Was it possible he had the ability to simply use his hand to dowse for water?

If that were true, neither she nor Aunt

Lizzie would want her to be in the employ of someone who had such powers. But since she didn't know for certain just what the doctor had been doing, she ought not be too hasty in judging this man who had been ever so kind to her. Still, the way he'd stood up so suddenly, as if taken aback by her question—apparently anxious to answer the phone—made her shiver, even though the room was plenty warm compared to the frigid weather outdoors.

Chapter Eighteen

Sadie was truly astonished at Dat and Preacher Gid's unexpected visit two days after Leah's. The knock at the Nolts' door came midafternoon Friday, and she was thankful there was no one else in the house at the time.

Dat and Gid agreeably stepped inside when she opened the door and welcomed them, and her father got right to the point. "Our preacher, here, went to plead your case to the bishop this past week . . . and I'm mighty happy to tell ya, I believe his news to be ordained of the Lord God."

"What news?" she asked, eager to know.

Her father turned toward Gid and nodded his head, as if prompting him to reveal all. "Jah, 'tis true . . . it's something of a miracle, I'd have to say." He looked down at his black hat before continuing. "Seems the bishop's willin' to give ya another chance at the Proving, Sadie. But only if you come clean before the brethren."

Carefully she listened as Gid explained further. "The requirements will be even more rigid than before, and you must repent to three of the brethren—the bishop, one preacher, and a deacon."

Dat went on to say that all this must be agreed to before the new time of scrutiny would ever begin. If, and only if, Sadie agreed to adhere to this even stricter Proving, which was to be extended to the beginning of June, instead of to the middle of April, she could return home.

Sadie could scarcely believe her ears. "A longer Proving, ya say?"

" 'Tis the price for disobedience."

She hung her head. "Jah, I was awful foolish."

Gid's face brightened, apparently heartened by her words. Dat, on the other hand, moved to her side, and she sensed his zeal for what he'd taken as an admission of her guilt.

"So embarrassing all this is," she said, her mouth dry as can be.

Dat's voice was thick with emotion when

he said, "We'll welcome ya home with open arms . . . when the time comes."

She knew she could not now keep making offhand remarks about getting a job out in the world. Truly, she did not desire to leave her life with the People, even though her short time in a modern house *had* been warm and wonderful-good in many ways.

She reckoned Leah's return of the butterfly handkerchief to her to be a symbol of providence ahead. Something far beyond her was calling her back to the straight and narrow, where she felt she might find peace if she simply did not fail in following the Old Ways.

———————◆———————

The heavy snowfall partially obscured Leah's view as she watched Dat and Gid from the kitchen window. The men cleared off the buried path to the woodshed, and then dug out the high drifts near the barn doors.

Soon here came Lydiann, piling on outdoor clothes, saying she was going out to help Dat "no matter how deep the snow," and with that was out the back door.

Red-cheeked Dat came in for some hot coffee after a while when Gid ran back up to his house for breakfast. With Lydiann still out in the snow, Leah and Dat found themselves alone in the toasty warm kitchen.

"I best be tellin' you first," he began.

Leah was struck by the radiance of his gray eyes, but she said not a word. "Somewhere along the way, I fell in love with Lizzie, and I plan to marry her come next Saturday." His gaze searched Leah's following this declaration. "I'm hopin' this won't come as a shock, nohow."

"I guess I'm not too surprised," she said, meaning it. "The twinkle in your eye for Aunt Lizzie has been perty obvious at times."

He nodded awkwardly as if there was much more he wanted to say.

"Goodness knows, I couldn't be happier for you two."

To this they both laughed. "Wanted you to know directly from me," Dat said, looking more serious again. "It'll affect you more than any of the others in the family, I 'spect."

She understood what he meant and held her breath as she waited for him to continue.

"Lydiann and Abe look to *you* as their mamma, which mustn't change a'tall be- cause of this," Dat said. "You'll always be that to them. Wouldn't think of meddlin' with that, not one iota, and Lizzie agrees whole- heartedly."

She felt ever so grateful to this man who'd loved and sheltered her as his own during her growing-up years, just as she was now doing for his children. To think he was planning to marry Leah's own natural mother. "Aw, Dat, you'll be ever so happy with Lizzie," she found herself saying. "I know you will be."

There was a merry light in Dat's eyes. "I'm awful glad Lizzie and I don't have to wait till fall to say *our* vows."

"Like the young folk."

He chuckled and added, "Bein' an old widower ain't so bad when it comes to some things, jah?"

Leah went to the wood stove and poured him more coffee, and he sat by the fire drinking it silently. Meanwhile, she headed upstairs to awaken young Abe as joy flooded her heart. She felt she ought to pinch herself at the thought of Aunt Lizzie becoming Dat's wife. At last dear Lizzie would have a husband of her own!

———◆———

Monday morning Leah hurried upstairs after making the pancake batter and while waiting for the griddle to heat up. Through his doorway, she spied Abe sitting on the edge of his bed, looking up at her with squinting eyes, as if his vision was still blurred. "It's me, Abe," she said, going to sit next to him.

"I'm awful mixed up," he whispered.

"That's all right. The doctors say you'll get better each day, jah?"

"No, I mean 'bout something else."

"Oh, what's that?"

He scratched his head, frowning to beat the band. "Just who's gonna be my mamma when Dat gets married again?"

She smiled and put her arm around him. Dat had announced the happy news to the rest of the family at suppertime last night. "Well, I am, silly. Who'd ya think?"

He shook his head. "I can't figure out how that can be. Won't Aunt Lizzie become my mother?"

She could see how confusing all this would be, even without the lingering effects of a traumatic blow to the head. "Let me tell you again all about the day you were born, Abe."

"Jah, I'm all ears for that."

He settled against her, and she let him relax that way as she shared the precious things Mamma had said, even prayed, over her beautiful baby boy as he was entering the world and she was leaving it for heaven. "Mamma must've surely prayed a special blessing over you at your birth," she told him. "By the sweet look on her face as she lay dying, I believe she did."

"Our mamma loved us, ain't so?"

Leah nodded. She would always think of his mamma as her own and felt sure she was smiling down on all of them as they looked ahead to the happy wedding day.

———◆———

Monday, January 21
Dear Diary,
    I feel as if I must write down my feelings or sink deeper into despondency. Abe doesn't seem to be getting better

quickly enough to suit anyone. Leah was here to see Mimi again yesterday afternoon, and she admitted to still being most anxious about him. I've thought of asking Gid to call for the hex doctor one day when Dat and Leah are away from the house, maybe, to put an end to this misery for poor Abe. For Leah, too. I hate to think this, but I wonder if Dat's refusal to have the Amish doctor come hasn't been some sort of a curse on his only son. Yet Gid doesn't think so when I talk to him of this, though I can see he is as wide-eyed with worry as the rest of us.

We've been awful careful not to discuss Abe's ailments in front of our girls. Even so, the notion young Abe will never be right disturbs me round the clock. Maybe all this never-ending worry comes from the baby blues I'm having something awful. I might just need a visit from the hex doctor myself. Oh, I just don't know, really. Mary Ruth seems to think I should throw myself on the mercy of the Lord God, but I honestly don't see how her "saving grace" can help me.

Poor Gid isn't in control of his own household . . . much less the household of faith. But I really can't lessen the amount of tears I shed, sometimes for no real reason at all . . . though I feel just terrible when Gid comes home to find me in a heap on the floor, sobbing while I hold tiny Mimi as Ida Mae and Katie Ann play. Is this what it feels like to lose one's mind, I wonder?

I must keep my tears in check for at least Dat and Lizzie's wedding. Gid's going to marry them in the front room at Dat's house. Since Dat's a widower and Lizzie, at age forty-five, is much older than most brides, this will be a small gathering of family and close friends.

Plenty of changes will take place in the Ebersol Cottage with this new marriage. Sadie has already returned home—on her best behavior and with the blessing of the bishop—and will move to the Dawdi Haus this next week to look after Dawdi John. Leah, of course, will stay put in the main house, because she is helping raise Lydiann and Abe, who will have had the love of three mothers in one lifetime.

Well, I best be tending to Mimi. Truly, her cries slice right through me—at times I am startled, even put out by my own flesh and blood. Whatever is wrong with me?

Respectfully,
Hannah

———◆———

The deep cold made itself known in the crunching creak of work boots on hard-packed snow as farmers headed for the barnyard, or in the solid thump of horses' hooves on wintry roads. A stiff northern wind swayed the towering trees in Abram's backyard as Gid made his way into the lower level of the bank barn, ready to shovel out the manure and redd up the stable.

Still ringing in his ears was the sound of Mimi's crying into the wee hours of this morning, and he wondered why it was that Ida Mae and Katie Ann had been such easy babies for Hannah to tend to. He recalled Hannah had actually been cheerful when the older girls were but newborns.

Picking up the shovel, he set to work, beginning the smelly yet needful job. All the while, he couldn't get his wife's gloominess out of his mind. The joy of motherhood had flown out the window with the arrival of Mimi. Nearly all Hannah wanted to talk about these days was one worry after another, concerns that revisited her during the dark night hours in her increasingly frequent nightmares.

Gid shoveled all the harder, glad for the quiet of the barn, not looking forward to returning to the log house for lunch. Fact was, he was often tempted to slip in at Abram's table and enjoy the peace of his father-in-law's house and Leah's tidy kitchen, come noon. Naturally he had never succumbed, always heading up the long mule road to the cabin where he'd made a home with Hannah. It wasn't that he regretted his choice in a bride—Hannah had been his all in all, his everything, from the first day he'd invited her for a ride in his courting buggy. He just wished he could somehow lessen her emotional burden. Maybe tonight he'd offer to walk the floor with inconsolable and colicky Mimi, if necessary. A good night's sleep might be all Hannah needed, he thought. Either that or a visit from one of the hex doctors. *Jah, might just do all of us some good along about now, including young Abe.*

He would have to check with Abram on this first, of course, because Abram had not called for a sympathy healer when it had been most critical. What had made Abram change his mind on something he'd long held important? Would Abram, in fact, agree to set things right by having the hex doctor come and work his magic as should have been done in the first place?

Just today Hannah had pleaded with him to ride for the powwow doctor not but four miles away. "Have him calm Mimi down with his potions or chanting. And me, too!" she'd said.

He recalled how uneasy he'd felt around the older man, how he could hardly wait to send him packing once Hannah's baby was born safe and sound. Never in his life had he felt such a cold presence—like a blue haze draped over all of them in the room. He could remember only a handful of times as a boy being taken to visit the man with healing powers . . . and only by his father. Mamma would sooner have seen them all perish than summon the Hexedokder, he knew.

Thinking back on his breakfast conversation with flustered Hannah, he wondered how she'd gotten to the place where she so strongly desired help from powwowing, especially since both her mother and Aunt Lizzie had resisted it.

◆

That evening following supper, Gid offered to look after the girls. "Hannah, go 'n' rest a bit," he instructed, following her into the bedroom to make sure she did indeed lie down.

Hannah nodded, brushing tears away, and he pulled up a quilt to cover her, hoping she might be able to console herself in the silence of the room.

His wife had caused him alarm on plenty of other occasions—if the ministers knew the full extent of her suffering, just how would it set with them? The preacher's wife was to be an example, not a hindrance to the People, so Gid must see to it that Hannah was surrounded with joyful folk like Leah, Aunt Lizzie, and his own mother and

sisters. There was plenty of support awaiting Hannah . . . and himself.

Meanwhile Gid had his first wedding to
prepare for, and after morning milking tomorrow, he must pay another visit to the
bishop about the procedure. The thought of
yet another face-to-face talk with the man
of God put a chill in his bones, especially after the grueling encounter he'd borne on
behalf of Sadie, but there was no putting it
off. Abram Ebersol was mighty eager to
wed, and the bride-to-be was happily willing.

Chapter Nineteen

Leah heard Lizzie stirring next door in the Dawdi Haus midmorning Tuesday. She could see the top of her aunt's head near the cookstove in the cozy kitchen, where she found Lizzie leaning down to remove a large sheet of chocolate-chip cookies from the oven. On the way over, she'd noticed the front room was empty. *Dawdi John must be upstairs resting,* she decided.

"Oh, hullo," Aunt Lizzie said, noticing her right then.

Leah joined her as Lizzie sat at the table to scoop warm cookies from the cookie sheet with a spatula, carefully placing them to cool on brown paper. "They smell wonderful-gut," she said.

"Your father's favorite, ain't so?" Aunt Lizzie smiled broadly as she mentioned Dat.

Leah breathed in the tempting aroma. "I'll

wait till they cool a bit before having a taste. But I'm having only one."

"Ach, goodness, you could stand to eat a whole handful." Lizzie eyed her curiously. "You ain't tryin' to lose weight, now, are ya?"

In all reality, Leah hadn't gained a single pound in more than ten years; she had been cutting her dress and apron patterns the exact same size since she was coming into her time of rumschpringe. "I just best not be eatin' more than one" was all she said.

"Some sugar will do ya gut," Aunt Lizzie pressed.

"Makes me droopy after a time, though." Leah supposed it did that way with many people. She'd noticed the same in Lydiann when she ate lots of cookies in one sitting or had too much cake or pie. Lydiann had a surge of energy—too much, really—and then she'd become whiny and worn out. The same wasn't true of Abe, though. Like Dawdi John, he could eat and eat desserts and never be bothered.

"We'll have plenty of goodies and pies and things for the wedding," Aunt Lizzie spoke up. "I've asked Miriam and your aunt Mary Ebersol to help with the baking."

Leah's ears perked up. "I didn't realize there would be more than just the immediate family invited."

Lizzie broke out in a wide smile. "Abram and I got to talkin' and we changed our minds 'bout that. Peacheys—Smitty and Miriam—will come, as well as most of your father's siblings. I've mailed handwritten invitations to my brother Noah and his wife, Becky, as well as all my siblings over in Hickory Hollow. We'll see who shows up." Suddenly her smile grew a bit cunning. "I even stuck my neck out and invited Peter and Fannie Mast."

"What on earth?" Leah couldn't believe her ears. "They'll never show their faces, ya know."

"No, prob'ly not. But we can keep extendin' the hand of friendship."

Leah wondered if her father had been in favor of this, but she was more interested in something else. "Since most people don't know about you and me bein' mother and daughter, I've been wonderin' what we— Sadie, Hannah, and Mary Ruth—oughta call ya, once you and Dat are wed."

"Well, now, I'll always be Aunt Lizzie to you girls, I'm thinkin'. Lydiann and Abe, too, of course." Lizzie's eyes narrowed. "Did ya have something in mind?"

To this Leah had to smile. "I wondered if Dat might want us to call you Mamma, out of respect, maybe." She paused. "I doubt any of us would mind that, but . . ."

Lizzie patted her face. "Nothing much 'tween you and me or your sisters and me will change when I marry your father. There'll always be a shoulder to cry on and plenty of love to go round. No need to alter any of that, right?"

Leah could feel herself relax a bit; she had wanted to honor Lizzie as her father's new wife, yet she longed to keep separate the special place dear Mamma still held in her heart.

Hannah dropped off Ida Mae and Katie Ann at the Peacheys', eager to slip away from the house and go with Mimi to visit one of the hex doctors. She'd gotten to thinking that perhaps all her ceaseless worrying about everyone and everything was more *her* problem, really—something unique to her. She seemed to turn near all the little things in the life of her family, immediate and otherwise, into an overwhelming haystack of issues. As she had tried to rest last night between Mimi's bouts of colic, she couldn't stop thinking about wanting to fall asleep forever, never to wake up. She didn't know why she would think such a thing, when it would appear she had the kind of life any Amishwoman would envy— a handsome, kind, and loving husband and three beautiful little ones. So what was wrong?

Well, she was on her way to find out, and with baby Mimi tucked snugly in a makeshift cloth carryall next to her on the buggy seat. Hannah rode as fast as she could to the only woman powwow doctor in the area: Old Lady Henner, as old as Gobbler's Knob itself, some said.

Hannah's mental road map proved to be absolutely accurate, even though she had visited this doctor only one other time in her life. The place was a quiet and unassuming white three-room cottage, set back from the road and lined on either side by lilac bushes and other flowering shrubs, which, as she recalled, were always more abundant in blossoms than any others in the area come springtime.

She made her way up the short walkway

and, holding her baby near, she rapped on the screen door, heart pounding as she did so. The elderly woman hobbled to within a few feet of the door and waved her in, not bothering to come and open it, almost as if she'd been expecting her.

"I hope it's all right to visit today," Hannah ventured.

"Come in, come in." The white-haired woman nodded. "What can I do for ya, Hannah?"

"I'm here for help with three ailments," she replied, thinking of the troubles of baby Miriam, herself, and her brother.

The nearly toothless woman gave a swift smile and peered into the small basket where Mimi, miraculously, was fast asleep. "Oh . . . you've brought your littlest one. Well, now, she looks something like your husband, ain't so?"

Hannah readily agreed. "She has Gid's eyes and hair."

"Ah, our youthful preacher . . ." The old woman looked at her, gray eyes cloudy, and Hannah wondered if she might be going blind. "This one's got herself a quick temper, and so awful young at that. Ain't that a big reason why you've come?"

Hannah removed Mimi from the basket. "I'd hoped Miriam wasn't a bad seed, so to speak. I'd hoped she simply had a long bout with the colic."

The old woman leaned hard on her gnarled walking stick and backed up and lowered herself into a rocking chair. "Now," she sighed, "give the wee babe to me."

Hannah lowered Mimi into the old woman's frail arms and lap. She wasn't exactly sure what Old Lady Henner began to softly utter while holding sweet, sleeping Mimi, but the short chant sounded mighty strange.

As she finished, the baby's eyes flew open, and Mimi reached her tiny hand up to the old woman's face and cooed contently.

"Now, then, Hannah, what can I do for you?"

Reaching down, Hannah picked up Mimi and placed her back in the basket, noticing how limp her daughter felt. Quickly she turned back to the old woman. "I'm afraid I have the mother fits, and there just ain't anything to stop 'em." She struggled with the lump in her throat. "Honestly I think I might be losin' my mind some days."

The old woman looked up at her. "I'll see

to all of that. Don't you worry your perty little head." And Old Lady Henner motioned for Hannah to sit cross-legged at her feet.

Eager for relief from the gloom that tenaciously enveloped her, Hannah went willingly to the floor and sat like a child, closing her eyes.

When the chanting was through, Hannah felt so relaxed she wanted to stay sitting there, without budging an inch.

But Old Lady Henner was eager to move ahead to the third ailment, so Hannah began to describe Abe's symptoms as best she could.

Then, for the longest time, the older woman squeezed her eyes shut, concentrating on something, her lips moving slowly . . . silently. After a while, though, she opened her eyes and shook her head, wearing a look of consternation. "Ach, I'm havin' me an awful time breakin' through for Abe, no matter how hard I try."

Hannah found this to be ever so peculiar, as she'd never heard of such a thing. Evidently Old Lady Henner's powers were fading with her age, but Hannah said not a word about that.

Abram swallowed his intense nervousness. He had never before thought of doing what he'd just done. The strongest urging had come to him—from the Lord God, he felt certain. "What do ya think of me placin' my hands on Abe's head to pray for him?" he'd asked Leah.

"For his healing, ya mean?" Leah's hazel eyes had shone.

He had nodded, reverently whispering the Scripture he'd committed to memory: "They shall lay hands on the sick, and they shall recover. . . ."

With Leah accompanying him, they had gone to Abe's room. There, Dat had knelt beside Abe's bed, placing his hands on his sleeping son, and fervently prayed, "O Lord God and heavenly Father, I come before you to ask for my son's healing, in the name of your Son, the Lord Jesus. . . ."

◆

It was Abe who broke the news to Leah, just as she was encouraging him to lie down for an afternoon rest, following the noon meal. She had been thinking about all the schoolwork Lydiann was gladly carrying home each day for her brother, worried the boy might never catch up, even a little fearful that he might lose a year and have to be held back. She doubted Dat would ever hear of such a thing, not for his bright-eyed and smart son, and she wouldn't let herself cross that bridge till the time came. Truth was, Abe was a determined sort of youngster. He'd not only survived the struggle of his own difficult birth, but he was pronounced to be "as healthy as they come" by Annie, the Amish midwife—something for which Leah was grateful each day.

"I can see better today," Abe told her as they headed up the stairs.

Leah noticed his speech was less garbled, too. "Of course, you're gettin' better. I knew you would." She followed him to his room and stood in the doorway, wanting to share with him what Adah had said in the hospital, that with God all things were possible. "Our heavenly Father's lookin' after you," she told him. "I've been askin' almighty God to heal you. Dat has, too."

He looked at her quizzically. "Ya talk to the Lord God 'bout me? 'Bout my hurt head?"

She couldn't help herself; he was such a

dear boy. She rushed to his side and squeezed him good. "Of course I do. You're the apple of His eye, just as you are your earthly father's."

When she released him, he looked up at her, his eyes clearly focused. "God must care for me an awful lot."

"I'd have to say that's ever so true." She pulled back the quilt and top coverlet on his bed, and Abe climbed in, having just removed his shoes. "By takin' it easy and not complaining, I believe you're doin' your part. Now let the Lord do the rest."

He smiled up at her from beneath the blankets. "You're downright smart," he said. "I'm glad you're my mamma."

She leaned over and kissed his forehead gently. "Have a nice sleep now, ya hear?"

Tiptoeing out of the room, she smiled at Abe's sweet remark, ever so glad God had given her the opportunity to care for him and Lydiann. Glad, too, that Sadie was back home and would be on hand for Dat and Lizzie's wedding. She dearly hoped Hannah would be able to attend, as well—Leah was deeply concerned about her sister's present mental state.

Heading to the kitchen to begin preparing

supper, she wondered if, like Hannah, Lorraine Schwartz might not also be a melancholy sort of person. There had been times when, upon entering a room, she'd discovered Lorraine's eyes red, a handkerchief in her hand. Leah's heart went out to her and Hannah both. It seemed to her there was much to be joyful about in life, but obviously Lorraine didn't see it that way, at least not since her younger son had forsaken his family. As for Hannah, she had every reason in the world to be happy.

◆

Blushing a bit and wearing her new blue cape dress, Aunt Lizzie stood before Preacher Gid on Saturday morning with Dat near and looking sober yet happy in his clean black Sunday trousers and coat. The front room of the Ebersol Cottage was packed to the windowpanes with wedding guests. Leah watched and listened ever so closely, not wanting to miss a single word as Dat and Lizzie promised "nevermore to depart from each other," but to faithfully care for and cherish each other, till that time when the dear Lord God should separate them by death.

Leah sat between Sadie and Lydiann, glad to see such a large gathering of folk on hand to witness the wedding service, aware of the sunny faces of Dat's relatives and a good many of Lizzie's, too—most coming by horse and sleigh because the roads were packed with plenty of new snow. Sadie was all smiles today, too, a sight Leah hadn't seen in some time, although she and her sister had enjoyed a long heart-to-heart talk upon her return, when Sadie shared that she was going to see it through *this* Proving "no matter what. I won't disappoint my family—or God—this time." Glancing at her now, Leah reached for her dear sister's hand as the People began to sing in unison three wedding hymns from the *Ausbund.*

The one and only thing to cast a faint cloud over the day was the obvious absence of the Masts, though neither Leah nor Lizzie—nor Dat especially—had expected Mamma's cousins to grace them with their presence this day of days.

When the time came Bishop Bontrager rose and took Preacher Gid's spot before Dat and Lizzie. He placed his big hands over theirs and solemnly recited, "I say to you: the God of Abraham, Isaac, and Jacob be present with you and aid you and carry out His blessing abundantly upon you, through Jesus Christ. Amen."

They were pronounced husband and wife moments later, and Leah found herself thinking right then of the mother who'd raised her. *Oh, Mamma, if you're looking down on all of us now, surely you know how happy Dat is this wonderful-good day.*

Lydiann looked up at her, eyes glistening. "This holy moment is ever so special, ain't so?"

Reaching over, Leah clasped her darling girl's hand and nodded slightly. Lord willing, there were not too many more years before young Lyddie and Abe would also be standing before the brethren with the dear young man and woman of their choosing, waiting to say their lifelong vows before God and the People.

Jah, not so many years hence, thought Leah through joyful tears.

Part Two

♦ ♦ ♦ ♦

*To appoint unto them that mourn in Zion,
to give unto them beauty for ashes,
the oil of joy for mourning,
the garment of praise for the
spirit of heaviness;
that they might be called trees
of righteousness,
the planting of the Lord, that
he might be glorified.*

—Isaiah 61:3

Chapter Twenty

Spring 1963
The sky was barely light and every bird in Gobbler's Knob was warming up for a grand daybreak chorus when Lydiann hurried downstairs, hoping to make it to the kitchen before either Mamma or Aunt Lizzie awakened. She wanted to surprise the family this morning with a great big breakfast, which she was planning to cook all by herself.

Ever since her sixteenth birthday last week, Lydiann had been planning the breakfast, this being the day before her first-ever Sunday singing. After all, if she met the right boy soon, it wouldn't be too many years from now she'd be cooking in her own kitchen. She and Mamma had been talking about this season of her life for quite some time now, Mamma encouraging her to simply "have fun during rumschpringe—get acquainted with plenty of nice fellas."

In other words, don't settle down too quickly with one boy and rush into getting serious.

Lydiann knew Mamma's intended message, all right. It was more than clear where she was going with her concerns. After all, having babies out of wedlock seemed to run in the family, and, well, she wasn't going to make such a mistake with *her* life. Mamma and Aunt Lizzie both had nothing at all to worry about, as she'd told them in so many words. Maybe more words than necessary, truly.

As for Dat, he wanted to get his say in, too, what with all his talk of "now, make sure Abe's the one to be takin' ya to the barn singing come Sunday night." Her first time at a singing was turning into a family concern—definitely not the way things were supposed to be.

Sighing, she contemplated all of this over the sizzling skillet, ready to pour fresh eggs and milk, mixed together and salted, into the pan. Naturally, once she did begin seeing different boys, coming home with them in their spanking-new courting buggies, not a soul under Dat's roof would be privy to anything at all. She just hoped she could tell the difference between a nice boy and one who wasn't so nice. Mamma had talked with her about some of the telltale signs to look for, one being about the way a young man looked at a girl.

She'd felt she had seen the right kind of look in Carl Nolt's eyes over the years, having attended the Georgetown School with him and all until two years ago, when she finished up eighth grade and came home to work alongside Mamma, Sadie, and Aunt Lizzie. Carl had long since forgiven her for her bold remarks about his adoption and happily gone off to high school, because there was no limit put on education by the Mennonites. She knew this from Mary Ruth, who was quite content to have married her preacher husband, Robert Schwartz, three years ago—a bride for the first time at the age of twenty-seven, of all things! The happy couple was living in a small rental house between Quarryville and Gobbler's Knob, and Mary Ruth was teaching Sunday school at the church where Robert was the associate minister, as well as conducting a weekly home-quilting class while waiting for their first baby, due in late October.

Setting the table and hearing footsteps in the bedroom directly above the kitchen, Lydiann was aware of Aunt Lizzie and Dat just getting up. She scurried about, hurrying the pace of her preparations, recalling as she worked how Dawdi John used to make hints about what a good Amish boy was supposed to look, sound, and act like . . . but that was more than a year ago, before he passed on to Glory. With only the memory of her wise grandfather to cherish, she hoped and prayed she might remember everything of utmost importance now that she was courting age and "ripe for the pickin'."

I do hope to have a wonderful-good time, she thought, looking ahead to tomorrow's singing, to be held near Grasshopper Level.

Abram rose out of a deep sleep, stumbling across the room toward his work clothes hanging on the wooden peg rack high on the wall. Such heavy slumbers—stupors, really—always hit him this time of year. He sensed it was going to be one of the warmest days of May thus far, with not a hint of a breeze coming in through the open windows. The dawn felt balmier than any in recent weeks.

Quickly dressing, he looked at Lizzie, still asleep. He grinned to himself and went over and poked her till she was awake. "I smell ham and eggs already." He chuckled, watching her drowsy face as she slowly opened one eye and then the other. "Best be gettin' up, or someone's gonna replace you as the breakfast cook," he teased, then leaned down and kissed the tip of her nose.

"I must've overslept," she said softly, stretching now.

He nodded. "And all well 'n' gut, since we had something of a late night, didn't we?"

"Oh, Abram." She sat up with a big smile on her pretty face, and then reached for the pillow as he backed away. She flung it straight at him anyway.

He tossed the pillow back and, when she caught it and leaned backward onto the bed, he hurried over to her and planted kisses all over her face. "Lizzie, Lizzie . . . look what you've gone and done to me. I feel like a young buck again." These years with his second wife had been joyful ones, despite a few ups and downs. He was altogether surprised they'd gotten along as well as they had, considering the many tiffs they'd had over the years they'd known each other. Lizzie, still his dear bride at fifty-one, kept him smiling, and he would have told almost any John Zook on the street how grateful he was to be so happily married at the ripe old age of fifty-nine.

Of course, there was more to happiness than being with someone who made you feel the way Lizzie did. If only Ida could see him now, she'd be amazed at his spiritual transformation, as well. *She'd be ever so joyful to see the answer to her many prayers,* he thought. Truth was, he and Lizzie were followers of the Lord Jesus in every respect, though they did not parade or air their beliefs. His own faith had helped him to accept Mary Ruth's choice of the Mennonite life . . . and husband. Sure, he wished she'd stayed Amish and married a good man right here amongst the People, but Mary Ruth and Robert delighted in walking with the Lord, adhering to the teachings of His Word, and holding firm to the assurance of salvation—all frowned upon by Bishop Bontrager and others in the Amish church here. Yet such strong faith could be found among the People, Abram's own having come about because of Ida, initially. Truly, the Holy Spirit had been at work in his life all those years.

———◆———

With a lump in her throat and a sense of foreboding, Leah stood at the edge of the walkway, waving as thirteen-year-old Abe drove Lydiann to her first singing. She wasn't certain just how long she held up her hand in a somewhat motionless wave, but when the horse and carriage reached the end of the lane and made the turn west, she realized her arm was still high over her head. *Goodness me,* she thought, feeling like a persnickety mother hen at thirty-two, worrying her head over Lydiann. But she knew why she felt so hesitant about Lydiann entering the time of rumschpringe—her darling girl was almost too eager to meet boys and begin her courtship years.

Dear Lord, be with her always, Leah prayed, wondering if she might not just stand here and wait for Abe to return from his brotherly duty. Still, she did not wish to behave the way Aunt Lizzie had when Leah and her sisters were courting age, although she knew Lizzie had meant well. She refused to get too caught up in guessing who was seeing whom, even in jest. *I'll treat Lydiann with respect and trust, the way Mamma always did me,* she decided then and there.

Turning toward the house, she felt nearly exhausted. Without a word to either Sadie or Aunt Lizzie, she hurried through the kitchen and to the stairs. She had long since purchased her own Bible, not wanting to borrow Mamma's once Dat and Lizzie had begun to read aloud from it every day, as well as from the old German Bible downstairs in the kitchen. The latter was still used for evening and morning family prayers, which, not surprisingly, Dat insisted on doing without fail.

In the quiet of her room, having moved back to her childhood bedroom years ago when Dat first married Aunt Lizzie, Leah settled into the chair near the window. Opening her Bible to Psalm Thirty-four, she read silently, *I sought the Lord, and he heard me, and delivered me from all my fears.*

Again she read the fourth verse, wanting to memorize it . . . realizing how essential it was for her to do so. *I must give Lydiann and her running-around years to you, Lord.* She made a conscious effort not to fret another minute from now until the wee hours, when Lydiann would be escorted home by her first beau, whoever that might be.

From where she was working in her little kitchen, Hannah couldn't hear everything being said in the front room, but she'd caught several words and sentences that almost made her wish she'd heard nothing at all. Gid and the bishop were talking about trading Gobbler's Knob young men for some in Ohio. She'd heard tell of switching boys between St. Joseph, Missouri, and places in Pennsylvania for the purpose of bringing fresh blood into the various Amish church districts, but never had she thought such a thing would happen here in Gobbler's Knob. All the same, she knew of several recent instances where babies had been born with severe physical or mental problems because of close intermarrying. As for her own healthy threesome, she and Gid both thanked the Good Lord daily for them, even though she wished she might conceive another child one day soon.

Just now, though, she wanted to inch forward and hear what on earth Gid was helping the bishop plan for some poor, unsuspecting souls—more than a dozen fellows, is what she'd thought she had heard. But she resisted the temptation and set about making a cake for supper, glad that the girls were off at school and nowhere around to hear the kind of talk their preacher father was involved in. More and more, Gid was succumbing to Bishop Bontrager's spell. It was as if the bishop were God himself to Gid these days—no matter what the older man said, her husband seemed to go along with it. The strangest thing, really, especially since Gid had always been his own man when it came to opinions.

Mixing the flour, sugar, and baking powder for the cream cake and filling, Hannah contemplated what such a trade of men might have meant for her had Gid been offered such an adventure. A chill ran up her spine and she shook her head. "For pity's sake," she whispered.

When she heard the front door close—an altogether odd occurrence when everyone else entered by way of the back door—she kept busy with her cake and hoped Gid might wander out to chat with her. Much to her surprise, he did, though here lately he seemed to be refraining from any church talk with her.

"Makin' supper?" he asked, avoiding her eyes.

She nodded, not so eager to say a word, hoping he wouldn't realize she'd overheard bits and pieces.

"Bishop's downright worried," Gid said.

Not as worried as I am, she thought.

"He thinks what he wants to do might cause a real stir amongst the People." Gid went and stood by the back-door window overlooking the flower beds she and the girls had planted not too many weeks ago.

"Oh?"

Gid came right out and asked her, "Did ya happen to hear any of what we talked 'bout?"

"Only a little."

Gid turned and came to sit at the table, where he watched her blend together an egg, some cornstarch, and milk for the filling. "I can't stand up to him on anything," he admitted. "He has such a powerful way 'bout him. There's just no gettin' through to the man."

"The man of God," she said softly.

"Jah, exactly. How do ya deal with that?" He went on to say exactly what the bishop wanted to do: that he was mighty eager to bring new men into this close-knit community. By the time Gid finished, his hands were over his face, covering his eyes. "This'll bring such heartache to our families. I can't begin to say . . ."

She felt the pain for those boys Gid had just mentioned. "Sweethearts will be torn apart, too, no doubt."

"Jah, with all of them courtin'-age fellas." He rose and went into the front room again without saying another word.

'Tis an awful sad day for the People, Hannah decided then and there, knowing, if the bishop had made his choice, nothing could halt the course of those boys' lives.

An idea popped into her head just then, and she left her cake batter to hurry to Gid's side. "Why not make the tradin' something the boys could choose to do? Appeal to the adventuresome, maybe. Wouldn't that make much better sense than makin' it required?"

Gid was studying her face now, reaching out to embrace her. "That's a wonderful-gut

idea, Hannah. This may be just the answer!"
He kissed her cheek and then released her
to rush out the back door, no doubt hoping
to catch up with the bishop.

Chapter Twenty-One

"That's a right perty sight," Sadie said as she and Abe rode together to market in nearby Bartville on the first day of summer. She motioned to the colorful arrangement of petunias around a large birdbath as they passed one farmhouse.

"Do ya know who lives there?" asked Abe, gawking over his shoulder as they passed.

"Somebody with a green thumb, that's who." She had to laugh, thinking about Aunt Lizzie's amazing talent for coaxing flowers of all colors and kinds to flourish under her tender care.

"*You've* got yourself a green thumb, Sadie."

"That's awful nice of you."

"Well, 'tis true." Abe grinned at her.

It was good of her brother to offer to ride

along and help her sell the produce and other items today while Lydiann and Hannah's older girls, Ida Mae and Katie Ann, tended the roadside stand at home. "We'll bring in a gut amount of money for all our work today, Lord willin'."

Abe nodded and hopped down out of the buggy, going to tie up the horse.

Sometimes she couldn't get over the kind and generous helper Abe was. His accident on Blackbird Pond all those years back had worried everyone nearly sick, especially Hannah, but it was clear there was nothing at all wrong with him now.

Abe was quick to unload plenty of fresh-from-the-farm vegetables, including Swiss chard and snap peas. There were also baked goods, dried nuts, and homemade tartar sauce from Aunt Lizzie, along with pepper jam, corn relish, and hand-dipped candles from Leah. Hannah had sent along embroidered handkerchiefs and table linens, and Sadie had canned chowchow and home-cooked stews. Everyone had pitched in the past few days to make this Saturday market day an extra good one.

Sadie was glad they'd gotten themselves settled in long before customers began to arrive. She had always liked to get there well ahead of time, allowing ample opportunity to chat with other standholders, most of them farmers' daughters and wives.

Among the newcomers were several youth from the Grasshopper Level area. One in particular who seemed to hit it off with Abe was a tall and slender young man with dark hair several aisles over from them. Being an outgoing fellow, Abe had gone wandering up and down the rows during a few lulls in the normally steady stream of buyers, talking to nearly everyone at each of the produce tables. Sadie couldn't see if the dark-headed young man was tending his table alone, but she certainly heard his catching laughter and, in the midst of all the marketplace chatter, she thought she heard Abe's, as well.

This is good, she thought, having been a little concerned, along with Leah and Aunt Lizzie, that Abe had been spending far too much time with Carl Nolt rather than other Plain boys.

When the volume of customers picked up again, here came Abe once more, rushing back to help Sadie, taking charge of hand selling and making change. Between customers, Abe mentioned the young man across the way, saying he'd given Abe a homemade peppermint stick made by his twin sister.

"How interesting," Sadie said, lowering her voice so as not to be heard by anyone but Abe. "You might not know this, but Mary Ruth may be having twins come fall."

"Ya don't mean it." Abe laughed. "I might have both a nephew and a niece?"

"Or two of either," she replied.

"Ain't it 'bout time Dat had himself a grandson? Goodness knows how much he'd like that!"

Sadie thought yet again of Dat's one and only grandson thus far, gone to heaven sixteen long years ago. It still surprised her how often she thought of that wee boy, all shriveled and blue, never having made a single sound, not even a whimper. Yet she loved him, he and his stillborn half sisters . . . all being cared for in heaven by Mamma, Harvey, and Dawdi John. *And the angels, too,* she supposed, because Aunt Lizzie had always said God's ministering servants cared for the babies who went to Glory before their parents. "Jah, maybe Mary Ruth will give Dat a grandson or two," she replied, standing to greet the next customer.

"That'd be right nice," Abe replied.

———————◆———————

When the end of the day came and it was time to say good-bye to the folk on either side of their table, Abe suggested Sadie go with him to meet his new friend. "No, that's all right. I don't have to meet all your friends, for goodness' sake," she said, feeling suddenly shy. Having observed from afar the way the two boys had gotten along, talking animatedly together, she didn't feel the need to barge in, and she told Abe so.

"But, Sadie, you'd like him. He's the nicest fella and downright easygoing." Abe motioned with his head, nearly insisting Sadie walk over there with him.

"All right, then," she agreed. "If ya do all the talkin'."

Abe said he would, and he led her to the almost empty long table. "This is my oldest sister, Sadie," Abe said. Then, turning to Sadie, he said, "Meet my friend Jacob."

The handsome teen reached out a firm

hand and shook hers. "Hullo, Sadie. Most folks call me Jake."

She smiled, surprised by his relaxed manner, just as Abe had described. "Nice to meet you, Jake."

Grinning at them both, Jacob volunteered that his next-oldest and twin sisters had gone to Central Market in Lancaster today, so he'd offered to come tend to the table here. "Tending stand ain't what I do best, though," he said, the color rising in his face. "I'd much rather help my father in our apple orchard."

Suddenly, at that moment, everything clicked. *This must be Peter and Fannie Mast's boy,* she thought. If so, he was right now talking to the cousins his own father had chosen to shun. Well, she didn't dare spoil things for Abe—she simply acted as if she had innocently met an acquaintance of her brother's.

Yet all during the ride home, Sadie couldn't get Jake's enormous dark eyes and his winning smile out of her mind. He reminded her of someone. A young man in the Millersburg, Ohio, church years ago, perhaps? And there was a certain resemblance to big brother Jonas, too. "Have ya ever met Jake before today?" she asked.

"Seems to me I did, maybe, quite a while back. But honestly, I can't remember where." Abe looked at her curiously. "Did you think you knew him from somewhere?"

She leaned back in the buggy seat, glad Abe held the reins to the horse. "Well, maybe so. Was it that obvious to you?"

He nodded, grinning. "You just were starin' at him," he admitted. "I felt a bit embarrassed, truth be known."

She didn't want to blurt out that they'd just run into Peter Mast's youngest son—at least she hadn't heard that Cousin Fannie had ever birthed more children after her fraternal boy-girl twins, but how would she know? Peter and Fannie had cut themselves off from the tiny world of Gobbler's Knob simply because the Abram Ebersol family lived there.

"I'd hate to embarrass my handsome little brother," she said, reaching up and touching his blond hair.

"Ach, keep your hands to yourself," he said playfully and clicked his tongue, urging the horse to a trot.

She laughed, glad to be heading home

even as the memory of Jake's countenance stirred up bewildering feelings.

———◆———

A nesting robin in the nearby maple tree sang with such clarity, Mary Ruth raised her head from the feather pillow, hearkening to its call. She was keenly aware this morning of the early bird's song, so anxious was she to greet the day. *This* day! How long had it been since her last Sisters' Day? She had been passed over far too long, yet she understood and had no business questioning why Sadie and Leah—Hannah too—had not included her at Adah Peachey Ebersol's and others' homes for canning bees and work frolics. A lingering sadness had pricked her heart, though she'd never shared any of this with her husband, who now lay asleep next to her. It was obvious why she had been treated so in the past.

It had been years now since Gid had taken it upon himself to ask her to stop coming to his household's little log home. Naturally Dat had felt she had done wrong in leaving her Old Order Amish life behind, yet she knew there was no benefit in rethinking any of that, especially when she would never give up her precious beliefs. Still, she did feel like not only an outcast from the community of the People, but also somewhat estranged from her family—especially her twin. Hannah was not behind the decision by Gid, Mary Ruth was sure, for she often saw the look of sorrow in her sister's eyes when at the Ebersol Cottage, where she *was* permitted to visit with Hannah and the rest of her family. "Just never talk with Hannah alone," Gid had said privately, making things heartbreakingly clear that day so long ago.

So the invitation to attend Sisters' Day at Leah's best friend's place was something of a breakthrough, at least in Mary Ruth's mind. Her heart was gladdened at the thought of seeing her sisters and Aunt Lizzie all in the same kitchen working together.

Getting up quietly so as not to awaken Robert, she gently placed a hand on her stomach and walked downstairs to the kitchen, turning her thoughts to the baby, possibly more than one, growing inside her. She offered a prayer for the safe and normal development of this, their first little one. Or two. And she prayed she might be a cheerful blessing today as she attended the work frolic, sharing in all the talk that grown women—married and single alike—seemed able to prattle on about on such a fine late-June day.

———◆———

As the sun was breaking over a dark string of trees, Lydiann hurried outside, barefoot and still wearing her nightclothes. She'd awakened with a hankering to spend some time with their new German-shepherd pups, especially sleek and pretty Boo, who reminded her quite a bit of their former dog Sassy. Lydiann sometimes still missed Blackie, King, and Sassy, who'd lived out their lifespans a few years before, but Dat had been eager for more dogs, so they'd purchased another two from Brother Gid.

Presently, Boo was making high-pitched sounds, the way some dogs did when a storm was brewing. Seemed to her that dogs could hear storms in the distance long before people—Dat had always said as much. It had to do with more than their keen hearing; perhaps they had a special sense for such things. From Boo's behavior,

Lydiann was ever so sure there'd be a thunderstorm later that day. She just hoped the weather cooperated with her handsome beau's plans for them to meet down Georgetown Road in his open buggy. But knowing him, she was quite sure he'd have the forethought to bring along an umbrella, though if the weather was too bad, he simply wouldn't show up. He *had* thought ahead the last time they'd gone riding in his courting buggy, reaching down and pulling an umbrella out from beneath the front seat just before the first droplets of rain fell on them.

Oh, she could just pinch herself with all this happiness, having met such a wonderful boy at her first-ever Sunday singing back in May. It had been obvious he'd had no interest in any of the other girls that lovely evening. In fact, after her ride home in his open carriage that night, she hadn't really noticed any of the other boys at the following singings, although she was sure they were awful nice and fine looking, too. Already she and Jake had seen each other more times than she could count on one hand, which was quite frequent given that courting couples were really only supposed to see each other every other Sunday night at barn singings and the Saturday nights in between those—usually four times a month. But here it was only one month later and she'd nearly lost track of how many moonlit buggy rides they'd enjoyed.

She and Jake Mast had done a good job of keeping their budding romance hush-hush—difficult to do when many of the young people whispered behind each other's backs about who was seeing whom. But Jake and she were exceedingly cautious, and it was a good thing, too, since neither of them had ever dated and they were, as Dat would surely say, too young to settle down just yet. Of course, there was also the prickly matter that Jake's family had chosen to shun her family—Jake had overheard his older sister Becky telling someone exactly that. Just why this was, Lydiann had no idea, but she took comfort in Jake's emphatic determination to continue seeing her, no matter what. "We'll get my father's blessing in due time," he'd told her recently.

"There ya be, Boo," Lydiann said, discovering the noisy dog in the warm hay of the stable area, not but a few feet from one of the two milk cows, as if he thought he was a new calf. "What on earth are you doin' whining and fussin' out here? Is a storm comin', do ya think?"

The pup looked up at her with kindly eyes as she knelt next to him, rubbing his neck under his ears. His eyes instantly glazed over as if with pleasure, and she smiled. "You're no help at all!" In a bit she got up and went in search of Brownie.

One of the mules neighed loudly as she moved through the lower level of the barn, which was already warming with the dawn of a new day. *It'll be a hot one today,* she decided, still searching for Mamma Leah's favorite of the two dogs. In fact, just last night Mamma had talked about what a gift of joy all their pets had been—both past and present. Secretly, though, Lydiann wondered if Mamma Leah didn't prefer cats to dogs now, since especially the barn kittens seemed ever so drawn to her.

When she finally located Brownie, he was standing up and pointing his nose toward the north like a living compass. She had to laugh, slapping her leg through her cotton nightgown and robe. "Come here," she said. "You're a silly one." But she knew she'd found her weather forecaster. "It is gonna storm today, ain't so?"

Brownie looked up at her as if he were smiling his answer. "I'll take along my shawl tonight, then . . . in case you're right," she said, deciding it was high time to hurry back to the house and dress for the day before Dat and Abe came trotting out to the barn for milking. What would they think if they found her in her nightclothes, of all things?

Chapter Twenty-Two

"Of course I do," Leah answered when, following breakfast, Lydiann asked her if she remembered her own running-around years.

"Then, why are ya worried 'bout me, Mamma?"

Leah paused. Had she mistakenly given that impression to her dear girl, or was it actually true? Was she too concerned about all the nights Lydiann was leaving the house after dusk and returning home before dawn? *Too much like Sadie's wild days,* she had been thinking, hoping Lyddie hadn't met some English boy somewhere. She felt she ought to ask, though, just for good measure. "You're not seein' fancy boys, are ya?"

Lyddie's eyes grew wide at the question. "For goodness' sake, Mamma, what would give ya that idea?"

She didn't want to say she'd had a nagging feeling, but she did wonder how on
earth Mamma had faced four daughters'
times of rumschpringe. Truly, she felt sym-
pathetic for any mother with a courting-age
daughter.

"There are rules to be followed during
the running-around years, Lyddie." She
reached for her hand. "Spendin' time with a
boy following Sunday singings is all well
and good. But ya shouldn't see each other
too often otherwise."

"But what does it hurt to see each other
more than that?" The light of love, or something close to it, was evident on Lydiann's
sweet face.

Leah's heart sank. *Just what I've worried
about.* "Ach, dear one, I daresay you're a bit
young to get serious."

Lyddie's brow knit into a frown. "But
didn't you like a boy long before you were
sixteen? Sadie told me so once when we
were up in the high meadow last spring,
gathering willow twigs to weave into
wreaths." She stopped a moment. "I . . . I
hope I'm not speakin' out of turn, Mamma.
You fell in love when you were young, didn't
ya?"

This moment Leah wondered why on earth she hadn't gone along to the pastureland when Sadie had invited her that day. What had she been thinking, allowing Lydiann to go off for hours alone with Sadie? She gathered herself, torn between her present feelings and what she knew she ought to be saying about all of this. It wasn't really Sadie's fault that such a sensitive topic had come up. Better Jonas and her romantic tale than for Sadie to have revealed hers with Derry Schwartz.

"Mamma, you all right?" Lydiann asked, staring at her.

"Oh sure, I'm fine. And about bein' in love and all . . . I'd have to say it was such a long time ago I've nearly forgotten." But she had not forgotten how much she'd loved Jonas . . . and how she'd felt the autumn day Sadie had revealed he was not the man her sister had married after all. Leah honestly believed she might never forget the bolt of shock that had ripped through her upon hearing the stunning news.

"Do ya remember how it felt when the first boy you ever loved reached for your hand and held it for miles on end?" Lydiann's words were coated with honey, but it didn't make them any more pleasant for Leah to hear.

Lyddie and her beau are farther along than I thought. . . .

"Oh, Lydiann, I oughta remind ya to be ever so careful. Don't fall too quick, too soon."

"Fall?" Lyddie gasped. "You make it sound dangerous, Mamma. Don't ya trust me?"

Of course she did—she had believed in her heart that Lyddie was eager for romantic love, though perhaps not the kind that involved devotion and commitment to one person for a lifetime. Leah tried to explain the difference, saying all the things Mamma and Aunt Lizzie had told her back when *she* turned sixteen.

At one point Lydiann seemed a bit peeved, and Leah couldn't help but worry this time of courtship might cause a rift between herself and her girl. Well, she would move heaven and earth to make sure that didn't happen. If it meant stepping back and praying about it more, she'd do that. The fact Lydiann was willing and almost excited to discuss such things was a comfort, a reminder they indeed had as close a mother-daughter relationship now as always. Leah earnestly desired to preserve their good relationship until such a time as the two of them would become equals. More than anything, it was essential for her to keep the talk flowing. She must attempt to keep an open mind, as well—try to know and understand what Lydiann was thinking, if at all possible, even though the People expected the courting years to be secretive.

———◆———

Just as their dogs had seemed to indicate earlier, the weather began to change around midafternoon, and a storm blew up. Lydiann watched the gale from her bedroom window, high on the second floor in what had been Hannah and Mary Ruth's bedroom when they were her age. She observed the storm whip the row of maples lining the pasture and lift and twirl the barnyard dust. A single bird flew for cover, heading home to the four-sided birdhouse Dat had erected.

Let nature get this out of her system, thought Lydiann, not happy about the prospect of meeting her beau in the midst of such a gust and rain. Surely, though, this fast-moving storm would pass by nightfall. She hoped so, because she wanted so much to ride next to him, talking into the wee hours. And who would've thought she'd like the first boy she'd ever spent time with. Well, that wasn't necessarily true, because she'd developed something of a crush on Carl Nolt a few years ago, and he on her, too. Discussing their differences, his being Mennonite and all, had made for several long walks between his house and hers, but no one in her family knew about them. She'd always felt she wouldn't be happy if she wasn't Amish, unlike Mary Ruth, who seemed to thrive in the Mennonite church.

But since Lydiann had met Jake, there had been very little space in her mind—or her heart—for Carl or for remembering fondly their school years together or his once-frequent visits. Truth was, Carl was the sort of fellow whom any girl might enjoy having as a kind of brother, but she couldn't imagine feeling about him the way she did about Jake, who was not only good-looking and fun-loving, but able to look at her with an expression that made her heart melt but good. She didn't know if falling in love was supposed to feel this way, but scarcely could she wait to ride through the night with Jake, eagerly listening to his voice, feeling secure and ever so happy while leaning her head on his shoulder, her heart nearly bursting.

If this blustery weather continues, Jake won't come for me, she thought sadly. They'd made this agreement early on since there was no way for him to contact her beforehand. So she sat down on her bed and prayed, asking the Lord God to bring a swift end to the wind and rain, dearly hoping she might see her beau this night.

———◆———

The busyness of the Sisters' Day work frolic in Adah's kitchen was a welcome relief to Mary Ruth. Beginning at midmorning the group of women had gathered at Adah's to put up canned peas. She worked alongside her twin and ten-year-old Ida Mae, pleased to have this time with Hannah and her oldest girl. She listened intently as her sister shared some of her daughters' latest antics, all the while happily anticipating the sound of children in her own home.

"Katie Ann's been collectin' butterflies lately," Hannah said. "Gid and I can't figure out how she catches them without damaging their wings, but she does. And she's got herself quite a collection now."

Ida Mae nodded, her blue eyes smiling. "You oughta see it, Aunt Mary Ruth. Ach, I wish you could . . ."

By the sound of things, evidently young Ida Mae wished her auntie might be allowed to visit their home. Mary Ruth was drawn to Ida's demure face and strawberry blond hair. *So similar to Hannah's,* she thought, wondering whom *her* baby—or babies— might favor in looks.

"I'll ask Dat if you can come up to the house after the frolic, maybe," said Ida Mae.

To this Hannah frowned quickly and changed the subject. "Where's Lydiann today?"

"Best be askin' Leah," said Mary Ruth. "I thought for sure she'd come, but she may be workin' with Dat."

"She sure seems to like workin' with the barn animals," Hannah replied. "She's a lot like Leah was at that age."

Mary Ruth hadn't thought of that before, but she could certainly see what Hannah meant. Lydiann did love the outdoors, and she liked working alongside Dat and Gid, too, though she hardly did so as often as Leah had.

"I, for one, am glad to keep my girls round the house, especially these summer months," Hannah said, smiling warmly at her Ida Mae as she reached for another jar.

"Not so much falls on your shoulders now, right?" Mary Ruth said.

Hannah nodded. "It's lots more fun, too, than when they're off at school all day long."

Feeling suddenly dizzy, Mary Ruth went to wash her hands at the sink, then stepped outdoors for a breath of fresh air.

———◆———

Leah wished Lydiann had come along to the Sisters' Day work bee, but she hadn't pressed the issue. If Lyddie wanted to stay behind and help Dat in the barn and the fields, then so be it. Still, she couldn't help but think Lyddie was probably daydreaming about her beau again, though she mustn't let herself get caught up in anxiety over Lydiann's rumschpringe.

Long before Mamma had died, before

she'd ever asked Leah to bring up Lydiann and Abe as her own, Leah had often contemplated notions of fate and a person's destiny, wondering if it was possible that a single spoken word or one misdeed could change the course of a person's future. She wasn't so sure about such farfetched youthful thoughts these days. All the same, the notion lingered in the back of her mind that she must step lightly where things of the heart were concerned.

She worked alongside Sadie, Adah, and Adah's younger sister, Dorcas, trying her best to think about other things. She was thankful when Dorcas began telling how her young sons had been going on "adventures," as she put it. "They're havin' themselves a great time roamin' the acres, goin' exploring. But yesterday Little Joe wandered off alone and, when he did finally come home, he said he'd found what looked to be a little grave."

Leah perked up her ears.

"Where on earth was it?" Sadie asked, looking quite surprised.

"Wasn't on Pop's property, that's for sure . . . it was south of us, a way over on that vacant lot. Honestly I think Little Joe must be dreamin' but gut."

Leah had sometimes wondered if someone else might also discover the grave one day. After all, it had been years and years since she and Jonas had first discovered what had then been a tiny mound, clearly trimmed of grass, although they were sure, at the time, that it was simply the well-tended plot of a beloved pet. But Dr. Schwartz had denied it was a grave altogether.

"Little Joe was both upset and confused, truth be told," Dorcas was saying. "He couldn't understand why the plot wasn't in the cemetery."

Sadie spoke up. "Best be tellin' Little Joe not to worry. No need to, really, is there?"

Dorcas shrugged her shoulders. "It bothered him . . . 'twas clear."

"Why's that, do ya think?" Hannah asked, having come over just in time to overhear the conversation.

"Not being in the cemetery, for one. And he said he saw flowers on it, like someone had just been there," replied Dorcas.

So Dr. Schwartz did lie to me when I asked, Leah thought, knowing he was the only one who knew the truth. In her heart, she knew she must approach him on this again; this time she would refuse to let him pull the wool over her eyes. *Dowsing for water, indeed!*

———————◆———————

The night air was good and fresh from the earlier storm, and Lydiann was delighted to be sitting next to Jake in his open buggy. "I almost thought we might not see each other tonight, what with the rain 'n' all."

He looked at her, eyes smiling his pleasure. "I'm mighty glad it stopped, too."

They talked about the next singing and how his twin sister, Mandie, had been asking him who he was seeing. "But Mandie's easy to distract," he said, "what with her interested in a couple of boys. I think we can keep her from finding out about us till the time is right."

"Do ya know who the boys are?" she asked.

He bobbed his head. "I have an idea, but I could be wrong."

"Your twin sister mustn't want you to know her business, then?"

He laughed softly. "Ya might say that."

They rode quietly, passing a good many roadside vegetable stands, all of them cleared off for the night. "Ever notice how busy the roads get this time of year?" she said. "They're nearly a public marketplace during daylight hours."

"Well, jah, and isn't it gut for the Plain families up and down Georgetown Road?"

"I don't mind tendin' vegetable stand, but it does get awful hot out there of an afternoon. And there's never a lull, it seems."

"When you're my bride, I'll see to it you have a nice big awning over our roadside stand," he said.

Stunned, she wondered if she'd heard him right. Had he just said what she thought—that he hoped to marry her?

Jake turned to look at her, and then reached over to touch her face. "I didn't scare ya, did I, Lydiann?"

To be truthful, she had been a bit taken aback by his boldness. "My mamma would be concerned." She paused, thinking she needed to say more. "And . . . I think it's best we . . . well, be careful not to get too close, ya know."

He smiled. "I understand, Lyddie. But I

want you to think 'bout us being together
soon . . . getting married."

None of her family would be much in favor of their wedding anytime soon, particularly since she and Jake were both only sixteen.

"Don't ya think we oughta wait a while
before sayin' our vows?" she asked softly,
trying to think the way Mamma would want
her to right now.

"I knew when I first laid eyes on ya that
you were the girl for me. If you feel the same
way 'bout me, why should we wait?"

"I do like you, too, Jake. A lot," she
replied, enjoying the nearness of him.

His smile returned. "Well, I happen to *love*
you, Lydiann. And I want to marry you come
wedding season."

She was further surprised by his outspoken announcement. "Ya mean, this year?"

"In five months . . . an eternity away,
wouldn't you say?"

With them having come along this far in
just one month, four more months of courting might seem like forever, especially if
they kept taking so many nighttime buggy
rides.

"This has all come up so quick," she whispered. "Mind if I think on it?"

"You've got yourself, say, ten minutes?" He was grinning to beat the band.

She knew he was teasing her now and was glad for the sweet smell left by the rain and the sounds of chirping insects as they rode under the stars and half moon. If she felt the way she did after such a short time as Jake's girlfriend, how on earth would she feel about him by November's wedding season? Deep in her heart, Lydiann was sure she knew the answer. She already loved him dearly, for sure and for certain.

Chapter Twenty-Three

"Your father says the bishop's got somethin' up his sleeve for some of the menfolk," Aunt Lizzie told Leah as they rolled out pie dough the day following the work frolic. They'd decided to use up the rhubarb on hand and make a dozen strawberry-rhubarb pies to be served at the common meal following Preaching service tomorrow at Jesse Ebersol's house.

"Oh?"

"An unusual plan, really . . . to help bring new blood into our community. And it doesn't seem to be a big secret. At least Abram didn't say it was."

Leah couldn't believe her ears when she heard what was supposed to happen before the harvest—young men from Lancaster County were being swapped with a few from Holmes County, Ohio. "This sounds outlandish. Who'd ever think of goin' along with it?"

Aunt Lizzie raised her eyebrows. "Evidently it's up to individual families which boys go and which stay."

Leah shook her head. "I doubt there'll be anyone volunteering, truly."

"Well, Gid's all for the idea." Lizzie looked up just then, staring right through Leah. " 'Tween you and me, there's no way he'll stand up to the bishop." Lizzie didn't continue; she let her expression finish her thought.

Leah wondered if this had all come about because of several babies born with severe handicaps in the past few years . . . and more than a handful with webbed feet, too. She shivered. "Maybe tradin' men isn't such a bad idea, really," she found herself saying.

"Well, no, I can understand the why of it. But think of the heartbreak . . . boys leavin' their families behind only to marry and settle down in a new, faraway place."

Like Jonas. It astonished her that she would suddenly think of him as a prime example. "Obviously the boys who've already joined church won't go, right?"

"Bishop Bontrager wouldn't think of doin'

away with his own ruling. Those baptized boys'll stay put or the Bann would be sure to follow."

Very few churches held to such strict guidelines, Leah knew. She was just glad she hadn't ever had any desire to leave the Gobbler's Knob community, wanting to honor her vow—not only because of the bishop's decision, but because she loved her dear family and the People here.

---◆---

While cleaning up after the Sunday common meal in Aunt Mary Ebersol's kitchen, Leah overheard several older women talking. One particularly gray-haired *Mammi* was saying something about "so-and-so livin' under the shadow of another's sorrow." When the woman turned and caught Leah's eye, she hushed up right quick, looking the other way.

Surely they're not talking about me! But as she minded her own business and helped dry the many plates, she couldn't get the comment she'd heard out of her mind. *Do the People think I'm living under the gloom of Sadie's less-than-spotless life?*

For sure and for certain, they could take one look at her and know she was as happy as any mother around here. All the same, the idea of folk whispering about her made her feel uneasy. Were the two older women feeling sorry for her? Did they happen to know of her former connection to Jonas Mast or, later, to Gid?

Leah couldn't abide the notion of anyone's feeling unwarranted sympathy for her, especially when, more than anything, she had been determined to be joyful in all she did, serving her family under God all these years. There was no need for such a thing to be whispered, yet she felt sure the comment had been about her, otherwise why the embarrassed look?

Fact was, she was as delighted to be alive as the next person, glad to be witnessing the maturing love between Dat and Aunt Lizzie, for one, as well as the love between Hannah and Mary Ruth and their spouses. If there was any fret showing on her face, she figured it had to do with raising two teenagers at the moment. Lydiann was out all hours and moping around like a love-sick puppy, of all things, and Abe was feeling his oats because Dat had allowed him to go with a group of older boys on a lark, raising a bit of tomfoolery at Root's Country Market.

Even so, the older woman's remark plagued Leah all the way home. She honestly didn't feel alone or lonely, neither one. Surrounded by the extended family she loved so dearly, there was scarcely any time to feel that way.

———————◆———————

Once home Leah decided to take the horse and carriage out for a drive, to give herself some quiet time. It would have made sense to simply turn around a full mile or so after she passed the Nolts' and Schwartzes' places, but she felt inclined to drift along on this pleasant and sunny Sunday afternoon, letting the horse pull her farther, not caring where she was headed. For certain, Dat might eventually begin to wonder where the world she'd taken herself off to, but for now she had plenty of time.

Sighing, she leaned back in the buggy seat and watched the clouds float by, feeling nearly as light as a chicken feather. She contemplated the sermons today, having

heard similar ones, if not the same, from
Bishop Bontrager more times than she
could count. But lately Preacher Gid's were
somewhat more interesting to her, and she
wondered if he'd gotten to reading the Holy
Bible, maybe. Since he spent so much time
around Dat, that might be a possibility, what
with Dat reading God's Word twice a day
and even studying it. So just maybe some
of that was rubbing off on their young
preacher—unbeknownst to the bishop, naturally.

She might have turned around about then
and headed home, but she saw two young
people walking her way. Without meaning
to, she found herself staring at the boy and
girl as they walked, who turned now and
then to glance at each other and smile or
laugh. The girl was shorter than the boy, and
Leah might've guessed them to be twins
except that the girl was quite blond in com-
parison to the young man, who had deep
brown hair.

As they approached the horse and
buggy, she waved to them and they waved
back, calling out a greeting to her. *"Wie
geht's?"* the boy said, smiling and raising

his straw hat. His face seemed rather familiar.

"Good day for walkin', jah?"

"The way from Grasshopper Level is all
uphill to here," he called. "But the return trip
is much easier."

She slowed the horse, pulling onto the
dirt shoulder.

"Are ya goin' far yet?" asked the girl.

"Looks like your horse is awful hot," the
boy said, briefly touching the bridle.

At that moment she recognized them.
"Say, aren't you Jake and Mandie Mast?"

"I thought ya seemed a mite familiar, too,"
Jake said with a quick look at his sister.
"Didn't we meet once over at Dr. Schwartz's
clinic? A long time ago, seems now."

"What a keen memory you have," she
said. "And jah, it's ever so nice to see the
both of you again."

"Same here," Mandie replied politely, appearing rather shy.

"I always wondered why we never
bumped into you and your family again,"
Jake spoke up, glancing a bit sheepishly at
Mandie. "But when I asked Mamma, she
said you were the sort of folk who kept to
home."

Homebodies, baloney! Leah thought sadly, quite sure the twins knew more than they were saying about their father's imposed shun of the Ebersols.

"Well, have yourselves a nice afternoon walk. I guess I oughta be goin' now."

"So long!" Jake called to her.

"Good-bye, Cousin!" Mandie said.

Even once the horse started moving again and she got him turned around in the narrow road, Leah could scarcely stop looking after the Mast twins.

Something's terribly familiar about Jake....

But she decided it was her memory of his childish face that tugged at her so, and as she rode farther away from the chance meeting, she felt quite sure that Jacob Mast must simply remind her of his father.

◆

Leah wasted no time Monday morning, after the laundry was washed and hung out to dry, heading off to work on foot. Once at the clinic, she went promptly to the waiting room and stood before the lineup of framed photographs on the wall. One in particular caught her eye—Derek Schwartz wearing a sports uniform and holding a baseball bat.

She sucked in her breath as she stared at his face. If she remembered yesterday's encounter correctly, Jake Mast and Derry Schwartz were nearly twins in looks.

But how can that be?

She thought back to the last time she'd seen Peter Mast, recalling his dark brown hair and distinct jawline. Both were akin to Jake's hair and the shape of his mouth and chin.

I'm borrowing trouble, she thought and set to dry-mopping the floors.

Dr. Schwartz noticed Leah standing in the waiting room, intently looking at a picture of his son Derek. That in itself wasn't so odd, perhaps, but her facial expression was one of discovery. He was well aware of the pounding of his own heart, his nerves suddenly on edge.

Turning from the doorway, he hurried back to his private office, closed the door, and began to pace. Would Leah approach him with more questions?

No longer could he attempt to fool himself into thinking his deceitful plan was forever safe. On a subconscious level he had been in a state of perpetual worry for these sixteen years—Sunday mornings spent tending the tiny grave, hoping to atone for this, his worst sin. Yet had he purposely set himself up to be found out? Putting flowers on an obvious grave . . .

Did he, in all actuality, long to be found out, the crime dealt with . . . himself punished?

If Leah was as bright a woman as she had thus far proven herself to be, no telling how long before she'd put two and two together. Or maybe she already had. What *had* he been thinking bringing her into his circle of acquaintances, hiring her to work for him, allowing Lorraine to put her to work as part-time housekeeper? She had even seen Derek in the flesh one Christmas quite a few years back. To think he had been remiss, even reckless, in protecting his awful secret.

The logic behind the treacherous deed he had committed now completely escaped him. Hadn't he thought it best to protect his good name?

What good name? he thought, sick with self-disgust.

A wave of dread seized him and he

leaned over, resting on his desk. *Breathe, Henry . . . take slow, deep breaths.*

———◆———

Mary Ruth perked up her ears when her father-in-law brought up the subject of his land Monday evening at supper. "It's a nice big property south of the Peacheys' farm," he said. "If ever you were thinking of building a house for your growing family, Robert—and now's as good a time as any— it would be ideal." He paused a second, his eyes blinking fast as he continued. "I'd like to offer you this as a gift . . . since your first child is on the way. We could begin excavating right away."

"Why, Dad, this is a surprise," Robert said, eyes wide at the news.

Lorraine spoke up next. "Your father and I have been talking this over for some time now."

Mary Ruth enjoyed watching Robert's handsome face light up at the prospect of owning land and a house, but he quickly went on to say they were comfortable in their small rental home for now.

"Well, if you should ever decide otherwise . . ." his father said.

"We appreciate the offer," Robert assured him.

Mary Ruth agreed. "What a lovely thing to contemplate for our future." She imagined Henry and Lorraine both were hoping for more than the one or two grandchildren they were expecting, and their growing family could surely use more space in years to come.

———————◆———————

On the drive home, Robert slipped his arm around Mary Ruth. "You know we probably won't take my father up on his generous offer, don't you?"

She was amazed at his response. "Whatever do you mean?"

"I'm not interested in handouts, even from my father."

"Your parents mean well, Robert."

"All the same, we will make our own way, under God. I feel strongly about this, dear."

She could understand Robert's position well enough—after all, she had been raised with a strong work ethic, too. It had been one of the things that attracted her to Robert in the first place. Her husband studied the Scriptures diligently—his first calling—also putting great care into his second job of planting trees and shrubs, beautifully landscaping folks' yards. *A preacher and a gardener both till the soil, in a manner of speaking.*

Smiling, she shared the thought with him.

"Well, aren't you clever?" He gave her shoulder a quick squeeze as he drove.

"Would you marry this Amish girl again if you had the chance?" she teased.

"In a minute I would. And, by the way, you aren't so Amish anymore."

She smiled back at him. "Oh, I don't know about that. They say, 'once Amish, always Amish,' you know."

———◆———

While Lydiann helped Leah clear the supper dishes, she mentioned having met a girl named Mandie Mast at the singing the night before. "She's the same girl we met years back, Mamma, over at Dr. Schwartz's clinic. I remember her so clearly because her eyes are blue as can be. Do ya know who I'm talking 'bout?"

Leah nodded. "Jah, I believe I do." She found Lydiann's comment about Mandie to be rather curious, because there were too many times when Lyddie simply could not keep track of having fed the chickens of a morning, let alone recall something that had happened years before.

Lyddie went on. "Mandie said she and her twin brother happened to see you out ridin' yesterday afternoon. So she must've re-membered *you,* too."

"I stopped the horse and talked with them a bit, jah." She didn't divulge Jake's com-ment about the Ebersols keeping "to home," though, or how peeved she had felt at hearing Fannie's untruthful explanation.

"Anyway, Mandie told me the most inter-esting thing."

Leah braced herself for some remark about the rejection Mamma's cousins had made of all of them.

"Mandie said her and Jake's birthdays aren't on the same date, even though they're twins. Isn't that downright peculiar?"

Lyddie had her there. "Whatever do ya mean, dear?"

"Mandie was born a few minutes before midnight on April *ninth* . . . and Jake came along in the wee hours the next day, so his birthday is April *tenth*." Lydiann laughed softly. "Now, what do ya think of that? Bein' twins but not havin' the same birthday."

April ninth?

"Are ya awful sure of this?" Leah asked, her pulse pounding in her temples.

Lydiann appeared confused. "I have no reason to think Mandie's lyin'.'"

"No . . . I didn't mean . . ."

So . . . Mandie and Jake were born mere hours after Sadie's first baby. The thought tormented Leah, and she couldn't stop her brain from spinning, her mind on her encounter with Cousin Fannie's twins yesterday afternoon—how she'd fixed her gaze on Jake, nearly staring a hole in him. He did not resemble Mandie; she recalled he never had, even as an infant. In fact, he didn't much resemble any of his brothers or sisters, though he did remind her of Peter Mast . . . but only if she thought enough about it.

Helplessly she thought of Jake's nearly black eyes . . . identical to the eyes that haunted her from a recently framed photo of

Derek Schwartz as a teen, a favorite of
Lorraine's she'd pulled out of an old scrap-
book. Leah had dusted it weekly for the
past few months, aware of her resentment
each time she considered again what he'd
done to Sadie . . . to all of them.

*The news of Sadie's baby—that he was
our grandson—would have caused Lorraine
tremendous sadness . . . even embarrass-
ment,* Dr. Schwartz had told Leah years before.

Once again she contemplated Jake's
dark eyes and shock of hair. But she shook
herself and hoped she was imagining
things.

———◆———

That night Leah lay still in her bed, reliving
the meeting with the Mast twins. She
thought of the striking similarities between
Jake and the new photo of Derek, as well as
those of his childhood photos she'd been
dusting in the front room of the Schwartz
home these years.

Tired as she was, she let her mind wander
into a whirl. Lyddie's comments about the

Mast twins' birthdays had gotten her all stirred up.

In her drowsy yet troubled state, Leah suddenly recalled the butterfly handkerchief Sadie had used to cover her dead baby's face after his premature delivery—and the strange comments Dottie Nolt had made about it years ago, upon its return to Sadie. Hannah had made only one such cutwork embroidered handkerchief, yet Dottie had said she'd seen Fannie Mast with one exactly like it. Was there in fact only one handkerchief . . . and had Fannie dropped it at the clinic, where it was retrieved by Leah?

Was it possible Sadie's baby had not died at all? Could it be that he was actually *alive*? She had seen his lifeless blue body with her own eyes. Had she been deceived? But Dr. Schwartz had left so quickly . . . and why was that?

Leah knew she must pay a private visit to Dr. Schwartz at the next opportunity—there would be no getting around the truth this time. She would not budge from his clinic all night if it took that to get his attention . . . or Lorraine's. She would do what she had to in order to drag an honest answer out of the doctor. She would give it her Amish best.

She tossed about in bed, dreadfully aware of Sadie, probably asleep now in the Dawdi Haus. If any of what she suspected was true . . . *Poor, dear Sadie . . . .*

On the other hand, Leah thought, what if she were completely wrong? Until she knew the truth, she dared not share her misgivings with anyone, even in speculation.

Chapter Twenty-Four

From time to time, Jonas ventured out and away from his woodworking shop, especially on auction days like today or when stifling afternoon temperatures and high humidity made it nearly impossible to keep his mind on his work. Today he'd taken himself off to the neighboring town of Berlin, where, due to the sale in town, he knew there'd be plenty of farmers congregating at Boyd and Worthman's Restaurant and General Store for a grand slice of pie, if not a generous lunch to go with it. At breakfast he had kindly asked Emma not to bother packing him a sack lunch as he'd had it in his mind that he wanted a chance to chew the fat a bit, needing some male companionship.

He paid the Mennonite driver quickly when he was let out at the stoplight on the main street, and then he headed off on foot toward the old restaurant that looked out onto the road. Inside he found a good many Amishmen already feeding their faces. Glancing about, he happened to see young Preacher Solomon Raber, or Sol for short. At only thirty-three, the newly ordained preacher was as pleasant a man as any he knew, with a contagious smile and big brown eyes.

"Hullo, Jonas!" Sol called to him, leaning up out of his chair a bit at a table not so far from the long wooden counter. "Come 'n' join us."

Jonas nodded and hurried to take the only vacant seat with the preacher and two of his friends, Gravy Dan Miller and Peach Orchard Levi Troyer, their nicknames distinguishing them from the dozens of other Dan Millers and Levi Troyers in the area. "Hullo," Jonas said, removing his straw hat. "What's gut on the menu today?"

"Oh, just everything." Sol tapped the sandwich section of the menu. "Like hot beef with some broth to dip it in?" He fairly grinned at the suggestion.

"Sounds fine to me." Jonas put down the menu, not bothering to look at the price or even what came with the sandwich.

They began to talk of the weather and local happenings, but when Sol commented, "I've heard tell of more than a handful of our young men volunteering to move to Pennsylvania," Jonas paid close attention.

"Just what do ya mean?" he asked.

"Well, now," Preacher Sol explained, "I guess one of the old bishops back east got this crazy idea to trade some of his boys with ours."

Jonas scratched his head, trying to recall if ever he'd heard of such a thing. "Whatever for?"

"Guess there's been too much intermarrying—the blood's gettin' weak or something, and it's affecting babies."

Gravy Dan nodded and spoke up. "Same thing's goin' on in some places out here, too. That's what happens when a fella falls for his first cousin and marries her, I 'spect."

"Jah, makes sense to me," Peach Orchard Levi said, his face blushing red at the sensitivity of the topic, no doubt.

Jonas hardly knew what to make of the idea. "So a few of our teen boys plan to go to Pennsylvania and marry and settle down, in exchange for the same number of fellas from back east?"

"More than a dozen are comin' here," Sol said, "from someplace in Lancaster County."

Lancaster . . . The mere mention of the area set his mind to turning. So many years had come and gone since he'd laid eyes on Leah Ebersol . . . Abram's Leah. And his parents and dear old grandparents—were they even still alive? His brothers and sisters . . . all the happy days, growing up and helping his father in the apple orchard, working the soil, preparing for market day week after week in the summer, the harvest and apple cider making. Remembering the beckoning smell of homemade applesauce, he felt he was right back in his mother's kitchen at this moment, even while he sat here in the heart of Holmes County, Ohio, in this wonderful-good restaurant catering to Plain folk.

He retraced the steps of his boyhood and teen years. Leah had been such a big part of those growing-up days, and for just a moment, he found himself reflecting on her warm and pleasing laugh, her gentle smile—nearly constant, it had seemed.

Although such memories were not improper, he refused to dwell on the past. His life was more than happy here. He had made the best choice for his future.

Still, the thought of young men passing between the states as a way to bring in fresh blood struck him as downright strange, yet he guessed he could see the need for it. He was just glad the Grasshopper Level bishop hadn't thought up this idea back when *he* was sixteen or seventeen. It would have meant having to leave behind his family and the girl he planned to court and marry. He had been quite young then; he and Leah both were. Just how would he have felt if the brethren had decided to start switching men around back then? He might have had even fewer years with his former beloved.

When the waitress came with his sandwich platter, Jonas felt strangely relieved, glad to dive into his lunch and abandon futile memories.

———◆———

Saturday, July 6
Dear Diary,
    Today, while the girls took turns tending the roadside stand with

Lydiann, I headed over to see Old Lady Henner. It's been a few weeks since my last visit, but I wanted to check in on her, see how she was feeling, especially since I think she might be dying. She's the oldest person living in the county at the present time, and she looks it, too. When I saw her pale face and frail condition, I asked if there was anything I could do—maybe call on another Amish healer. I wish she might live on forever, though I know that's impossible. She's only human, after all.

Another reason I went to visit her was to make sure all my ailments, physical and mental, were tended to, in case she should die in her sleep here before too long. That might seem selfish, but I've come to depend on her and don't see how I'll manage when she goes. The dear thing has been such a comfort.

Dat and Aunt Lizzie have not been privy to my frequent visits over the years, and I don't plan on telling them. They would not approve, though there are many amongst the People who do put great stock in our Amish hex doc-

tors, *Gid* and the bishop included. *Thankfully Dat has not been able to persuade my husband differently.*

Mary Ruth and Robert stopped in at Dat's the other day, and Mary Ruth looks as healthy as I've ever seen her. When I spied them from the rose garden, I called to the girls, and all of us ran down for a nice visit under the shade of the linden tree, where we sipped cold lemonade. It was such fun seeing the way Robert and Mary Ruth smiled so fondly at each other, as if they share a special secret . . . which, of course, they do. Goodness, Dat has made it clear he's just itching for a grandson, holding out hope for Mary Ruth to give him his first. As for me, I've given up on having more than three children, and all girls at that. Seems to me the Lord God has closed up my womb, and probably a good thing, too, after what I went through with Mimi—though, of course, following her first visit to Old Lady Henner, there was never another sleepless night due to colic. I know Gid and the older girls were ever so happy about that. Gid came right out and asked if I'd taken Miriam off to the hex doctor, and I told him the truth. He probably wondered why I'd waited so long.

Well, it's an awful hot July, but I can't complain. Living up here with tall shade trees sheltering the whole back of the house, we enjoy our evening hours on the porch, looking out over the flower gardens and laughing at the girls' cute antics, enjoying one another's company like nobody's business.

Respectfully,
Hannah

———◆———

Lydiann hung on Jake's every word as they rode slowly together beneath the dark covering of sky and trees. He had a big talk on tonight, telling about the times his mother would read to his twin and himself, both of them squashed into a single large hickory rocker by a flickering fire in the wood stove.

"Mostly she read Bible stories to us, but sometimes she would read poetry about animals and nature by one of Dat's Amish friends," Jake said.

She found that interesting. "A *man* who's a poet, ya say?"

"Jah, and a real gut one, too."

"What sort of poems . . . rhyming ones?"

Jake laughed a little. "What kinds of poems don't rhyme?"

She tried to explain that there were, indeed, poems where the phrases and lines rambled along without any rhyme at all. She had come across them one day when she and some of her school friends had taken themselves off to Strasburg to the library there and stayed for hours reading all different kinds of books. Mamma Leah had never known of it, but Lydiann had happened into Lorraine Schwartz out on the street, and Lydiann remembered feeling as if she'd been caught doing something wrong, even though Mrs. Schwartz had merely eyed her curiously.

Lydiann shared with Jake that she sometimes felt she craved books, just as Mary Ruth told her she had at this age. Sometimes she felt as if she had a little piece of each of her older sisters in her, and, all in all, she was mighty glad the Lord God had made her the way she was. She could scarcely wait to get on with her life, particularly when Jake was ever so near, as he was right this minute. "I love ya, Lyddie," he whispered, reaching for her hand.

She wondered how much longer it would be before he might kiss her cheek, though she knew courting days were a time to "get to know one another," as Mamma always said, and not about smooching.

So when Jake leaned near, their heads almost touching, she held her breath, fearing she might fail Mamma tonight, for sure and for certain.

Just at that moment a hoot owl startled her with its nocturnal cry. "Ach, Jake!" she hollered.

"It's only a barn owl," he laughed.

But the sound from high in the tree had altered the intensity of the moment, and in one way she was glad, thankful she had been careful to stay pure during their courtship. On the other hand, she almost wished his lips *had* found her face. Who was to ever know, after all? In fact, from what she heard from girlfriends and distant cousins, some parents expected their teenagers to do a bit of necking now and then. "It leads to marriage," said one, "which is just what the deacons, preachers, and the bishop hope for."

More marriages mean more babies, she knew—the way the Lord God intended them to populate the community of the People. Thoughts of marriage and babies made plenty of good sense to Lydiann, especially tonight. Except that now the romantic moment had passed and Jake was back to talking about his twin sister.

Puh!

◆

Leah decided to go on foot to visit Dr. Schwartz on Monday afternoon so that she could contemplate his answer all the long walk home. For now, she took her time, listening to the peeping of birds and insects in the dense woods, trying to calm her frayed nerves. She'd planned to arrive at the clinic a full hour before he resumed patient hours, well aware of Dr. Schwartz's daily schedule.

What will he say? she wondered. *Will he brush me off again?* She could only hope she was able to stand her ground this time . . . persevere until she was satisfied that what he revealed was the full story.

She was growing increasingly anxious to get the confrontation behind her. Doing such a thing went against her grain, yet the accumulation of unasked-for clues now made it impossible to avoid.

The road ahead wavered and blurred into watery colors as Leah finally allowed herself to let go angry tears. She felt strongly that if there was any truth at all to what she suspected, she had every right to lash out at Dr. Schwartz. Just how she might reveal her fury, she was undecided, because, fact was, the good doctor was probably not good at all, and she'd been schnookered, working for him and his wife all this time.

Sighing, she raised her head to the sky and tried her utmost to enjoy her morning walk—the birdsong, the gentle rustle of trees, and the vastness of God's world. At this moment she felt as small as the tiniest insect. A feeling of helplessness nearly overtook her, and Leah stopped walking and turned around quickly, staring back at the long road from whence she'd come. *Lord, are you with me in this?*

Her tears ebbed a bit, and she realized

then and there she had nothing to fear, nothing to be ashamed of. She would turn herself right around and walk forward . . . for Sadie's sake. No longer did it matter what Dr. Schwartz thought of her. Most important was discovering if Sadie's child was alive or not.

Chapter Twenty-Five

As Leah made the turn left off Georgetown Road toward Dr. Schwartz's clinic, the wind gusted, and she found herself thinking of the Scripture in Philippians chapter four, which she had read just this morning: *I can do all things through Christ which strengtheneth me.*

She began to whisper the Scripture, surrounded now by a marked sense of confidence. She felt undeniably convinced she was doing the right thing. *I am my father's daughter. . . . I can do this,* she assured herself, aware of her rising optimism. *With God's help.*

Dr. Schwartz was in his office, poring over a pile of papers, just as she assumed he might be, and when she knocked on the doorjamb of the open door, he looked up immediately. His eyebrows shot up. "Well, good morning, Leah. Aren't you here early?"

"I came to talk something over with you, Dr. Schwartz, if ya don't mind." Somehow she managed to get the whole sentence out without breathing.

The pause between her statement and the time involved for her to inhale deeply was long enough for the doctor to murmur, "Ah." The way he frowned and rapidly blinked his eyes made her feel somewhat hesitant, but she did not lose heart.

She began by asking right out the most urgent question of all. "What happened to Sadie's baby after you left with him the night he was born?"

The doctor's frown deepened and he rose quickly to close the door. When he turned to face her, he wore an odd look. He sat back down at his desk and gazed intently at the ceiling, seemingly aware of something she could not see. "Leah," he said, lowering his eyes to her, "*you* saw the baby. He was as blue as can be."

"Jah, ever so blue. But is it possible he turned pink sometime between his birth and now?" She breathed again. "What I mean is . . . could it be Sadie's son actually lived that night . . . that he lives even now?"

Calmly, his hands folded on the desk before him, Dr. Schwartz replied, though nearly in a whisper at first. "I'm afraid these may be the most startling words you've ever heard. Absolutely no one else knows this about my own dear grandson—your sister's son—until now. . . ." He paused, looking down at his desk. Then, biting his lip, he began again. "Sadie's premature baby *did* live that night. Quite a miracle, even though I've heard of similar things happening. The night air apparently revived him . . . as phenomenal as anything I've witnessed." He studied her attentively.

Leah breathed hard at the matter-of-fact way in which he had revealed the life-changing news. "You kept Sadie's baby, then?"

"I weighed the consequences, Leah. My son's future . . . the fact that, at the time, Sadie had kept her pregnancy a secret from her family . . . except for you and your aunt. My reasoning was sadly skewed, you must know. I wanted what was best for my family, our good name . . . the baby's future. I was terribly selfish."

"You should have returned him to Sadie— to us. You never came back and told my grieving sister her baby was alive." Leah was nearly overwhelmed at the reality. "What happened to him? Where did you take my sister's son?"

"A good family gave him a home . . . once he was strong enough to leave this clinic."

"So *you* looked after him? You tended to Sadie's baby until he could be placed in the loving arms of . . . a new family?"

He nodded, eyes glistening. "I was torn between right and wrong . . . didn't consider the ultimate consequences. I didn't know the torment my poor decision would eventually produce in myself. In others . . ."

The doctor wept, not with sobs but with great sighs and tears coursing down his face. "I would go back to that night in a minute, if I could, and I would do everything differently. Believe me, Leah . . . I would change everything."

She sat shaking in the chair across from his desk, trying hard to remain seated, fearing she might simply storm over to Dr. Schwartz and shout at him in Amish.

Holding on to the chair, she attempted to speak her mind without losing her temper.

"How could you do such a thing? You stole my sister's baby from her." Suddenly she sprang to her feet. "If Sadie knew this, it would rip her heart in two!"

"My life was altered forever that night," he whispered, seemingly struggling to get the words out.

"*Your* life?"

He remained silent for an awkward span of time. At last he spoke again, "I have offered my continual remorse to God." He brushed sorrowful tears from his face, wiping his chin hard with his folded white handkerchief. "I deserve no mercy. Do as you must with what I have told you." He turned away from her.

You know what I'll do, she thought angrily. *The People don't press charges. It isn't our way.*

Inhaling, she demanded again, "Where'd you put Sadie's son? Where *is* he?"

"Fannie and Peter Mast's youngest son is Sadie's boy. They are raising him as Mandie's twin brother."

Jake Mast . . . the mirror image of Derry Schwartz. Her suspicions had been well founded.

Sighing with a tremendous sense of sadness, Leah stood next to the beautiful desk, leaning her hands flat on its highly polished surface to support her weight, lest her trembling cause her to fall. "Does Fannie know who her young Jake really is?"

Dr. Schwartz picked up a pen and stared at it, then absentmindedly pressed it against a piece of paper. "Neither Peter nor Fannie has any reason to suspect Jake is not their flesh and blood. You see, Fannie did birth twins—the first was born well before midnight, after I returned from delivering Sadie's baby the same night. And up until the moment when Fannie's stillborn second baby came, I had no idea what I would do with Sadie and Derry's frail little one. He was barely alive." He hesitated for a moment, apparently pained at the memory. "You must believe me, Leah. I felt then as if God almighty had made it possible— inexplicably so—for Fannie to nurture and mother Jake, for my grandson to be raised in an Amish family, his rightful heritage. And at the same time I knew sending him home with the Masts would protect my family from shame."

He went on to say that switching Fannie's dead baby son with Sadie's own premature one had seemed sensible, if not the right thing to do at the time, and the Masts had never been the wiser. "In doing this, I've been fortunate enough to watch my grandson grow up . . . a luxury I've denied your sister."

"You took it upon yourself to do that which is only for the Lord God to do!" Leah's rage was fanned by his explanation, and she was helpless to quench it.

The doctor stared blankly at his desk, tear stains evident on his face.

She had to stop to collect herself—so many thoughts assailed her . . . nearly too many to consider. "If I'm understandin' what ya just said, Fannie Mast has given Jake all the love my sister gladly would've offered him. . . ."

Dr. Schwartz forlornly nodded.

She clenched her fists and turned to stare at the wall. "So you must've buried Fannie's dead baby in the grave on your property, then." She swung around to face him again. "Is that what ya did?"

Again he nodded. "The least I could do for the Masts' full-term baby was give him a proper burial."

"And I'll bet you thought it would soothe your conscience."

He rubbed his face and kept his hands over his eyes for the longest time before looking at her again. "I could be arrested . . . sent to jail for this crime, if word gets out."

"Jah, for certain."

"Do as you see fit," he said flatly, as though resigned to his just fate.

"The People are forgiving and generous . . . nearly to a fault." She struggled to continue. "Even if Peter and Fannie came to know this horrible thing, they would not condemn you. I'm quite sure of it." Part of her wanted to see him squirm, but it was evident that the guilt-ridden years had already taken their toll, transforming him into the dejected man he now was.

With a great sigh, she said, "It might be best if I not continue workin' for you and Lorraine." Then, before he could answer, she excused herself from her expected hours of labor this day. Leah hurried out of his office, not looking back at the clinic established by the man the community had wrongly trusted . . . a man who had deceived them all. Sixteen precious years had been lost to Sadie—to all of them—forever.

Hot with anger, Leah headed down the road, plagued by the terrible truth that Mamma's cousins had unknowingly raised Sadie's child—Dat's only grandson.

Jacob Mast.

How bitterly ironic it was that Peter and Fannie's youngest son belonged to the cousins they'd chosen to shun.

◆

As if the news of Jake Mast's being Sadie's only living child wasn't enough, Leah began to feel under the weather. She was painfully aware that she must hold close the disheartening information, lest she weaken and pour out her shock, sadness, and exasperation to either Dat or Aunt Lizzie. *It's Sadie who deserves to hear it first. When I can muster the strength. . . .*

Sleep refused to come that night, and Leah stared at the dark windows, wishing the moon were out in full to spread its white light into the room—the same bedroom where she had ofttimes wondered where

Sadie had taken herself off to back when her sister was in the midst of rumschpringe. As it was, Leah felt the murky room was dreadfully silent with Sadie sleeping next door in the Dawdi Haus.

Sadie surely slept soundly still, having dreams of the little ones she'd lost . . . longing in the very depths of her soul for the babies she'd birthed but never held long enough to truly love or know.

A breeze blew in the open windows, gentle yet strong enough for the shades to flap slightly. *When should I tell her?* Leah wondered, knowing it would be heartless to keep the information from her any longer. Yet she struggled with the idea of coming right out and saying Jake was Sadie's son, especially since the Masts had kept all of them at arm's length and worse. Considering the commotion this could cause between the two estranged families, she shied from revealing such news to anyone. Still, the thought of being privy to what Sadie did not know caused Leah a wakeful and troublesome night.

———————◆———————

By the noon meal of the next day, Leah was in such turmoil she could scarcely keep her attention on serving the large pot roast to the family, let alone interact normally with either Lydiann or Abe as they sat chattering at the table, eager to enjoy the dinner she and Sadie had prepared together. All Leah could think of was how she had been kept from the truth about her own birth mother until adulthood, thereby having missed out on the extra-special closeness she might have experienced with Lizzie had she known differently as a little girl. Though her Mamma had always loved her, they had not shared the strong bond Sadie and Mamma had always had, seemingly so closely linked, and understandably so, Sadie being Mamma's firstborn and all. Indeed, had Leah known about Lizzie, she might have had that with her.

At last Leah concluded she could not, *would not,* keep back the near-sacred news about Jake from Sadie, who had been dreadfully wounded so many times over. It was time for her sister to hear the facts of the matter as both Dr. Schwartz and she knew it.

Leah contemplated the afternoon ahead,

thinking she might invite Sadie to take a walk someplace where they could be perfectly alone, once their gardening work was complete. Perhaps the woods? But no. How much better it would be to have the sun shining on them as they walked and talked. With the strong emotions that were sure to surface, she definitely wanted to be where they could see the openness of sky and fields.

As she placed the heavy platter of roast and vegetables before her family, Leah settled in her mind on the best place for her most solemn talk with dearest Sadie.

Chapter Twenty-Six

Henry had heaved himself out of bed the day after the grueling confrontation with Leah, floundering to find his robe and house slippers long before Lorraine might awaken. He had then proceeded to the bath, where he'd replayed the conversation as he lathered up his whiskers for shaving, fearing he had done the wrong thing in sharing Jake Mast's identity.

He recalled splashing on some aftershave and dressing before wandering downstairs to the sitting room between the front room and the kitchen. There he'd sat in the stillness for more than a half hour, pondering the probable destruction of his life until the newspaper had thumped against the back door. He had risen slowly to collect it, hungry for news of the outside world to choke out his own agitated thoughts.

All morning long he had gone back and forth about the wisdom of having revealed the truth. Now that he was sitting at his office desk, a sliced apple and a turkey and Swiss-cheese sandwich uneaten before him, he pondered again what he had done. *Such stupidity!*

Yet he had to hope his devastating confession was safe with Leah. Sighing, he could only imagine what she was going through now. His doing . . . all of it. Torn between the truth and the pain it was sure to inflict on her older sister, Leah was, no doubt, aggravated by the tremendous burden of her knowledge. He had done her a great disservice, and he was ashamed, not only of having revealed the deed, but of having committed it in the first place.

He tried to picture Jake growing up in Abram's household, being looked after and loved by his real mother, surrounded by his rightful family.

Leah won't contact the authorities, will she?

Even if she did not, Henry wondered if word might eventually get to Peter's and Fannie's ears. What then? He would be compelled to be straightforward with the

Masts, if it came to that. And what of poor Jake? The innocent young man would be forced to come face-to-face with not only his unsought birth mother but the entire Ebersol family. Would Sadie's family ever accept Jake as their own? Would Jake embrace them?

Questions wrenched him every which way, and he felt as tired when he reached for his sandwich as he had upon slipping into bed last night. Although he had experienced no trouble falling asleep, he had awakened repeatedly throughout the long night, even startling himself with the sound of his own miserable moaning. And Lorraine, saint that she was, had slept through the many thrashings and turnings he felt unable to control.

My life is in ruins, Henry thought, realizing that if his wife discovered *this* offense, he would have to daily atone for every wrongdoing he had ever committed . . . and there were many. Not that she would purposely hold it over him—that wasn't her way. His reluctance for her to know about their grandson now had more to do with Lorraine's keen interest in God, which made him feel even more culpable.

———◆———

Leah suggested she and Sadie take a walk following noon dinner, to which Sadie heartily agreed. She simply went along, enjoying the wispy clouds softening the rays of the sun, bringing the slightest bit of relief from the hottest part of the afternoon.

"Did ya know that Dat doesn't believe the English know anything 'bout how to gentle a horse?" Sadie had been thinking on this, having heard Dat say to Gid earlier that morning that he thought their approach was an insult to the horse. But the lack of a response from Leah made Sadie doubt she was any too interested in talking about horses. No, it was fairly obvious, now as they'd made the turn onto the main road and were heading southeast toward the Peacheys' place, that there was something very important on Leah's mind.

Leah slowed the pace and turned to face her. "Sadie, I don't honestly know how to tell ya . . . what I must say to you, but I'm gonna try."

She could see Leah was struggling as they continued walking, coming up on the area where the road opened up and the field

on the left stretched out to a pretty pond—
a small one, to be sure, but one that made
for a lovely verdant setting, nonetheless.
"What's on your mind, sister?" she asked,
feeling breathless and almost perplexed at
the tone of Leah's voice.

"Oh, Sadie, this is the hardest thing I've
ever had to do . . . but I want you to know
that if I could keep this back in order to
spare you—if I thought it wouldn't hurt you
worse to never know—well, I wouldn't utter
a single word." Leah was absolutely shaking with emotion.

"You're frightening me," Sadie said.
"What on earth is it?"

They walked for too long in total silence,
but Sadie decided not to pressure Leah. It
seemed best for her sister to take her time
with whatever was troubling her, even
though Sadie couldn't begin to think what
that might be.

Along the road, a green fringe of pasture
flourished where thin feelers on sheaths of
grass turned purple, then sapphire, then a
deep gray-lavender as the sun shifted in
and out of the faint cover of cirrus clouds.

Leah spoke again, a near whisper. "Sadie,

your baby . . . the son you birthed in Aunt
Lizzie's cabin . . . he didn't die that night."

Sadie stopped walking and felt as if her
heart might stop beating. "What are you
sayin'?" Her voice cracked.

Leah reached to hold both her hands.
"Come with me. I'll tell you all that I've just
learned."

They turned a sharp left, and she followed
Leah down through a vacant and large
piece of land, her mind and heart screaming
to know more even as her sister quietly
shared the astounding story.

At last they stood at the grave where Dr.
Schwartz had buried the Masts' *real* son.
Sadie was scarcely able to see for her tears.
Leah held her as she sobbed with both sor-
row and joy.

My son's alive! she thought, and when
she turned to look at her sister, she saw on
her face a reflection of her own emotions.
Sadie hardly knew what to think or say. She
felt almost ill, and a cold shiver ran up her
spine. "Dr. Schwartz has known all along?"

"Jah, I'm sorry to say."

"Well, I must tell Jake . . . I must meet
with him privately. Right away."

"Oh, Sadie, think on this a bit. Think what

this knowledge might do to him, to Mandie . . . to the entire Mast family."

Sadie shook her head. Obviously Leah didn't understand and had no idea what she was asking. Jake was a fine young man with a gentle nature—she knew this sure as anything, having watched him with Abe, shaken his hand at market, and witnessed the lighthearted expression in his eyes. "I can't wait any longer, don't you see? I've already lost all this time!"

Leah's head drooped, and when she looked up at Sadie, she was crying. "Please think about your son, Sadie. Peter and Fannie are the only parents he's known. For you to go to him now and reveal this . . . I just think, well, I s'pose I wouldn't have ever told ya if I thought you'd press ahead without thinkin' things through . . . ya know?" Leah reached over and touched Sadie's elbow.

Sighing, Sadie whispered, "Jah," choking back her own tears. "Maybe I'm bein' awful hasty, but I want to get to know him. . . . The years have flown from me."

Why is all this happening? Why now?

The entire story was as strange as can be, yet she would not doubt it for a minute, for Leah could be trusted. And looking into her sister's eyes, seeing her concern, as well as her sadness, Sadie knew something else: She must do Leah's bidding and simply wait. But when would be the right time? She had no idea, and all she could think about now was that she had already looked into the face—and felt the hand—of her only living child. Her son.

Leah was speaking again. "I think it wise to keep this just 'tween us till we carefully consider what we ought to do next, if anything. Till we seek some wisdom from above."

"Jah, from the Lord God."

Leah nodded her head, eyes still glistening. "We mustn't rush into something you'd surely regret later."

"And you don't think we should ask Dat or Aunt Lizzie 'bout this?"

"Not just yet, no."

Sadie, though terribly frustrated, began to slowly understand the reasoning behind Leah's words. At least in this solemn moment she did. Later today she did not know how impulsive she might feel, how eager she might be to hitch up the horse to the buggy and drive over to the Masts' orchard house to tell Jake the good news—that his real mother had come to take him home, where he belonged.

Ach! I mustn't do any such thing! She imagined the potential scene she would make with Jake's family, his close twin, all his older siblings—and him. Sadly she began to think that if she truly loved her flesh and blood, she might need to leave him in ignorance, never knowing he was the illegitimate child of one of the Ebersol cousins his family had shunned.

As they rose and walked back toward the main road, Sadie thought of the night she had told Leah of her youthful pregnancy and how the roles on this day were, in a peculiar way, quite reversed. Today it had been for Leah to share the truth that Sadie's own son was very much alive, instead of Sadie revealing her secret about the wee babe growing inside her. Truly, this child of hers had been veiled in secrecy from the time of his earliest beginnings.

Chapter Twenty-Seven

The days slid together, hot and muggy, the mid-July heat rising like a deep green tide in the open pasture. The intolerable temperatures brought with them sultry, restless nights for all the residents of the Ebersol Cottage, particularly Leah and Sadie, who had agreed that, for now, it was best Jake not be told of his true family roots. At only sixteen, he was too young for such jolting news, they reasoned, and the strained relations between their two families only compounded the problem.

Leah was prayerful, even watchful over her sister, hoping Sadie might somehow manage the emotional trauma she was now experiencing with some seemliness, keeping her feelings in check, at least while in the presence of other family members. And even though Sadie and Leah had endured several rather tense days, going so far as to exchange angry words in the vegetable garden one afternoon, Leah was quite sure no one suspected them of having had a fuss over something as earthshaking as Jake Mast's being Sadie's son. Such a secret to keep!

───────◆───────

With tomorrow a "no-church" Sunday, this Saturday night was an evening when most courting couples were out riding together. The traditional arrangement ensured their staying out all hours didn't cause stress in the family if the daughter or son of a household decided to sleep in a bit on Sunday morning.

Having hunger pangs in the middle of the night, Leah crept downstairs for a glass of milk and a cookie when she happened upon voices in the kitchen. Never having expected to encounter Lydiann entertaining her beau here in the house on a warm and moonlit night, of all things, Leah halted in surprise. She could see both Lyddie and a tall young man in the shadows, over in the corner where Dat's hickory rocker usually sat in the summer, out of the way of the wood stove, which was used for cooking even during the heat of July and August. She could see the two standing quite close together, talking. Not so eager to listen in, she decided to go and sit on the steps leading to the second floor, hoping Lyddie might have the common sense to send the young man on his way fairly soon. Yet even there, she could hear their voices.

"We'll get hitched as soon as the harvest is past," the young man said, startling her. "We'll be the first couple published at Preachin' this year."

Lydiann laughed softly.

"I'd marry ya tomorrow if we could."

"But we're underage," Lydiann said. "Will your father sign for you to marry?"

There was a long pause; then Lyddie's beau replied, "Somehow or other, I'll get him to say he will."

Leah felt terrible sitting there eavesdropping, yet she realized her girl was in over her head with this boy. Just what on earth could she do? Speak to Dat, maybe? But no, thinking back on her courting days with Jonas, she would not have wanted such interference, although there had certainly been enough of that coming from her father, for certain.

She rose and thought of heading back upstairs to simply wait for Lyddie to say good-bye to her fellow and head for bed. Just as she moved to do so, she heard Lydiann talking again. "Oh, I love ya so." And suddenly Lyddie burst out crying, as if her heart might break, saying she didn't see how her father would agree to let her marry so awful young. "You just don't know what you're askin', Jake . . . you don't know Dat."

Jake.

Leah froze in place, unable to make her legs move forward. She knew she'd heard correctly, and her heart was pounding much too hard. Could it be Lydiann was seeing Jake *Mast*?

"Ach . . . Lyddie, don'tcha worry your perty head," Jake was saying. "Things'll work out; you'll see. We're meant to be to-gether."

Calm down, Leah told herself. *There are oodles of Jakes round these parts. Nothing to fret about.*

Even so, she knew she would not be hur-rying back upstairs yet. No, she'd wait right here all night long to find out which tall Jake her Lyddie was crying over like there was no tomorrow.

———◆———

Sadie stared in the little hand mirror on the dresser that quiet Sunday, trembling as she dressed. She looked much as she had a week ago, although she *had* lost some inches, since the waist of her apron was quite loose. Staring at her features, she noticed her eyes had an almost distant look to them. *Will I ever know Jake Mast the way a mother knows her son? Will I ever be allowed to love him . . . share my life with him?*

She feared she might never lay eyes on him again, let alone speak privately with him. The droop of her mouth gave away her fears as she studied herself in the small mirror. Mamma had always said to look at the eyes of a person to know what they were really thinking, but now as she pondered that, Sadie felt sure it was especially the mouth that betrayed the truth about a person's happiness or grief. She let her face sag, without forcing even the slightest smile, and she was surprised at how terribly alone she seemed to appear—alone and weary of life.

I have no choice now but to keep this quiet, she thought. *I gave Leah my word.*

She went downstairs, through the small front room of the Dawdi Haus to the connecting door to the main house. In the corner cupboard of the big kitchen, she pulled from its shelf a large volume, *Martyrs Mirror or The Bloody Theatre.* An account of seventeen centuries of Christian martyrdom, including one of her father's own great-grandmothers, Catharina Meylin, Dat frequently read silently from the book. Leah had been the one to tell Sadie about their special relationship to this courageous woman following Sadie's return home. Not so long after that, Sadie had read for herself the heartrending tale of the great-grandmother who'd given up her life for the Lord Jesus.

Today the final recorded words of this godly woman, mother to many children, comforted Sadie's heart as she held the big book ever so close, almost cradling it.

———◆———

All that long morning Sadie kept wishing Dawdi John were still alive; she could sit with him and talk about most anything—even, she was sure, about her long-lost son. But Dawdi could no longer lend his kind, listening ear . . . gone to heaven, where Sadie had thought all her little ones were, up until a few days ago. It seemed so strange, nearly like a dream, to think her only son lived—and with Mamma's cousins. She had to remind herself repeatedly of the reality of it.

Since the house seemed deathly still, she decided to visit Hannah and the girls. She hurried out the back door of the Dawdi Haus, wishing she didn't have to reside alone in an addition typically meant for older relatives. Still, she knew she ought to be grateful for a place to live so near to those she loved.

Hurrying across the wide backyard, she walked toward the mule road, waving to Dat, who was stumbling out of the barn, rubbing his eyes like he'd just awakened from a catnap in the haymow. It was so hot she almost wished she'd stayed indoors fanning herself with the colorful paper fans Lydiann had made a while back at school.

Thinking of her own school days past, she was all the more anxious to see Hannah's girls—so cute they were when they stood together all in a row. Young Miriam, already six years old, had become a surprisingly cheerful sort—nothing at all the way she had started out. Though she'd never come right out and asked Hannah, Sadie guessed her sister had taken her youngest to one of the hex doctors for that, since she'd seen such a drastic change in not only the baby but in Hannah herself.

Ida Mae and Katie Ann must have seen her coming from their back porch, because they ran down the steps and hugged her hard. "Mamma, Mamma! Aunt Sadie's here for a visit," they called.

Pretty soon, Hannah and Mimi joined them. "Well, it's gut ya came up today, or we'd start thinkin' you a stranger."

"Never that." She followed the girls to the porch, where they all sat down, full of smiles. "It's sure cooler up here."

"Jah, under all these trees," Hannah replied. "Gid says it's a right nice place for a house."

"Where's Gid today?" Sadie asked.

"Over yonder, visiting an uncle."

Ida Mae asked if Sadie wanted some lemonade or something else cold to drink. "We have sun tea, too . . . sweetened with honey."

"Tea sounds gut," she said, glad to get her mind off herself . . . and Jake.

But when Ida Mae returned with a tall glass of tea for her, she was struck by how very dear each of Hannah's daughters was. *To think what life might have been like without even one of them. . . .* Sadie felt as if she might cry, contemplating each of the wee lives lost to her. Even the one that had just been found was still so far out of her reach.

◆

Following breakfast Monday morning, Leah went out alone and began hoeing weeds in the vegetable and flower gardens, not caring that by now Dr. Schwartz would be missing his former housekeeper. Truth was, she wanted to have nothing to do with the man, and the best way to avoid him was simply to stay as far away from the clinic as possible. *Let him explain to Lorraine why I'm not coming back,* she thought, still beside herself with anger.

Meanwhile, Sadie was inside, moping about, although no one was in the house to inquire of her sister's dark mood—at least not at the present time.

Leah took out her intense frustration, even fear, on the vinelike weeds that had determined to choke out the staked tomato plants. All the while she mulled over what on earth would happen if Jake Mast—who was indeed Lydiann's beau—somehow obtained his father's permission to marry young . . . assuming his father wasn't privy to his son's courtship of one of Abram Ebersol's daughters, that is. Her imagination ran away with her regarding Lydiann and Jake's courting relationship, revealed by Leah's Saturday-night kitchen vigil. Sadly she thought of the strong possibility of deformed and mentally retarded babies such an aunt-nephew union might produce. And dear Lydiann—what would she think if she discovered she was in love with her sister's son? The emotional implications alone were enough to cause serious problems for Lydiann and Jake.

She wished the dilemma might simply disappear, but there was no escaping what she now knew must be swiftly dealt with. Even so, she must carefully contemplate this and ask God for help in knowing what she should or shouldn't do.

And there was the matter of Sadie, too. If Leah were to tell her of Lydiann and Jake, would she become distraught at this devastating news? Leah recalled all too well the hopelessness and the long, sad nights that had beset Sadie following the loss of her son all those years ago. Sadie had sniffled into the wee hours each night, competing with baby Lydiann's own fits of crying. Most likely Sadie was already reliving all of that, the wounds having been reopened by Leah herself. And now this latest discovery . . .

Leah didn't know what to do. She longed to run to the house and check on her sister, embrace her, but maybe it was best she chop away these nasty weeds, though it would likely do Sadie some good if *she* were the one out here hacking away at the pesky vines. *Goodness, how she must need something to pound on right about now!*

Aunt Lizzie wandered over from the barn, looking pink in the face. "It's too hot for weeding, Leah," she said, wiping her brow. "But if I know you, you'll keep on workin' no matter what I say."

Leah had to laugh at that. "I think ya know

me too well," she replied, leaning on the hoe. "I don't quit till the job's done."

Lizzie turned and glanced toward the house. "Where's Sadie?"

"Inside."

"Tryin' to keep cool?"

Leah said nothing, hoping Lizzie wouldn't take it upon herself to fetch Sadie just now.

"Is something the matter with your sister?" Lizzie frowned and shielded her eyes with one hand. "For the past couple of days she's been down in the mouth."

"Seems so" was all Leah would say. All she *could* say.

"I'm thinkin' it's time we made us some ice cream. Chocolate, maybe. Might put a smile on all our faces, ain't so?"

Leah nodded and watched Lizzie head toward the house, hoping Sadie might be sheltered away in her bedroom, except with its being so hot, she hardly thought her sister would want to be upstairs in the Dawdi Haus.

Returning to her weeding, she forced her thoughts to the upcoming farewell for the teenage boys headed out to Ohio. She wondered how the mothers, sisters, and even sweethearts would ever manage saying good-bye. Gid had mentioned to her and Dat last week that it would be nice for some of the women to bake cakes and serve them on the first Sunday in August, following the final Lancaster Preaching service for more than two handfuls of boys. Since the church meeting and the subsequent singing would be held at Old Jonathan Lapp's house, Leah had already talked with his unmarried daughter about providing several hot-water sponge cakes for the common meal.

Just then the thought popped into her head that she ought to talk to Gid about somehow getting Jake Mast included in the group of young men headed to Ohio. *A solution, maybe?* she wondered, realizing it would mean having to share the truth about Jake with her brother-in-law. *I'll have to talk to Sadie, too . . . tell her about Lydiann being in love with Jake—wanting to marry a close blood relative!*

But the thought of the awful heartbreak such a plan would cause Lydiann, as well as Sadie, kept her from marching right up to Gid and Hannah's place. How on earth could she be responsible for setting such a thing in motion? With a shudder, she realized that what she was thinking of doing was nearly equal to what Dat had done about Jonas Mast, arranging to have him work in Ohio as a cabinetmaker's apprentice.

Feeling distressed, Leah left the garden and headed back to the house for some ice-cold lemonade.

Chapter Twenty-Eight

Dense storm clouds, which before Tuesday's noon had threatened rain, had all but dissipated when Leah met Sadie on the small porch off the Dawdi Haus, where Sadie was beating rugs.

"Sister, I'm afraid I have something mighty difficult to tell you," Leah began softly, hating to find herself the bearer of sad news as she explained how she'd stumbled onto the late-night conversation in the kitchen between Lydiann and Jake.

Sadie's eyes widened as she promptly abandoned her chore, draping the rugs over the porch railing. "Ach, are ya ever so sure?" Shaking her head in apparent disbelief, Sadie's face turned ashen, as if she might be ill. "This can't be."

"But it is, and we must do something to put a stop to it—and right quick."

"Why must this be happenin'?" Sadie moaned. "On top of everything else!"

Leah leaned on the banister. "If we don't do anything, they prob'ly will end up married. We can't stand by and merely hope they change their minds 'bout each other."

"We have to think more on this," Sadie said. "Let's walk up to the high meadow— go somewhere more private."

Agreeing, Leah hurried off with Sadie, the two of them talking through the ins and outs of this almost unthinkable quandary.

When they'd exhausted all possibilities, including telling Lydiann privately of Jake Mast's parentage—something both feared would come to no good end—Sadie tearfully begged Leah not to mention a word to anyone. "Not even to Gid," she said. "I'm just not ready to think 'bout having Jake sent away."

"Well, honestly, it's the wisest choice we've discussed," Leah said.

"Jah, I see that." Still, Sadie said she couldn't bring herself to agree to anything, least of all something that would take her only living child farther away from her.

◆

All that day and the next, Leah went about her chores and responsibilities, hoping a better solution would present itself. She wasn't too surprised when Lorraine Schwartz stopped by the vegetable stand, asking for her, and Lydiann sent the doctor's wife up to the house, around to the back door.

Lorraine's eyes were full of concern. "We miss you terribly, Leah. We can't be without your wonderful help."

So as not to open up the troublesome topic with the doctor's unsuspecting wife, Leah promised to return to work the following day, saying she had not been feeling well lately—which was entirely true. Surely Dr. Schwartz, wretched man that he was, would understand the source of Leah's illness should Lorraine relay this exchange to him. As justified as her decision had been, Leah felt sorry about having stayed put at home, leaving innocent Lorraine in the lurch.

When Lorraine had gone her way, Leah turned her attention to Sadie. She understood why her sister wanted to keep quiet about Jake, wanting nothing to hamper her chances of bumping into him—a selfish but unsurprising reaction, for sure. Sadie's present grief, along with her hope for at least one more encounter with her son, caused Leah to consent for now to keep mum about Jake and Lydiann's romance. Yet each day that passed brought opportunity for Sadie's sister to fall more deeply in love with Sadie's son.

———◆———

A full week had passed since Leah had heard Jake's declaration of love for Lydiann, and she felt increasingly anxious. She was aware that this Sunday there was to be another singing across the cornfield at the Peacheys' place, where Dorcas and her husband, Tomato Joe Zook, lived with their young family now that Smitty and Miriam had moved to the Dawdi Haus. There was no question in Leah's mind that Lydiann would go, particularly with the singing this close to home. Lyddie wouldn't even need to bother asking Abe for a ride when she could simply walk over there.

Leah wished she could approach Lydiann with her concerns about Jake, but neither she nor Sadie felt that was wise. Leah in particular had a strong desire to shield Lyddie from the truth about her forbidden courtship with Jake, and undeserving as Dr. Schwartz might be, she felt concern for him and especially his good-hearted wife, as well. Truth be told, Lyddie wasn't so good at keeping secrets, and in the wink of an eye, everyone might know that the doctor, whom so many had trusted, was responsible for this horrible deed. Worse still, Jake's relationship to the only family he had ever known could be placed in jeopardy as Sadie's past reputation was once again brought to light. *Ach, but such a revelation would be a devastating blow to Dat and Aunt Lizzie, too!* Leah dreaded the thought of telling anyone at all, though Gid might actually be able to quietly help do something about the mind-boggling *Druwwel.* And what an entangled problem it was!

She had prayed all week long there might be a better answer. If she could just convince Sadie how essential it was for Jake to leave . . . to help her understand that what Leah assumed her sister wanted most desperately—a private encounter with Jake— most likely wouldn't happen anytime soon, and in a few months the wedding season

would be upon them. No, they couldn't simply mark time when something this important was at stake. Leah must act immediately.

———————◆———————

The hayloft had often drawn Sadie as a
small girl when she was sad or miffed. She
much preferred the sweetness of the hay to
the lower level of the bank barn, where the
enduring reek of the animals saturated the
air. But this night, she'd felt terribly alone in
the Dawdi Haus; the heat had been stifling
as she tossed about in her bed in the room
where Aunt Lizzie had slept before she'd
married Dat. Sadie had gotten up and stood
near the open window, yearning for even the
slightest waft of a breeze, and then headed
downstairs to the kitchen, where she'd
opened the screen door. There she had remained for the longest time on the little
square porch, looking out toward the top of
the Peacheys' farmhouse and their big barn.

It was close to two o'clock in the morning
when she made her way out to their own
barn and gingerly climbed the ladder to the
haymow just under the eaves. Tired as she

was, she wouldn't think of allowing herself to sleep there, with the mice and the insects crawling about. Despite the presence of the barn cats, she was ever so sure the pests were there, just out of view. Late as it was, Lydiann was probably still out riding under the stars with Jake Mast, and Sadie was determined to see for herself exactly how it was between the pair.

Sighing, she thought back to the day she'd first heard her child with Derry was actually alive. How could things have changed so radically for her in one respect, yet nothing else had seemingly changed at all? She sat in the hay, having imaginary conversations with Jake in her head, trying to guess what another face-to-face meeting with him might be like now that she knew he was her flesh and blood. Would he appreciate knowing that she, not Fannie Mast, was his real mother? Would he be upset? Would he even believe her?

Tormented, she rose and began to pace the upper level, going back and forth in her mind. And what of Jake's love for Lydiann? Wasn't it probable he was simply experiencing something akin to puppy love? If Leah would simply bide her time and not speak to Gid, as she'd promised, there was always the possibility Jake might become disinterested in Lydiann and move on to a new girlfriend, as many young men in their middle teens were known to do. Sadie could only hope so, because the thought of Jake's being sent away was almost more than she could bear.

———◆———

The tickle of kitten fuzz against her bare foot awakened Sadie with a start, and she realized hazily that, despite her intentions, she must have settled down on the threshing floor, amongst the various mother cats and their kittens. But now she was quite awake and aware of the sound of a horse and buggy . . . and voices wafting through the darkness.

"Oh, Jake, I'm nervous 'bout askin' Dat for his permission."

"We mustn't fret, Lyddie. Mamma always said the Lord God moves heaven and earth for those in love." It was Jake's voice, but if Sadie hadn't known better she might've thought Derry was speaking.

Let Jake have pure motives, Lord. . . .

Sadie was ever so anxious to lay eyes on him again, even in the dim light of a half moon—the faintest silhouette would satisfy her heart—so she moved to the window and peered into the night.

Lydiann's voice was muffled now as she pressed her face against Jake's shoulder. Sadie watched them embrace near the buggy and then gaze into each other's eyes.

The scene told Sadie just how serious they were. This was most likely not the puppy love she'd hoped to witness.

With tears in her eyes, she could only wonder what it would mean to her sister and Jake—and their future children—if no one stopped them. *Spared them, truly.*

Sadie knew beyond all doubt she must tell Leah it *was* for the best to confide in Gid and see that Jake was somehow included among the boys traded.

Poor Lydiann, thought Sadie, moving from the window. *How will she ever survive such a loss? How will I?*

◆

Leah happened upon Gid as he was rounding up the cows for afternoon milking.

She felt awkward, his being alone and all, but she knew it was necessary, what with Sadie not feeling up to coming along.

"Nice day, ain't?" She folded her hands in front of her.

Gid nodded. "We could use some rain, but, jah . . . a right fine day."

She stood still just then, realizing she had little time to speak up. "I . . . uh, Gid, there's something awful important on my mind."

He turned his full attention to her.

"As you know, Sadie gave birth to a baby years ago, and she thought the wee one was born dead," Leah began, aware he had heard as much at Sadie's kneeling repentance at Preaching, nearly seven years ago. "Well, it's come to light that her son is actually quite alive."

"He's *alive*?" Gid was frowning as he held her gaze. "Oh, Leah, no wonder ya came to talk to me. Where's Sadie's boy now?"

"Growin' up as Peter Mast's youngest son." She spoke more softly now, explaining all that she knew as quickly as she could. "And worst of all, Jake's seein' our Lydiann . . . and quite seriously."

Looking even more puzzled, Gid squared

his shoulders. "How on God's green earth do ya know he's courtin' Lydiann?"

Somewhat embarrassed, she shared what both she and Sadie had overheard. She sighed, pressing on, hoping she might appeal to Gid's kindliness. "Honestly, what I have in mind will bring Lyddie much sadness, and she won't understand what's happened to her beau . . . but I've been wondering if Jake shouldn't be one of the boys approached about going out to Ohio. Ya know . . . to get him away from Lydiann, his aunt by blood."

Gid nodded his head emphatically. "I sure can see where you're comin' from. I can talk to the bishop about it right quick."

To this Leah shook her head. "Let's keep this 'tween you, me, and Sadie for now."

Willingly, Gid agreed. Leah was ever so sure he understood the impact such a revelation could have on the community of the People. No good thing could ever come of it.

◆

Hitching up his horse and carriage, Gid went straightaway to Grasshopper Level to speak with Peter Mast, mighty concerned. He found Peter in his apple orchard, puffing on his pipe and muttering to himself as he ambled along.

Catching Peter's eye, Gid introduced himself, though being a preacher for the district neighboring Grasshopper Level, he was fairly certain Peter knew who he was— at least by name.

"Jah, I know ya well enough." Peter's eyes narrowed. " 'Tis a mighty gut thing you got yourself loose from that Leah Ebersol . . . I daresay."

Gid wondered where Peter was going with such a snide remark, but bearing in mind his business there, he held his peace. "Look, I best be gettin' to the point of why I'm here," he said, anxious to put some distance between himself and this coldhearted man. " 'Tis a right touchy subject I'm here 'bout, but seems your son Jake is awful serious about Abram's Lydiann."

Peter coughed and removed the pipe from between his chapped lips. "Now, just a minute here. Did ya say one of Abram Ebersol's daughters?"

"Jah, that's what I'm sayin'. Seems Jake's determined to marry her, and as a preacher and Lydiann's brother-in-law, it troubles me that she is thinkin' of marriage at such a young age," said Gid, withholding the sensitive information that Jake was also an Ebersol himself. Being a man of his word, Gid intended to keep his promise to Leah on that.

"Marriage? Well, I'll be puttin' a stop to that!" There was instant fire in Peter's eyes at the mention of a possible wedding involving the two families.

Gid was aghast at Peter's vehement response. Such animosity he had scarcely seen on the face of any man, let alone a God-fearing Amish farmer. The rift between Peter Mast and Abram Ebersol was unmistakably enormous, and Gid cared not to get himself caught in the middle. He was quick to suggest that perhaps Peter might consider including Jake with the Gobbler's Knob boys heading out to Ohio in two weeks' time. "What would ya think of that?"

"Put *my* son in the trade for the Ohio men?" Peter asked, actually seeming to calm a bit as he contemplated the notion.

"Jah, to settle in and work out there . . . find himself a mate," he said, wanting Peter to be clear on what he might agree to.

Peter looked pointedly at him. "If it's true my son's courtin' an Ebersol, I'll be thinking hard on this."

Mighty eager to depart now, Gid remarked that Hannah was waiting supper for him and excused himself to head back to his horse and buggy . . . and home. *Back to the peace of my house,* he thought, shuddering from the intensity of the encounter.

Chapter Twenty-Nine

Lydiann's bedroom was tidy because she could not stand for anything less than perfectly clean. Her bureau was kept dusted, even polished, and the handmade doilies were washed and ironed frequently. She liked to make her bed just as soon as she slipped out of it of a morning, and her floor was free of dust bunnies and cobwebs, even beneath the bed, a fact she was very proud of. She'd often thought what an exceptional housekeeper she would be for her husband and family some fine day— a family she'd hoped to have with Jake. But now, as she held the letter from him in her trembling hands, reading it again for the tenth time since its arrival days ago, she felt that hope was dimmed . . . if not gone.

Dear Lyddie,

I'm sorry to write in a letter the things I want to say to your face, but I have no other choice.

First of all, I apologize that I couldn't attend the singing at your neighbor's place recently. I wanted to . . . really, I did.

Please, you must believe me, Lyddie. I have nothing to do with this painful separation. My father is entirely opposed to my hope of marrying this fall. Somehow he is privy to who you are, although I was not the one to inform him. It has come to his ears that I am seeing one of Abram Ebersol's daughters, and my father, who, as you know, has always looked unkindly on your father and your family, is insisting I go to Ohio. His response was worse than I feared—I see that I was right in wanting to keep our love secret from him till our wedding day, if necessary. I am so sorry.

Lydiann, I love you and always will. I know this as sure as my name is Jacob Mast. Please don't cry for me once I'm gone to Ohio, my dear girl, because I

will come back to Pennsylvania someday. For now, though, I am expected to
establish myself in the home of an
Amish family, begin working, and court
girls from that area. I know this is terrible to have to tell you. Truth is, I refuse
to either court or marry anyone but
you, my darling. You are the bride of
my heart. I will simply work hard in
Holmes County until I am of age; then I
will return for you.

Will you wait for me? I know this is
the most awful thing that could have
ever happened to two people so in
love.

I will not forget you. When I arrive
where I'm intended to go, I'll send you
another letter. Please pardon my father
for this. I must attempt to forgive him,
too. Meanwhile I must try to figure out
a way to earn his blessing on our future
marriage, years from now.

All my love,
Jake

Lydiann stared at the letter through her
tears. She already missed him and was feeling on the verge of collapse, as if someone

had chopped off a supporting limb. Her heart was wounded and forlorn . . . all because of an ugly problem between Jake's father and her own.

For sure and for certain, she could not begin to comprehend what would have made Jake's father choose to have him join the young men being herded off to Ohio. What sort of father would do such a thing? Would Peter Mast have decided to send his son away if *she* wasn't the girl he loved? Could Jake have been spared this terrible thing if he'd fallen in love with, say, Uncle Jesse Ebersol's daughter, maybe? All too well, she knew the answer.

Lydiann rose and went to the bureau and shoved the letter deep into a drawer, wishing she'd never turned sixteen this past spring . . . wishing she were still as young and naive as the day before she went to her first singing and fell hard for wonderful Jacob Mast.

◆

Hearing of Lydiann's dejection from both Hannah and Aunt Lizzie, Mary Ruth visited Lyddie every other day, offering her company, even going so far as to invite Lydiann to spend some time with Robert and her, "just to get away a bit."

But Lydiann refused, saying she wanted to stay close to home, near Mamma and Abe. Still, Mary Ruth couldn't get over how beside herself Lydiann was for one so young. *Her heart must be broken,* she thought as she sat on Lydiann's bed, looking now at her young sister's tear-streaked face.

"I can scarcely eat," Lyddie told her, sitting in the upright cane chair across the room. "I miss him so."

She sighed sadly, remembering well how troubled she had been when Elias Stoltzfus died. "I felt the same way once," she admitted.

"You did, sister?"

Mary Ruth nodded and began to tell Lydiann of her dear friend and first beau, explaining how he had been killed in an accident, though leaving out the part that Robert had been the one whose car had struck Elias's pony cart.

When she was finished, Lydiann was crying all the harder, and Mary Ruth went to her, reaching down to kiss her cheek. "Oh,

Lyddie, I never would've told you all this if I had thought it would upset you so."

"No, no, it's a gut thing ya did, prob'ly." She looked up at Mary Ruth with the saddest, bluest eyes. "I needed to hear that someone else had such a dreadful thing happen to them and yet could still smile, years later." Lydiann got up and put her arms around Mary Ruth, clinging to her as if she might slip from her grasp. "Denki, sister."

Holding Lyddie was the best help she felt she could offer, so she let her sister cry in her arms, for as long as need be . . . just as Leah and Mamma and Aunt Lizzie had always comforted her. All of them would continue to surround Lydiann with their love, if possible making up for the powerful sadness.

"The Lord Jesus cares for you," she whispered.

Lydiann moved her head as if to say she knew that was true. "Mamma Leah prays for me every day," she murmured.

"I do, too," said Mary Ruth, hoping God's love would touch Lydiann during her time of misery.

Chapter Thirty

Halfway to Smitty's, Abram felt the warm breeze on his face and breathed in a whiff of the barnyard. He fixed his gaze on Blackbird Pond, shimmering in the distance, and recalled the winter day he'd found Abe unconscious on the ice. His son had bounced back to normal, which had made him a believer in prayer all those years ago. That and his wonderful-good relationship with Lizzie. No question, the Lord had bestowed blessings upon him . . . upon each member of his family, really.

He just wished God might reach down now and pull up the sides of Lydiann's mouth, helping her to smile again. Abram was aware of her gloominess, yet knew from Lizzie only that a young man had gone off to Ohio, instead of staying home and courting Lyddie as he'd set out to do. Sadie, too, had seemed awfully down in the dumps recently, and although he'd asked Lizzie about that, as well, she hadn't offered any answers.

Truth was, his house was full up with women who had a whole range of emotions, and he'd learned over the years to keep a safe distance at particular times. It did seem, though, that if one woman was tetchy, there was bound to be at least one other of a similar mindset. The hitch was, of course, that he had three adult women and one courting-age daughter all living together under the same roof.

He grinned at the thought as he approached Smitty's pasture now, having reached the edge of the cornfield. It was a very good thing his twins had found themselves fine husbands. For certain, he didn't care to imagine what daily life would be like with all *six* of the women in his life residing at the Ebersol Cottage, for goodness' sake.

◆

Both Leah and Dat preferred to wait until the last possible minute before fetching a gas lamp on summer evenings, waiting till just past dusk for some artificial lighting in the house. Tonight Leah made her way out to the utility room to get one of the tall lamps, scarcely able to see as she went.

She had noticed Lydiann sitting clear back in the dark corner by herself as the rest of the family all sat around the table, enjoying Dat's reading from the Bible and the cake she'd baked for supper. She had been careful not to make hot-water sponge cake, which had been served at the farewell meal for the boys heading off to Ohio. She had no desire to remind Lydiann in any way of that particular Sunday, hard as it had been for all of the People. For the past three weeks she couldn't help but observe how crestfallen Lyddie had looked since Jake Mast had left with the others—all of it her doing. Yet what other choice had she?

Leah had always loathed self-pity, but she completely comprehended where Lydiann was coming from. The girl seemingly had no interest in battling her emotions, and she could not hide her anguish, especially from those who loved her. Sadie had tried to cheer her up to no avail; even Abe had asked Leah if there was something wrong with Lyddie—"She's just too quiet," he'd said.

She's entitled to be sad, since we pulled the rug out from under her. She, Sadie, and Gid had never bothered to consult with Lydiann but had, instead, taken matters into their hands and acted in what they all agreed was her best interest. Yet right now, looking at her, Leah questioned their approach—it seemed nothing could soothe her girl. And although Leah believed in her heart that Jake's leaving was for the best, she did worry Lyddie might never get over his seeming abandonment of her.

She began to clear away the dishes, thinking all the while of what might bring a smile to Lydiann's face . . . Sadie's, as well. She was reminded of some of the new boys from Ohio; several of them had taken an obvious shining to Lydiann at the first Preaching service after their arrival. Leah had been as sorry as she could be to watch the light in their eyes fade when Lyddie politely looked the other way. Of course, it was too early to encourage her girl in that direction—much too soon.

The glow from the gas lamp was altogether cheery now as it cast large shadows of each of the family members onto the far wall. The steady warmth of the lamp offered security and a bit of comfort.

Just as the presence of God's love lights our pathway, Leah thought.

———————◆———————

"O Lord God, help me understand why Jake left me behind," Lydiann prayed beneath the massive branches of the thornless honey-locust tree. She still remembered the first time Mamma had ever brought her and Abe up to these woods, to what she called her "special piece of earth."

"It's one of the most restful spots I know," Mamma had told them. Today Lydiann was finding out for herself yet again that most always what Mamma said was true.

I'm so alone, Lord . . . remembering when Jake was my own, and I was his.

She recalled those things Sadie had shared with her years ago regarding Leah's romance with Jonas Mast—how his joining the Gobbler's Knob church and then not staying put here had caused him to be shunned. Because of Jonas's subsequent estrangement from them, the Masts were still angry with Leah and all of them. Was that the only reason Peter Mast despised the thought of her being Jake's bride?

Lydiann was grateful to receive Jake's love letters—several each week. She answered each one of them often right here, beneath the tree that had so often comforted Mamma Leah in the past.

This day, she took out her stationery and pen and, once again, told Jake of her steadfast love. *I'll love you no matter where you are,* she wrote. *Ohio or Indiana,* or *Pennsylvania. Where you are doesn't matter as much as the state of our hearts, ain't so?*

She meant every word she wrote beneath the shade of this old and very rare tree, and she could scarcely wait for the years to fly, till Jake would send for her or, better yet, return home for her. An eternity away to be sure.

———————◆———————

By the time Jonas redded up his woodworking shop and closed for the day, he was eager to get home. A fine supper would await him, and he happily wondered what delicious dish Emma had cooked for him to-

day. Coming from a long line of terrific
cooks, Emma seemed to derive great joy
from preparing tasty meals, even feasts,
nearly every evening. He had frequently told
her that simple fare was fine with him, but
Emma thrived on cooking and baking—the
fancier the better. Most of their neighbors
took their big meal at noon, but since he
had quite a ride to his shop, which he rented
from an old farmer friend, Jonas was
satisfied with a good sandwich or two at
that hour. Maybe that was the reason why
Emma seemed to want to outdo herself
come supper. He smiled, thinking of her af-
fectionately. What a kind and generous
woman she was, always considering him.

It was as he reined the horse into the lane
that he noticed another buggy parked near
the side yard. His good friend Preacher Sol
Raber hailed from the house. "Jonas, hullo!"
the jolly man called.

Glad to see him, Jonas jumped out of his
carriage. "What brings ya all the way to the
sticks?"

"Oh, I thought ya might want to take a
young man under your wing, is all."

"Why, sure," he said, not waiting to hear

just who might be looking for some pointers in cabinetmaking.

Sol continued on to say he'd recently met one of the young men traded from Pennsylvania. "He's just hankerin' for some gut fellowship with a master carpenter, as he says. Naturally I thought of you first, Jonas."

"If he's hardworking, I surely could use some young help."

Sol grinned, showing his teeth. "Fine and dandy," he said. "I'll bring him out first thing tomorrow. How's that?"

"I'll look forward to it."

"I think the two of you will get along fine," Sol said. " 'Specially bein' he's a Mast, same as you."

"How 'bout that?" Jonas found this news altogether interesting. "Where's the young-ster from in Pennsylvania, anyway?"

"Lancaster County."

"Plenty of Masts round there." He reached for the bridle. "What's his first name?"

"Jake."

He stood up and scratched his head, suddenly bone weary. "Jake, ya say?"

"Jah, and this one's mighty young to be

gone from family." Sol took off his straw hat
and wiped his brow with his blue paisley
kerchief. "Honestly, he says he's downright
miserable—came out here against his will.
Guess his pop wanted to get him away from
the girl he loves for some reason or other."

Jonas turned just then, deliberately looking at the acres of tall corn across the dirt
road.

"You all right, there, Jonas?"

He patted his horse's neck. "I'll look forward to meetin' this Jake fella."

Sol pressed his hat back down on his
head and made for his own carriage and
horse. "See ya tomorrow, then."

"Have a gut evening, Sol." With that
Jonas offered a confident wave and set
about unhitching his horse.

Chapter Thirty-One

With the arrival of September, Lydiann found more relief in working alongside Abe outdoors than inside the crowded house. She was glad to help where she could, especially with Dat complaining more often about aches and pains. Besides, the other women of the house were far better at scaring up a dinner. Lydiann preferred to write wonderful-good letters to her faraway beau, reminding him of her love for him as often as he did her.

She found herself continually checking the mailbox, even tuning her ear for their postman, ever so eager for more word from Ohio. Jake had written in his very last letter that he was doing some work with a "right fine woodworker—one with the same last name as my own." He looked on it as quite providential, especially since master wood-

workers were few and far between here in
Lancaster County. His happiness at this
turn of events made Lydiann both pleased
and a little sad. Pleased that he was finding
plenty to keep his hands busy until such a
time as he could return to her . . . and sad
because she feared he just might get himself too attached to either Ohio or the
friendly Mast woodworker.

Today she intended to take twenty minutes from her morning chores to write another letter to Jake so she could get it
tucked into the mailbox before the mail was
picked up this afternoon.

"What're ya thinking 'bout *now*?" Abe
asked her when they'd hauled the milk cans
to the milk house.

"Nothin' much."

"Like foolin', you're not." He eyed her curiously. "You're thinking 'bout that beau of
yours, ain't so? The one who up and left
ya."

She sucked in air quickly. "Mind your own
business!"

Abe frowned, staring hard at her. "What's
a-matter, Lyddie? Ya don't have to bite my
head off."

She had a mind to ignore him and she did.

"I've heard things . . . from some of the other fellas, ya know," Abe said.

She nodded. " 'Spect you have." She tensed up, worried he'd come right out and ask her something about Jake specifically—make her admit to his knowing whom it was she loved.

"Some of my friends are asking 'bout ya," he said. "A few are downright sweet on you, Lyddie."

She turned and glared at him, the little brother who'd become a young teenager before her eyes. Tall like Sadie and nearly as blond, Abe was good-looking in anyone's opinion. She didn't know for sure if she ought to say what she was thinking, but she did anyway. "I know our cousin Essie Ebersol is sweet on *you,* but would I have come right out and said it without thinking?" she hollered over her shoulder. Then she blew out a long sigh. "Truth is, when ya start to learn 'bout such things—who likes whom and all of that—it's really not for you to be sayin'. Don't you know anything?"

He stuck out his tongue. "Puh!"

"The day you ever think twice before

talkin' . . . well, that'll be a right fine one, if I must say so!"

Before she might up and shed a tear, she started for the potting shed to cry her eyes out in peace. She wouldn't have been so easily upset, except she was missing Jake something awful.

When at last she'd pulled herself together, Lydiann headed for the chicken house, where she felt altogether hopeless as she scattered feed to the clucking hens and the solitary rooster.

◆

On Jake's second visit to Jonas's cabinetmaking shop, unlike the first, the two of them quickly got to talking. Jake seemed less perturbed at having been unwillingly sent so far from home. In fact, it appeared to Jonas that Jake settled in for the day as if he were visiting an old friend. With their mutual Lancaster County connection and same last name, Jonas was curious to know more about Jake's family. "What's your father do?" he asked.

"He owns an apple orchard in a place called Grasshopper Level. Ain't really a

town or a village—it's just a raised area between miles of farmland, southeast of
Strasburg."

Astonished, Jonas stared at Jake. *This
has to be my baby brother!* Looking at his
nearly grown sibling, he was painfully aware
of the passage of years, having been cut off
from his family for nearly sixteen years. Had
the Lord God truly brought his youngest
brother to his very door?

Jonas said nothing, only watched and listened intently as the sad-eyed teenager
went on. "My pop gave me no choice," Jake
said, reaching for a hammer and holding it
gingerly. "I had to leave home and come
here, like it or not."

Jonas found this altogether puzzling. "Did
you ever ask why that was?"

Jake laughed quietly. "You don't know my
father. He isn't one to be questioned."

Jonas knew someone like that well
enough, but the description wasn't one he
would have used of his father. Fact was he
knew *two* such someones: Abram Ebersol
and Bishop Bontrager. But there was no
sense bringing up the past with his young
friend—his brother!

"I'm here 'cause I lacked courage, I

s'pose you could say." Holding the hammer in both hands now and frowning down at it, Jake went to sit on the wooden stool near the table saw. "I'm in love with a girl my father doesn't like . . . doesn't approve of her family." He clenched his jaw. "How am I s'posed to feel 'bout that? I can't just stop loving her at his say-so."

Jonas studied him as he listened to the all-too-familiar account, drinking in the image of this dark-haired teen before him. Jake had been merely an infant when Jonas was still living at home, so he couldn't be of legal age to marry on his own just yet. No doubt he needed their father's permission to marry, something that had been denied.

"She couldn't be prettier, Jonas, with a down-to-earth sort of grace. Ever know someone like that?"

"Jah, I believe I do." He was thinking now of Emma.

"What do you do when love comes along clear out of the blue and nearly knocks ya off your feet? Do you follow with all of your heart?"

He nodded. "Well, I should say so. Lord willin', of course."

Later, after Jonas had shown Jake several

different tricks of the trade, he offered to take him back to the family with whom he was staying near Berlin.

"You sure?" Jake's big brown eyes were alight with the offer.

"Wouldn't mention it if I wasn't."

They had a good chuckle over that and headed out to hitch up the horse and buggy.

◆

Sadie headed on foot to Ivan and Mary Etta Troyers' place, keeping her promise to help with some heavy cleaning, even though several of the older daughters planned to be on hand to help, as well. Thinking about a family of twelve—a perfect dozen—she wondered what it would be like to raise ten youngsters as she made her way toward the Troyers' farmhouse not too far down from the Kauffmans' spread. Not only did it seem unfair that some women had no trouble giving birth to one healthy baby after another, but she had also begun to second-guess Jake's going to Ohio. As far as she was concerned, it might as well be China, or some other country halfway around the world.

She rubbed her neck, realizing anew how upset she still was—finding and losing her precious son all within the space of a few weeks. Every now and then, she recalled how she had "heard" her baby crying all those months after she birthed him. At the time she'd thought she was losing her mind, but presently she wondered if God had been trying to tell her all those years ago that Jake was very much alive.

Now she let her eyes take in the trees and pastureland, sighing crossly. Never would there be another chance to anonymously spend time with her boy, let alone talk with him one-on-one as she longed to. How she wished to share the truth of who she was with him. Who *he* was to her!

She refused to let herself cry—not here on the road in plain view of Englishers driving past in their fancy cars. Today she must be in control of her emotions, not allow her misgivings to take over again. She must try to demonstrate the kind of pluckiness Leah seemed to have cultivated over time, despite her own heartaches. Just last night Sadie had talked with Leah, who indicated that when sorrowful things happen to people who are the children of God, they can either run to the Lord and seek after His presence, or they can pray and plead for God to remove the struggles so their life might be happy once again. "But don't be mistaken," Leah had warned, "it is not the easy or contented life that makes folk hunger hard after the Lord Jesus."

Even so Sadie wasn't sure she was ready to fully surrender her wants and wishes to the Lord God. Feelings of anger and resentment still raged within her—toward Dr. Schwartz and toward God, too, for allowing the doctor to do what he'd done. Sure, she could observe Leah's joyfulness all day long, but she didn't understand where it came from. It seemed the more sorrow Leah encountered in her life, the more peaceful, even content, she was. Sadie wished she, too, might experience such a miraculous reaction to the sad circumstances swirling around her, but she wasn't convinced a closer walk with God was the way for that to happen. When she prayed at all, she much preferred to beseech Him to bring her son home to her. It was only in that event that her happiness would be restored.

———◆———

The lush green of grassy hills and treed hollows was never tiresome to Jonas, even though he took this way to work each and every weekday, and ofttimes Saturdays. He enjoyed the ride on the back roads of his second home in Apple Creek, though Grasshopper Level would always be first in his heart. The winding dirt roads led to one lumberyard after another, past Amish schoolhouses and white clapboard houses with sometimes three Dawdi Hauses built onto the main house, and clusters of mailboxes for as many Masts as Millers and Yoders. There, vast hayfields were frequently misty with gray fog at dawn, and golden fields were dotted with oat shocks, as well as large well-kept red barns with green roofs and miles and miles of whitewashed horse fencing. He never took a bit of this striking, colorful scenery for granted.

The road to town dipped and turned, making for some interesting conversation as Jake compared the landscape to that in Lancaster County.

"I'm gonna miss the apple harvest back home," Jake commented, and then said that another big reason he had despised being sent out here was having to leave behind his twin sister, Mandie. "Her name's Amanda, really, but she rarely gets called that anymore."

What should I say? Jonas's mind whirled mighty fast as his brother once again happened on the subject of their family. *How much does Jake know about me? Anything?*

Difficult as it was, he decided he would not reveal his identity just yet, for he feared Jake might not even know he existed, due to the Bann imposed by Bishop Bontrager. Even if Jake *had* heard of his wayward older brother, there was a real possibility the lad might not want to fellowship with him any longer, preferring to follow the strict shun slapped on Jonas. There was no way in this world he was going to ruin their growing friendship.

Yet again Jonas wondered what he had done to merit the divine blessing of being reunited with one of his family. So full was his heart, he could scarcely hold on to the reins.

Chapter Thirty-Two

Leah noticed almost immediately Lydiann's freshly scrubbed face and the combed hair neatly tucked beneath her head covering. Watching from the front room window, she was quite aware of the boost of energy in Lydiann's stride this afternoon as she hurried out to the mailbox. *She's surely eager for word from Jake,* thought Leah, wondering how long he would cling to Lydiann, especially when he had been admonished by his bishop, even Gid, to mingle with Ohio girls. No doubt Peter Mast shared the same desire. But if what she suspected was true, Jake had dismissed their urging, steadfastly staying in contact with Lydiann. Often, Leah had seen her, pen and paper in hand, heading off toward the woods after chores, just as she herself had when writing to Jonas so long ago.

When Lydiann came running in the back door, calling for her, Leah anxiously went to see what was on her mind. "Mamma, listen to what my beau wrote to me!"

Surprised, she asked, "Ach, Lyddie, are ya ever so sure you want to share this?"

" 'Tis all right, really. I know you'll keep quiet, ain't?" Lydiann began to read from Jake's most recent letter as soon as they'd settled down at the kitchen table.

Leah was taken with the expression in Lyddie's voice as she related one interesting thing after another, pleased that her girl should entrust this very personal moment to her . . . yet sobered that Lyddie's affection for Jake did not appear to have lessened.

As the letter came to a close, Lydiann's voice became softer. Then, she looked up, still holding the letter. "I best not read further."

Leah nodded, struggling with a lump in her throat. She loathed having to pretend as if she didn't know anything about how and why Lyddie's beloved had ended up being sent away.

"He cares for me, Mamma." Lydiann brushed tears from her face. "What am I s'posed to do 'bout that?"

Unable to advise, Leah merely reached out a hand. "I'm awful sorry, dear. Truly I am. I hope you can trust the Lord for your future."

"Is that what you had to do, too, Mamma? After Jonas left here?"

She inhaled sharply. "Jonas?"

"Remember, Sadie told me 'bout him— and you—quite a while back."

Leah didn't care so much to talk about what she'd put behind her. There was no need to rehash the old days, especially when Jonas was the last person she wanted Lydiann to be asking about just now.

───────◆───────

Lovely and peaceful, that's what Mary Ruth thought of this particular September morning as she drove the car to visit Lydiann. She hadn't stopped by to see her youngest sister in more than a week, and she wanted to gauge for herself how Lydiann was coping.

More than anything, she wanted to pass on the encouraging things she was learning in Scripture; she'd even tucked into her dress pocket a slip of paper with sermon notes from last Sunday. She wouldn't press the issue, of course, but she certainly hoped the Lord might make it possible for her to speak privately with Lydiann. That and maybe offer a quiet prayer for her.

When she parked the car in the driveway and switched off the ignition, Abe came running out from the barn to greet her. "Hullo!" he called, peering inside the driver's side of the car.

"How are you?" she asked, unable to open the door with Abe now hanging nearly inside the open window, reaching to touch the steering wheel, a curious grin on his face. "I think you best keep your eyes on driving horse and buggy," she said, lest Dat accuse her of promoting worldly interests in his only son.

"Aw, don't worry 'bout that. I know plenty of boys who have cars . . . hide 'em from their fathers."

She didn't like the sound of this at all and was glad when Abe stepped back so she could climb out of the driver's seat and head for the house. But Abe was trailing right behind her, not ready to let the topic drop.

"How fast do ya think your car can go?" he asked. "How quick can it get to top speed from a dead stop, I mean?"

"Now, Abe . . ."

"I'm serious," he replied. "I want to know."

She shook her head. "I have no idea about any of that."

Evidently disappointed, Abe sat down on the back steps, and she made her way inside.

In the kitchen she found Leah and Lydiann working side by side, stirring up two large fruit salads. One was to be served at dinner and the other was to take to Miriam Peachey, she was told.

Mary Ruth wondered about the latter, and Lydiann explained Miriam was under the weather. "That bein' the case, I wanted to do something nice for her and Smitty."

Sitting down on the wood bench, Mary Ruth was glad for a chance to catch her breath. Without asking, Lydiann brought her a glass of iced tea. "Denki," she said, glad for it, even though the day wasn't nearly as hot as it had been in past weeks.

"Won't be long now and school will be startin' up again," Lydiann mentioned, sit-

ting down next to her. "Will you be missin'
your students?"

"Well, yes and no."

Leah smiled and came over to the table
with some crackers and several varieties of
cheese on a plate. "You'll have one of your
own little pupils to look after, 'fore too long."

"A new little one in the family," Lydiann
said, eyes sparkling with her words. "I'll
baby-sit whenever you want—just so long
as it isn't twins. I'm not sure I could keep up
with two babies the same age." Suddenly a
shadow fell over her face, as if something
had brought back a sad memory.

Leah quickly changed the subject to
plans she had for making several crib quilts
for the new baby.

"That's real nice of you," Mary Ruth told
Leah—then to Lydiann, she said, "Rest assured I'm having only *one* baby."

"Oh? When did ya learn this?" Leah
asked, keeping her voice low and glancing
toward the back door.

"The midwife told me yesterday." Mary
Ruth sighed. "I do believe Robert is somewhat relieved, as well."

Just then they heard a sneeze coming
from the back steps, and Mary Ruth put her

hand on her chest. "Goodness, is Abe still sitting outside?"

Leah hopped up quickly and went to check, only to return with a grin on her face. "You guessed quite right," she said. "Abe took off runnin' toward the barn just now, but you can be sure both Dat and Gid will soon know it's a single baby comin'."

Mary Ruth reached for a second cracker with two small pieces of cheese on top. "That's all right with me." She looked at Lydiann, eager to talk with her alone, but the moment never presented itself, and after a piece of apple pie, she bid her farewell to her sisters.

"Come again soon," Leah called as Mary Ruth made her way out to the car.

"Oh, I will," she replied, noticing Lydiann making a quick dash toward the road.

The familiar squeal of brakes from out on the main road told Mary Ruth it was time for the mail.

Leah heard Lydiann run into the house, and when she turned, she saw her waving a letter, already opened.

"Listen to this!" Lydiann plopped herself back down on the bench and began to read, nearly breathless with excitement. " 'Dear Lydiann,' " she began. " 'I have the most interesting news. You know I've written in the past about the woodworking shop in Apple Creek. Well, I've made quite a discovery—one I think you'll be surprised at, too. You see, I've been working alongside my eldest brother all this time . . . and didn't even know it.' "

"Wait just a minute. Would ya mind readin' that last line again?" Leah interrupted, her heart in her throat.

Lydiann stared at her for a moment, frowning a bit, and then she raised the letter to reread it.

"Oh my . . ." Leah groaned.

"Mamma, did I upset you?"

"No . . . no. Is there more you want to share?"

Lydiann nodded. "I read this on the way in from the mailbox . . . and, honestly, if Jonas Mast isn't the one givin' woodworking pointers to *my* Jake."

Leah felt her hands trembling now. "Well, for goodness' sake," she whispered, not sure how to respond in the least.

"Can ya believe it?" asked Lydiann. "His own shunned brother."

Quickly Leah gathered her composure. "The Bann on Jonas is not for us to speak of." She wanted to say she'd never felt it was his fault . . . yet it wasn't for her to question the man of God, especially not in front of Lydiann. Truly, she had mixed emotions about the whole situation.

Trying to occupy herself, Leah offered Lydiann a glass of iced tea, but she was once again caught up in her letter. Leah sipped her own cold drink and breathed a silent prayer.

Chapter Thirty-Three

Hannah was anxious to write in her journal as her husband and girls lay sleeping soundly, bringing peace to the small house.

Friday, September 28
Dear Diary,
It is nearly nine-thirty tonight, yet I can't sleep—I'm ever so sure I am expecting another baby. We've waited so many years for this day, the thought doesn't frighten me in the least, especially because I made a good number of visits to Old Lady Henner before she died last week. The People turned out in large numbers for the funeral, but it was clear to me who was there paying their respects and who wasn't. Dat and Lizzie did not attend, nor did my sisters, all of them honoring Dat's stand

against powwowing except me. Gid did happen to say on the long ride over to the funeral that he was beginning to see Dat's side of things, but he didn't go any further than that. These days it sounds to me as if Dat has much more sway over Gid than his own father does—Gid talks often of "Abram this and Abram that." Seems to me Gid has embraced my father as nearly his own.

All the same, I don't think he knows how much my father and stepmother tend to read the Bible, even study it. But I figure what Gid doesn't know about that won't be a nuisance to him if the bishop should ever ask. It's best to leave things be as they are, just as nobody kept me from going to Old Lady Henner all these years.

If I truly am in the family way, I hope to have yet another baby not so long after this one so he or she can have a close-in-age sibling. But I won't fret about when the Good Lord wants to send along our children to us, though I would like to give Gid a boy this time.

And I am awful happy for Mary Ruth, who is looking forward to her first wee

*one at the end of next month. What fun
it will be to hold my twin's newborn in
my arms! Mary Ruth will be a wonderful-good mother, for she has always
had a strong leaning toward infants
and little children . . . and she had all
that practice with Carl Nolt when he
was tiny.*

*Well, with Old Lady Henner gone, I
don't believe I'll be seeking out a hex
doctor anymore. I never cared much at
all for the ones who are men—they
give me the jitters. Now it will be for me
to simply follow more closely the folk
medicine on my own.*

*Respectfully,
Hannah*

◆

An early October throng of ladybugs rose
like a great mist and then settled on the
sunny-most side of the barn the first
Saturday of the month. Leah had observed
them in flight while taking down some
washing that couldn't wait till Monday, all
sun dried and bright from hanging on the
line that morning and part of the afternoon.

At the sight of the insects, she wondered whether an awful harsh winter might be in store this year.

Lydiann and Ida Mae and Katie Ann were away at Central Market in downtown Lancaster, tending table to a host of yellow, orange, white, and lime gourds, along with piles of prized pumpkins slashed from the vines just yesterday. The trip was a good, long ride by horse and buggy, to be sure. Still, Leah wished someone other than herself might have witnessed the strange sight, knowing Lydiann and the girls would have been equally surprised at hundreds of ladybugs seeking out shelter for the coming winter. No doubt the insects had found it under the loose slats on the south side of the old bank barn.

Hurrying across the backyard with her wicker basket, its contents nearly spilling over, she spied the ladybugs again. Immediately she got to wondering if Dat and Gid had split and stacked ample firewood to carry both families through the cold days come late October and beyond.

October. The word played in her mind with the energy of a brush fire before it quiets down and begins to smolder. Dat and

Abe had lit the first such fire of the season just this morning, having spent hours raking up dead tree boughs and limbs in preparation, tidying things up in general. Sunlight seemed to leak out of the first weeks of autumn, and yet the vast woods to the northwest grew brighter by day, especially where the maples were set against ancient hemlocks.

Her thoughts flew to Lydiann, who continued to sulk around the house as though her last friend had died—when there wasn't a new letter to be had, that is. Faithfully Leah spent time in prayer each morning on the subject of Jake Mast, asking that he might stay put in Ohio. Asking, too, that Lydiann might eventually become interested in a different young man.

With the slowing down winter would bring, Lydiann would soon have plenty of nurturing from the whole family—long fireside chats with Leah, evening prayers with Dat, playing table games with Lizzie and Abe. And knowing Lyddie as Leah did, she had reason to believe the dear girl would not pine for Jake forever. At least she hoped not.

———◆———

Sadie was astonished when Lydiann came running in the back door saying she'd received another letter in the afternoon mail delivery.

In a whisper, Lydiann told her, "If you keep it quiet, Sadie, I'll tell ya who my beau is. I'll even read ya a bit of his letter."

"Aw, no, that ain't necessary," Sadie said immediately, glancing at Leah, who stood behind Lydiann. Sadie had recently suspected her youngest sister of sharing Jake's letters with Leah, although Leah had not revealed this in anything she'd said. Still, Sadie assumed she was right, as unusually close as Lydiann and Leah were. Certainly Leah had seemed to have more on her mind here lately.

"But I want to tell ya, honestly I do." And Lydiann revealed, right then and there, that the boy she loved was indeed Jake Mast. "And he loves *me*, too," she said, eyes twinkling.

Sadie was speechless at Lydiann's willingness to make known her beloved's identity, though she was grateful to have an opportunity to hear the kinds of things her son wrote and the way he phrased his thoughts. It was a small way to feel nearer to him.

Lydiann was already scanning her letter. At once she stopped reading to herself and announced, "Ach, listen to this. Jake writes that his eldest brother, Jonas, lives clear out in the country, where he boards and rooms with an older lady who is almost completely deaf. I guess he thinks of her fondly . . . as almost a family member, since he's never married and had a family of his own."

"What on earth?" Sadie said, bewildered. "You mean to say Jake knows of Jonas . . . and Jonas isn't married?" She looked now at Leah. Her sister's lips were parted, as if in shock, but she remained silent.

Lydiann refolded the letter. "Sure sounds like it, ain't?"

"Well, I should say this is quite amazing," she breathed. "If it's true."

"Jah, 'tis ever so surprising" was all Leah said.

"You all right?" Sadie placed a hand on Leah's slender shoulder. Evidently overcome with unexpected emotion, Leah bowed her head, and Sadie felt her precious sister tremble at the astonishing news.

Leah slipped away to the Dawdi Haus after Lydiann and Sadie had taken themselves off for a midafternoon walk at her
insistence and following her repeated as-
surances she was going to be quite all right.

Now, in the solitude of Sadie's small
house, she looked about her, taking in the
tiny front room, the hickory rocker, the simple maple side table and wood settee, all
the furnishings reminding her of Dawdi
John. This room where she'd spent much
time getting to know her grandfather, asking
him questions about his courtship days . . .
and sharing with him some about her own.

Incapable of grasping the implications of
what Lydiann had revealed not thirty minutes ago, Leah felt terribly restless and
walked to the open front door, welcoming
the scents and gentle breezes of early autumn. There she recalled how Jonas had
gently carried her into his father's house after she'd wrenched her ankle playing volley-
ball, how his strong arms had made her feel
cared for and secure. Truly, there was so
much to remember: The early years of
stolen glances at family get-togethers, the

summertime picnics on the lawn, the dear betrothal promise they'd made as young- sters, a love covenant to be sure. She re- membered fondly the day of their church baptism, the long afternoon afterward spent sharing intimately while sitting in the grassy meadow, his sweet kiss on her lips. Dozens of Ohio letters had traveled between them . . . followed by the heartache of the years when she had naively believed Sadie had stolen him away.

Early on in those painful days, she had met with the Lord God in a very personal way up in the woods, realizing that she was and always would be God's Leah, that the dear Lord Jesus would mend her heart in due time and fulfill His plans and will for her life. Now the unexpected news that Jonas had remained single, just as she had, was almost more than she could comprehend or bear.

Standing there, Leah was relieved to be alone with her thoughts. Glad, too, that both Dat and Aunt Lizzie had not been present in the kitchen earlier. It had been hard enough to hold her emotions in check with Sadie and Lydiann staring at and making over her.

Sighing into the stillness, she breathed

her silent questions. *My beloved, what things do you recall? Will you ever know that I am and always will be your Leah?*

In her heart she knew this was so. She had always loved Jonas, no matter how long she'd tried to fool herself into believing differently.

Yet even in this hushed moment of reflection and inner acknowledgment, she was not so sure Jonas would care that she was still a maidel. How could she possibly know what he was thinking . . . or if he was even aware that she, too, remained unmarried?

Turning, she wandered back into the house, to the kitchen doorway looking out to the barn and up toward the mule road.

All the happy days . . .

Through the simple act of faithful living, Leah had learned the most important thing—not to cling to or to chase after happiness. What she yearned for now was the heaven-sent joy that carried her through, even in the midst of suffering.

Jesus is the joy of my life, she thought anew.

She had come to know and live this truth from reading Mamma's Bible, and she'd attempted to teach it to Lydiann and Abe.

Dropping to her knees beside the small kitchen table, she thanked the heavenly Father for not only her many blessings, but for all of life's difficulties that had led her to this amazing moment . . . although she had no idea what to do with her knowledge of Jonas. But that was not for her to decide. She would do as the Scriptures instructed and wholly trust the Lord.

Chapter Thirty-Four

An enormous relief came over Jonas on Monday morning when he opened the door to the woodworking shop and there, once again, stood his youngest brother on the stoop. He had wondered if perhaps Jake had gotten his fill of instruction, so intense Jonas had been the last time Jake spent the workday here. Intense in part because he'd heard things from Jake regarding Leah, whom Jake's girlfriend referred to as Mamma. The notion Leah was now Lydiann's mother had completely baffled Jonas. How was it his former sweetheart could be raising Lydiann, whom Jonas knew to be *Ida's* daughter? Sadly there was only one way that could have come about, and he was anxious to quiz Jake about it to-day. He must be more patient in awaiting answers about the girl he'd loved in

Gobbler's Knob, yet his heart shouted to know all he could about her, especially since he had come to know she was not, in fact, married to Gideon Peachey. Was she Gid's widow, perhaps, helping a similarly widowed Abram raise Lydiann?

◆

Sadie hurried through the connecting door to the main house, to the kitchen, where she made coffee, began to mix eggs and milk for scrambling, and fried up some bacon. She wanted to do something nice for Leah, seeing as how her sister was probably still mulling over the surprising Ohio news.

She waited until the table was laid and Aunt Lizzie had gone outdoors before slipping out of the house herself, wearing only an old sweater for her wrap. Quickly she caught up with Lizzie on the other side of the barn, where she was out taking a short jaunt in the grazing land.

At once she opened her heart to the woman she'd often confided in as a young girl. "I'm hopin' ya might help me get word to Dat's ears somehow . . . about Jonas

Mast," she began. She did not plead with fancy words, nor did she fight back the tears that threatened to spill. She prayed silently and spoke honestly, hoping a gentle approach might work more effectively than dramatically beseeching Lizzie to do her bidding . . . for dear Leah's sake.

◆

Abram was dressing around for Tuesday morning chores when Lizzie sidled up to him and said, "I have an idea . . . and I want ya to think on it."

"Oh?" He leaned down and kissed her full on the lips. Then, when she tried to wiggle free from his tight embrace, he kissed her again.

"For goodness' sake, Abram!"

He looked at her, all fresh and sweet from a good night's rest. "How was I to know what you had in mind, dear?"

She smiled and went to sit on their bed, her arms folded now. "I've heard tell that Peter Mast's eldest son is as unattached as any man ever was."

He felt the frown crease his brow. "Well, how on earth would ya know that?"

Lizzie looked at him with love in her eyes. "My dear Abram, you best be trustin' me on this," she said. "But I know one thing—you could put a smile on more than one person's face round here if you'd be willin' to write one short letter."

He had no idea what she was suggesting and told her so.

"We've heard from someone in Ohio"— and here she looked at him, as if to make her meaning clear—"who knows for sure that Jonas has never married."

"And just who's that?" he asked, beginning to suspect the reason for the sadness in Lydiann's eyes.

"Don't know exactly . . . though I wouldn't tell ya, prob'ly, if I did."

Oh, he loved this spunky wife of his. He walked over to her and raised her up so he could hug the stuffings out of her.

"Think of it, Abram—Jonas not hitched up yet," Lizzie said in his arms. "And Leah still single . . ."

He figured out then he was supposed to put it together that the two of them might yet secretly care for each other. Leah's happiness, according to Lizzie, lay right in his own hands.

———◆———

Lizzie was adamant. "Peppermint oil in tea *does* fight colds!" She glanced up at Hannah's girls playing in the haymow as she talked with Lydiann below. "My mother and grandmother both said this, and I know from experience it's true."

Lydiann sniffled and then pulled out a handkerchief from her dress pocket and sneezed. "This always happens to me at the beginning of autumn," she complained. "What is it 'bout that?"

"Oh, the change of seasons, I 'spect. Some folk get downright blue when summer turns to fall, and others catch a cold, just like you are. But . . . ya really oughta try some peppermint oil in a cup of tea, I'm tellin' ya."

Obviously uninterested, Lydiann turned up her nose yet again.

"All right, then, but don't say I didn't try 'n' help."

"I won't." Lydiann shrugged and headed for the ladder to join her young nieces.

A stubborn sort, she is, thought Lizzie, wishing Lydiann wasn't so much like Sadie had been at this age. But then again, who was *she* to talk?

Seeing Hannah's girls so playful just now, she thought of Mary Ruth and Robert. She could scarcely wait for their first baby to arrive, another grandchild by marriage for her. She felt so full of joy each day, walking and talking with the Lord Jesus and enjoying the young ones growing up around her. Sometimes she felt she ought to pinch herself to see if all her dreams had really come true, though she knew they surely had.

Only one thing clouded her happiness, however infrequently. Still, she wouldn't let it rob her peace, but it *was* something she could never quite shake. She wondered when she ought to finally bring herself to sit down one-on-one with Leah and be done with it . . . reveal everything about her beginnings. Or at least all she remembered. She had been taking into account the sorrows and disappointments Leah had endured these years, not wanting to further hamper her dear girl's seeming contentment with the potentially burdensome knowledge. She'd thought of asking Abram his opinion on this—if he thought it a good time to consider addressing it with Leah—even though he himself was in the dark about the man who'd fathered her one and only child. Truth was, she couldn't bring herself to reveal this to Abram, either—not just yet.

——————◆——————

Leah had by no means endeavored to keep up with the English in the neighborhood. For one thing, talk of daylight savings time coming to an end here pretty quick made her laugh under her breath. Lorraine Schwartz loathed "losing light at the end of the day," as she liked to say, so it always fell to Leah to change back the settings on their clocks to "slow time" come the last Sunday of this month. Seemed odd to her, really, fancy folk wanting to go back and forth like that, especially since the People never observed "fast time" in the first place.

She did as was requested of her all the same, heeding the wants and wishes of her employers. Both Dr. Schwartz and his wife had become accustomed to her being altogether dependable, except for the few days, of course, when she had quit her job out of sheer anger. The problem with working for Dr. Schwartz, whom she'd long seen as an

upstanding man, was that she no longer
viewed him as so good, after all. Leah
sometimes wondered if there was something she might do to help point him toward
the Savior his heart undoubtedly longed for.

As Leah set about dusting the many
framed family pictures, taking note that the
pictures of Derek as a teen had been removed and replaced by wedding pictures of
Mary Ruth and Robert, she thought how odd
it was that the doctor's second grandchild
was also to be an Ebersol by blood, though
the circumstances were vastly different.

Sighing, she would not allow herself to
feel upset for having approached Dr.
Schwartz as she had. There had been ex-
treme frustration and sadness in his eyes
that day, but also absolute relief, as if the
man had been waiting all these years for
someone to condemn him!

Well, now that he had finally owned up to
the truth, she felt almost sorry for him. Leah
hoped she might share the love of the Lord
Jesus with him—if not in words, then by her
deeds.

———◆———

Jonas stared down at the unexpected letter Jake had thrust into his hands, quite stunned to see it was from stubborn Abram Ebersol.

Meanwhile Jake tried to explain. "Tell ya the truth, I was mighty surprised gettin' this letter from Lyddie's father, along with a short one from her, too."

Jonas ran his hand through his hair, saying nothing.

"You all right?" Jake stared at him but good.

"Never better." Jonas had to suppress the urge to chuckle, but nothing of what Abram had written had anything to do with Jake. Except without this mighty handsome brother of his standing here, how long might it have been before Jonas had heard *any* word about Leah . . . let alone that she was still a maidel? He slipped the paper into his pants pocket.

He paused, wanting to get the words out just right. "I think it's high time I find out for myself why you were sent away. Your being here makes no sense to me at all." Jonas placed a firm hand on his brother's shoulder. "Time I heard this straight from the horse's mouth."

Jake expressed his wholehearted enthusiasm for the idea, and Jonas hurried to finish the new desk he'd promised to complete by next week. The more Jonas deliberated on it, the more he pondered how Jake's inclusion with the men who'd been traded—none of the others had any complaints, evidently—appeared much like what had happened to him years ago, just as he was preparing to wed Leah.

While sanding and smoothing out the wood's surface, he recognized that he had no idea what his first step upon his return would be toward Leah. Could he actually show up at Abram's home unannounced and knock on the door? He was a shunned man. Even if he were to be so brazen, Leah would adhere to the Old Ways, he was sure. And knowing Abram, he had not consulted with Leah before writing this brief letter.

Rubbing the wood all the harder, he wondered if Leah would *ever* want to see him again. Abram had hinted as much, yet nagging thoughts continued in Jonas's head. Truth was, the two of them scarcely knew each other anymore. *Is a future for us even possible?*

Unjust as his shunning was, Jonas was

suddenly very eager to get home and set things aright. For Leah's sake.

He scrutinized the piece of wood intended for the desk top and immediately spotted the small yet visible dip where he'd sanded much too hard. Straightening, he stopped his work. *Outcast or not, it's time I correct the foolishness of the past . . . time I did what I should've done long ago.*

"This desk will have to wait for finishing," he announced.

Jake looked up, eyes blank. "What do ya mean?"

"I'm closing up shop for a few days. I'll explain everything when I return."

Feels like a lifetime of waiting, he thought.

Chapter Thirty-Five

The sun had already begun to make its way southward in Lancaster County. High in the sugar maple trees, birds preened and twittered contentedly, and, Jonas imagined, perhaps an ornery crow poked at an abandoned wasps' nest.

He was very aware of the many familiar landmarks as he rode in the backseat of the taxicab he'd taken from the train station in downtown Lancaster. Staring out the window, he made up his mind to do things the right way, with some semblance of propriety, at least. On the other hand, since he was a mere visitor, there was no harm done in simply putting off a visit to Bishop Bontrager.

While it was Leah he longed to see, he felt he must head straight to Grasshopper Level to speak with his father before entertaining notions of a visit to Gobbler's Knob. So the cab was traveling through the village of Strasburg, southeast toward Peach Lane with its tall trees and curving road dotted by Amish farms on either side, and then on to the Mast orchard house. He gazed out at roads he and Leah had not only ridden on together in his open buggy, but had walked on numerous times, enjoying the sun, the earthy smell of the fields, and their easygoing talk.

When he arrived at his father's house, Jonas hurried around to the back door, where he saw his mother in a green dress and old black apron standing by the cookstove, stirring a big soup kettle with a long wooden spoon.

Turning to look his way and seeing him just then, she let out a gasp and put her hand to her throat. "Ach, is it you, Jonas?" she said, coming quickly to the door, her eyes shining with happiness and tears both as she stared at his face and beard. "You've come home!"

But almost as fast as she'd expressed joy on her sweet face, the reality of his shunning must have set in, for her eyes darkened and she began to back away.

"Hullo, Mamma. Is Dat home?" His pulse throbbed with every breath, and he felt as though he were sleepwalking.

His mother struggled to hold back her tears, the thinly disguised longing evident on her dear face. "Your father's in the barn," she said softly.

"Believe me, I mean no trouble . . ." he managed to say, knowing full well he was required to speak to his father first, as was their custom when an excommunicated family member returned home.

Jonas hurried across the yard toward the large bank barn. The luster of orange and yellow trees captured his awareness yet again, but only for an instant. His stride was strong and he felt the determined set of his own jaw, his gaze steadfast on the open barn door.

He found Dat tending to the mules, talking low, slow words in Dutch, just as Jonas remembered his father doing when he was a boy. Standing there, he took in the old place and its noticeable barn stench, recalling all the years he'd worked alongside his father and younger brothers . . . the pranks they'd pulled on each other, the times when he was allowed to wear Dat's work boots and he'd gone clunking and falling through the haymow, kicking up a dust to kingdom come.

He waited to speak till Dat's back was no longer turned so he would not startle his aging father. "Dat, it's Jonas."

As tall and brawny as ever, his father inched his head up, taking uneven breaths, his large shoulders rising with each measured heave. "Son?"

"I've come a long way to speak to ya." He wanted to hurry to Dat's side, reach around the familiar burly frame and hug the man he'd missed so terribly.

Dat extended his hand. "Come here to me, Jonas. Let me look at ya."

Obediently he moved across the barn floor; his mouth went dry as the moment hit him hard. "I wish to talk to ya, Dat."

"You're a married man, jah?" His father chewed on a piece of straw he held in his callused hand as he studied Jonas's chin. "Where's your missus?"

Jonas felt the softness of his beard. "Oh that. Well, things are a bit different out in Ohio. We let the whiskers grow right away, followin' baptism. I'm still unhitched."

Dat kept staring, as if what Jonas had just

said and what Dat was seeing with his own eyes didn't quite register. "Jake wrote us a letter . . . said he'd run into ya . . . but I never expected him goin' out to Ohio would bring *you* back to us."

How can I tell him otherwise? Jonas wondered, but he didn't have to reveal his plans—not just yet. "I'm home to talk over some things with Bishop Bontrager," he volunteered. "In fact, I'm headed up to Gobbler's Knob after a while."

Dat seemed interested in hearing more, nodding his head quicklike. "Well, now, I sure hope you're goin' to talk about repentin' and returning home . . . where ya belong, after all these long years."

Jonas didn't have the heart to say differently when he took in the look of longing in his dear old father's eyes. "I have some questions to voice, for now." He didn't say what, but he added, "And I'm here to ask something of you, too."

"That's right fine, as long as you're goin' to repent." There it was again. Dat knew he best not be talking for too long with his wayward son unless the Gobbler's Knob bishop allowed it.

"I have to know something from you directly," said Jonas. "Why was my brother sent to Ohio . . . forced to leave behind his sweetheart-girl?"

Dat's eyes grew suddenly small and a deep frown tunneled into his brow. "Not your concern."

"I beg your mercy on this, Dat. Jake's awful *ferhoodled* . . . he loves a girl *here*. He wants to marry her—he told me so."

"Abram Ebersol's daughters are off limits to my sons. No exceptions," Dat bellowed, hands clenched. Jonas heeded the flinching muscles around Dat's mouth and whiskers, the fire in his eyes as he uttered the terse explanation. "The family's tainted. Leah's a bad seed, 'cause of her illegitimate birth. But I don't need to be tellin' you that. Look how she tricked you."

Jonas was shocked that his father could refer to one so lovely in spirit as deceitful, even wicked. "How can you say that?"

"The woman betrayed you by gettin' you to join church with her over there in Gobbler's Knob, that's what." His father made an attempt to explain his view of the entire problem: that Leah's deception— Jonas's taking the baptismal vow in her church—had set him up for eventual shunning, when "she dumped ya and went for that other fella."

"Gid Peachey, ya mean?" Jonas asked, knowing from Abram's letter to him that Leah had never married Gid. "Leah is, in fact, still a maidel."

The news was evidently not a surprise to Dat.

"You honestly blame Leah for all this?" Jonas asked.

"Abram, the skunk, carries the full weight of blame," his father replied, making it mighty clear that had not Abram opened his home, and Ida her arms, to "that witch of a sister, Lizzie Brenneman, back when she was in the family way without a husband, you would never have been put under the Bann. Never!"

Dat's shout startled the mules, and a small cloud of dust rose into the air as the animals' hooves stamped and dug into the ground. "That's enough talkin' for now. You best be headin' to see the minister!"

With that Dat turned away as one did to the shunned, although doing so did not conceal the rapid rise and fall of his father's shoulders.

Will he turn his back on me . . . yet again?

———◆———

"Ach, she's as perty as a rosebud," Leah breathed, cradling Mary Ruth's newborn daughter in her arms.

Mary Ruth nodded drowsily in the birthing bed, all smiles. "A gift from our Lord to us," she said, dabbing at her perspired face and neck with a damp towel.

"What's her name?" Leah looked down at this precious tiny person, holding her gently near.

"Ruthie," replied Mary Ruth, glancing up at Robert, who leaned his head against her own.

Leah kissed Ruthie's wee face and reluctantly passed her to Aunt Lizzie, who was clearly itching to get her hands on the sleeping bundle. "Suits her fine, seems to me," Leah said.

"It surely does," said Lizzie, eyes alight.

Leah stepped out into the hallway, glad for such an easy birth for her sister. She was also grateful to Dan and Dottie Nolt, who had insisted Robert and Mary Ruth come to their home for the midwife-assisted birth, although the idea behind that was so Mary

Ruth could be within "calling distance" of Dr. Schwartz should anything go wrong.

Whispering a prayer of thanksgiving, Leah donned her shawl and slipped out the back door, pleased to walk beneath the brilliant canopy of colors toward home.

◆

Blazing autumn foliage caught Henry's attention as he rose from his desk and stared out his window. He noticed the young Amishwoman strolling along the road, swinging her arms and enjoying the afternoon sun. He was intrigued by her grace and the lilt of her gait—back straight, head high, and feet bare, even though temperatures had turned chilly in the night. Leah was a beauty to behold, and he wished he had not disappointed such an upstanding person with his selfish stupidity.

The phone rang in his office, and he went to his desk to pick up the receiver. "Dr. Schwartz speaking."

"Dad, you're a grandpa!"

"Well, what good news, Robert! How's your little missus?" he asked first about Mary Ruth.

"Oh, she's fine . . . happy as can be."

"And the baby?"

"A little girl—six pounds, eight ounces, and only nineteen inches long. But she's real healthy and the prettiest baby I've ever seen."

"No doubt it's true." He chuckled, recalling Robert's own birth and the rapturous feeling of seeing his firstborn child for the first time. "Congratulations, son," he said. "And give Mary Ruth our love."

Robert urged him to come over right away. "Bring Mother along to see little Ruthie . . . her given name. It's not a nickname," he insisted. "This is Mary Ruth's idea, and I like it!"

Henry could certainly hear the joyous cadence of Robert's voice, and he assured him they would soon be over. "Thanks for the phone call," he said before hanging up.

He returned to the window, wondering if Leah was still in view. Staring into the near-neon oranges and golds of the expansive willow oak shade tree and silver maples, his thoughts returned to the secret Abram's second daughter had evidently chosen to keep from the world . . . at least for now.

I dare not press my good luck, he thought.

News of his first granddaughter mingled
with his former reflections on Jake, his first
grandson. In a second of momentous decision, he reached for a pen and wrote two
words on his note pad: *Early retirement.*

He determined his future right then—a future that would be his choice no matter
what Leah decided to do. He would turn his
clinic over to Ron Burkholder, the young in-
tern presently assisting him, and retreat
from his faithful patients. He would punish
himself, since no one else had . . . effectively locking himself up by withdrawing
from his greatest passion in life, however
much longer it might endure. He would announce this to Lorraine tonight at supper,
after they'd cooed over and held their new
grandbaby.

"Ruthie," he whispered, already fond of
the name Mary Ruth had selected.

Once more his thoughts returned to
Jake . . . and to Derry. *My son will never
know either his own son or his niece.* Henry
was again humiliated that Derek bore the
Schwartz name. Or perhaps, on further recollection, Derek was merely a reflection of
the worst part of himself. Henry shuddered.

Chapter Thirty-Six

Jonas was convinced he'd borrowed his father's slowest driving horse, but he wasn't in the mood to gripe, even to himself, though he was in a tremendous hurry. He had left his father in an awful bad way, back there in the barn, Dat having been both glad and reluctant to see him. Regrettably there had been no other way to handle that initial encounter, and the fact remained that he *had* needed transportation to get to Bishop Bontrager's.

The truth came home to him that his father believed Abram's daughters were at the very root of the problem besetting the Masts. First Leah . . . and now Lydiann.

Poor Jake, he thought, wishing he could do something to change things for his brother. But knowing their father . . . and hardheaded Abram, there was only one way to unravel such a thorny matter.

Hurrying the old mare, Jonas leaned forward in the Mast family buggy, as if doing so might encourage the horse onward, up the long, steep grade to Gobbler's Knob.

———◆———

Years ago Leah had memorized the tree that marked the halfway point between the Nolts' house and the Ebersol Cottage. She looked curiously at the bent old spruce, wondering what had happened to cause its deformity. Surely not lightning or hurricane-gale winds, although they'd had a few scares with such violent weather in past summers. Today the autumn air was as calm as the atmosphere encircling a new-born infant, and she felt as though she could still smell and feel Mary Ruth's new little one. "Ruthie Schwartz," she said, smiling at the memory of Robert's face upon holding his daughter for the first time.

I will enjoy everyone else's babies, she thought, though not sadly, merely accepting her own lot. *I'll love each one . . . spoil 'em, too!*

Watching the birds flit from tree to tree, several groups of them playing chase across the road and back again, she got to thinking about the days, not so long past, when Lydiann and Abe were completely dependent on her loving care. The years had flown away and both children had reached adolescence, eager to stretch their youthful wings. Especially Lydiann . . . *dear, heartbroken girl.*

She could only hope for the best where Lyddie was concerned . . . Abe, as well. She, Dat, and Aunt Lizzie had surely given their all to instill obedience to God and the church, along with a full measure of honesty, kindness, and a humble spirit. The children had heard more Scripture than *she* ever had growing up, and for this she was beholden to Dat. Leah was endlessly thankful he had embraced Mamma's and Lizzie's faith as his own. Really, it had changed his attitude toward a lot of things.

Feeling compelled to wander from the road a ways, she found a large rock beyond the shoulder and sat there still as could be, enjoying the birdsong that was certain to quiet with deep autumn and, soon to come, the cold winter. She remembered the surprise in Dat's eyes when she had shared about the ladybugs congregating on the side of the barn. "Jah, a right harsh winter this one'll be," he'd said, confirming her suspicions.

Pondering nature's splendor all around, she heard the sound of a horse and buggy but did not turn her head to look. Dozens of carriages and horses came and went up and down this road—sometimes she could almost tell which horse belonged to which family before ever actually laying eyes on it. Presently she concentrated on the rattle of the hard wheels, the *clip-a-clop* and gait of the horse. Whoever it was wasn't from Gobbler's Knob.

When the horse was but several hundred feet away, she turned out of curiosity. Squinting, she saw the features of a bearded man who seemed familiar some-how. She was drawn by his appearance but knew better than to stare at a married man, for pity's sake! Yet there was something more to him—the way he held the reins, the tilt of his head—than simply his looks.

The closer the horse pulled the carriage toward her, the more she stared. She ought to look away, but a sudden knowing flooded her.

Jonas? But surely she must be mistaken.

This man had a beard. Had Jake gotten his information off beam in his letters to Lydiann?

Her own indecision was resolved when the man glanced her way, a look of puzzlement on his face.

Suddenly he pulled on the reins and called out, "Whoa!"

When the horse had obeyed and come to a halt, he leaped down and walked toward her. "Leah? Is that you?"

This *was* Jonas. There was no mistaking his voice, or those azure blue eyes.

Removing his hat, he said softly, "I didn't expect to see ya out here on the road."

And I didn't expect to see you ever again, she thought in wonderment. It was her turn to nod, her turn to say something—*anything*—but she was unable to speak. Jonas was *here*! He stood only a few feet away, holding his hat, eyes shining.

"Nice day for a walk, ain't?" he said.

His casual tone took her off guard, and a thousand answers cluttered her mind, none of them making sense at all.

"Jah, a perty day, for sure," she murmured, still staring at his beard.

A long, awkward moment passed as

Jonas held his hat in his hands, turning it repeatedly. Neither of them seemed to know what to say.

"I'm on my way to see the bishop," he said at last, gesturing toward the buggy. "Would ya care to ride a ways with me?"

She was again mindful of his beard. "But . . . Jonas, you're married."

He chuckled a bit. "These whiskers don't mean what you think." And he explained the Ohio custom, apparently mighty eager to clear up that niggling detail.

She felt like laughing but squelched her giddiness. She wasn't a bit sure what she was doing . . . couldn't think clearly, not with those adoring eyes of his staring down at her that way.

"You must be mighty surprised to see me, Leah."

"Well, I'd have to say I am. Uh, but I best not ride with you," she said quickly.

He frowned for a moment and then smiled. "I'm here to clear up a few important things."

Jonas is a shunned man. . . .

"Are ya headin' to the bishop's to talk 'bout lifting the Bann on you, maybe?" she asked.

He paused, his eyes locked on hers. "He and I have plenty to discuss." His smile was the next thing to beautiful. "I came back right away when I heard. . . ." He shook his head, as if reconsidering his reply, nearly twirling his hat in his hands now.

Turning, he looked at the horse and carriage. "I say you and I have some catchin' up to do."

She eyed the buggy, wishing she could agree to go along and sit beside him in the first seat the way they used to in his open courting buggy when they were teenagers. *Lydiann's age,* she thought.

Was she willing to risk getting in trouble with the brethren, accepting a ride before the bishop had his say with Jonas?

"If the bishop or one of the ministers should happen along and see me ridin' in your buggy, wouldn't I be considered disobedient?"

He grinned. "All of that . . . and much more."

She couldn't suppress her smile. "I don't mean to be difficult—"

"Then don't." Again, the smile that made her heart flutter. "Please, won't ya get in the carriage, Leah?"

She took a deep breath. *I've waited forever for this moment.*

"I want to talk to ya further," he said more softly. "I've missed you terribly."

All reason flew away when his endearing eyes met hers. "Well, I s'pose it might be all right." She willingly followed Jonas past the horse and to the carriage, where he helped her up.

Once inside, Jonas picked up the reins, his voice suddenly earnest again, a concerned look in his eyes. "How's your family?"

She shared that her father was well. "But Mamma died giving birth to our Abe in 1949," she explained. "I raised my brother and sister Lydiann as my own, with help from Dat . . . and, more recently, Aunt Lizzie, who married my father some six years ago."

He expressed his sadness over the loss of her mother, and Leah was taken by his gentleness. Their talk grew more animated as she attempted to catch him up on the community of the People in Gobbler's Knob.

The years were melting away, as though nothing much had changed. And when her father's house came into view, Jonas didn't halt the horse or offer to make the turn into the long lane to the Ebersol Cottage.

Instead, he kept on, describing his Apple Creek cabinetmaking shop and telling her about Emma Graber, the deaf landlady who rented out an upstairs room to him. He talked of his years alone . . . and the many wonderful-good things the Lord had been teaching him.

Leah hung on to his every word, soaking in his presence, memorizing his every movement and expression . . . lest she wake up and discover this to be a fleeting dream.

When Jonas stopped talking of Ohio, an uncomfortable silence followed. And then, he turned to her, his eyes altogether serious. "Leah . . . I believed all these years . . . you were married to Smithy Gid."

She shook her head slowly. "I sent a letter right back—after you wrote me your questions." She paused, gathering her thoughts, her wits.

Jonas turned to look at her. "What letter do ya mean?"

In all her life, she could not have imagined this conversation and this moment, as the two of them came to grips with all the foolishness that had caused their wedding plans to go awry. She explained the mix-ups and misunderstandings as best she could, careful to keep dear Sadie out of her remarks. "I've honestly forgiven the past," she whispered at last.

Slowly Jonas pulled back on the reins, bringing the buggy to a stop on the dirt road south of the Amish cemetery, off Georgetown Road. "I didn't know for sure till just now," he said, "but I've waited years to tell you this, never daring to believe I'd have the chance."

She stared at his dear face. "What is it?" she asked, nearly breathless to know.

His eyes gently pierced her. "My heart has always belonged to *you*, Leah."

In that tender, yet revealing instant, she knew that no matter how busy her life had become, how important her responsibilities to Lydiann and Abe, or how many times she had been convinced she'd left the past far behind, she had never, ever stopped loving Jonas.

"If you should happen to have any feelings left for me," he said in a near whisper, "I'd like to spend time with you . . . get to know you again. Once the bishop gives me the go-ahead, that is."

She breathed in slowly and held the air in her lungs. Was he indicating he'd returned home to court her . . . was that what he meant to say? "I . . . it's . . . I'd like to get reacquainted, jah, really I would. It's just that . . ." Scarcely could she get the words out.

So many things to consider . . . to work through. The bishop's insensitive ruling on Sadie, for one. Wouldn't Jonas be put through a similar Proving? One even more trying, perhaps? And there was Jonas's father to reckon with, too. Wouldn't Peter Mast and Bishop Bontrager put their heads together and devise a way to keep Jonas and Leah apart? Possibly forever.

"I love you," Jonas whispered, his words close to her ear.

Tears sprang to her eyes, yet she nodded back, desperately trying to tell him that she cared deeply, too.

"I'll never leave you again, Leah. Never."

She could not speak for the rush of emotion, and when he moved closer still, she felt nearly helpless, yielding, at last, to his tender embrace.

Epilogue

I honestly marvel at the amazing things the Lord has done in my life—I sometimes have to pinch myself, for sure. Jonas still loves *me* . . . after all this time. But what is most astonishing, aside from my darling's plan to move back home, is that Sadie—with a little help from Dat—was the one to set the wheels in motion for Jonas to return in the first place. Aunt Lizzie whispered this to me while we were rolling out pie dough today.

The minute I could go and find Sadie in the Dawdi Haus, where she was sitting and reading Mamma's Bible, I leaned down and kissed her cheek.

She looked up at me and said with eyes bright with her own tears, "It was the least I could do for ya, sister, considerin' all the trouble I've caused."

Dear Sadie! She misses Harvey something dreadful, and I pray she might offer up her desires and longings to the Lord, for He alone is the answer to her lonely and broken heart.

Lydiann, too, seems caught in a fog of melancholy. She is miserable and restless, and more times than I can count, I've prayed that something or someone might come along to get her attention off Jake Mast.

It's still heartbreaking for me to think of Sadie's son being clear out in Ohio, though now with Jonas returning home, I also worry Jake might up and decide to come back, too. If so, what a pickle we will be in!

Dr. Schwartz surprised me by announcing his retirement, even though Lorraine says this won't happen for another six months or so—he'll have to turn his loyal patients over to young doctor Burkholder. If I want to, I'll still have plenty to do keeping house for them, though sometimes it's hard to work for Dr. Schwartz, knowing what I know. It does seem peculiar to me that he should want to simply travel round and "see the world," giving up his work at the clinic when he's still a relatively young man. Dat thinks it's an awful shame. "A man oughta work till he dies," my father likes to say. As for me, I think it *is* high time the village doctor packed away his stethoscope.

Thinking of work, Sadie, Lydiann, and I have been busy sewing dresses and aprons for Hannah's girls, as well as crocheting more baby blankets for sweet Ruthie. And it won't be long before Ruthie has herself a new cousin, for Hannah's told me privately that she's expecting another little one, as well.

Abe, the baby of *this* family, has been having plenty of fun at the expense of a good many rats and other farm pests here lately. With the corn harvest in full swing, he's been joining other young fellows round the area, going to pest hunts. So the suppertime talk is frequently filled with his chatter about such rambunctious things, but I do love to watch his expressive eyes light up with all the youthful excitement. And I can see by Dat's eyes that he, too, is delighted and amused.

Dat is also outwardly pleased at the prospect of Jonas's impending return to Gobbler's Knob, although I must admit to being quite fretful in waiting to hear how the bishop and the brethren will view all of this . . . and just when I'll see my beloved again.

For now, I simply thank our dear Lord for His merciful kindness, and I'm trusting Him no matter what the future may hold. I can only hope to marry Jonas one fine day, but even such a sacred end—and a joyous beginning, too—must rest in God's sovereign will, and that alone.

Watch for ABRAM'S DAUGHTERS book five,
The Revelation,
in summer 2005 at your local bookstore!